M000204842

HEART OF
A LION

Also by Stephen Zimmer

The Rising Dawn Saga
The Exodus Gate
The Storm Guardians
The Seventh Throne
The Undying Light

The Fires in Eden Series
Crown of Vengeance
Dream of Legends
Spirit of Fire

Hellscapes
Hellscapes, Volume 1

Chronicles of Ave
Chronicles of Ave, Volume 1

HEART OF A LION

A LION

Book One of the Dark Sun Dawn Trilogy

Stephen Zimmer

SEVENTH STAR PRESS

Copyright © 2015 by Stephen Zimmer
All rights reserved. No portion of this book may be copied or transmitted
in any form, electronic or otherwise, without express written consent of the
publisher or author.

Cover art: Bonnie Wasson
Cover art in this book copyright © 2015 Bonnie Wasson & Seventh Star
Press, LLC.

Editor: Scott M. Sandridge
Published by Seventh Star Press, LLC.

Stephen Zimmer's logo created by Elizabeth Lowery

ISBN Number: 978-1-941706-21-3

Seventh Star Press
www.seventhstarpress.com
info@seventhstarpress.com

Publisher's Note:
Heart of a Lion is a work of fiction. All names, characters, and places are
the product of the author's imagination, used in fictitious manner. Any
resemblances to actual persons, places, locales, events, etc. are purely
coincidental.

Printed in the United States of America

First Edition

Acknowledgements

I would like to thank Bonnie Wasson for taking on the challenge of creating the first image of Rayden Valkyrie. Bonnie is a wonderfully talented artist and a very dear individual to me, and it is a great honor to have her incredible talent on the cover of the first Rayden Valkyrie book. She delivered the magic just as I knew she would.

I would like to thank Scott Sandridge, my editor on this novel. Knowing how Scott has a passion for the genre and is very versed in it, I had the greatest of confidence in the care he had for this project.

I would like to thank Susan Roddey, whose encouragement and nudges during a difficult period leading into 2014 helped to get me back on track with my writing. The project I immersed into was this very book, as both Susan and Rayden helped me find my way forward again creatively. Susan is a true friend and I'm very grateful to have this special gal in my world.

I would also like to thank dear friends such as Robin Blankenship, Christina Butcher, Amanda Parks, and Eric and Kylie Jude, who helped me stay the course during times of storm.

I always will thank my mother, who I miss each and every day. She opened my eyes to the world of fantasy fiction and creative writing. Her encouragement and support throughout the years truly guided me to the path I am on now.

I want to thank my loyal readers. I put my best into any book that I turn into an editor as nothing less is acceptable for the readers who buy and read my work. My readers motivate me to push harder always to grow as a writer, as we take this wild and crazy storytale journey together.

DEDICATION

To the Power underlying this and all Universes.

To my mother and father for making my road possible.

To my sister for the gift of family.

To Elizabeth for bringing the sun back into my skies.

CHAPTER 1

Hooking her arm around his body, Rayden snatched the boy off his feet. Carrying him forward she dived to the ground, a massive set of jaws erupting from the waters just behind her.

Snapping down on empty space, the river predator found itself denied what should have been easy quarry. The creature swung its elongated head toward her and the child, locking its gaze upon them.

Rayden got her feet under her and with the boy in her grasp ran up the bank. She knew the great speed of the reptilian giants inhabiting the rivers of the Mystic Kingdom. The monstrosities could chase down a person on land.

Focusing all her energy on gaining distance from the river, she bounded forward with all the haste she could muster. She did not spare a glance over her shoulder until they were far away from the river's edge.

Seeing no sign of pursuit, she slowed, before finally setting the wide-eyed boy down on the ground. Catching her breath, she watched the monster turning and slipping back into the river. The creature drifted along the gleaming surface, beginning its search for other prey.

"Never trust the waters!" Rayden snapped at the boy, turning her attention back to the child. "You would have been eaten had I not seen that monster coming for you!"

"He doesn't know what you are saying," Ammanus said to her calmly, from where he had stood watching the entirety of the rescue.

"I am sure he understands the idea," Rayden replied to her companion with a surly edge. Adrenaline still raced through her veins and the chill of another close call with death lingered in her heart.

The boy was staring toward the river with eyes glistening from terror. His body trembled and she had no doubt he realized just how close his brush with death had been.

She had seen the giant crocodile from higher above, moving in slowly under the water's surface towards the unaware boy playing by the riverside. Had the water been cloudier, she might not have perceived the approaching danger.

Even then, she had gotten to the boy just in time. An instant later and one of them would have been dragged back into the waters, clenched in the massive jaws of the river predator.

Hot from the sun and exertion, rivulets of sweat ran down her face, stinging her eyes until she wiped it away with the back of her hand. She looked into the blue skies draped above. Barely a cloud to be seen, a few wisps of white drifted here and there.

"I won't be needing the pelt," she remarked, looking back to Ammanus. "You can keep it in your care."

A gift of the tribal people far to the south, the great desert cat's skin had been hard won in battle. Killing the long-fanged beast had been difficult enough. Surviving the massive battle that took place soon after had been nothing short of miraculous.

The dark-skinned people of the far southern lands had been fascinated with her lighter complexion, having never seen anyone from as far to the north as Rayden. By the time she departed they called her the White Lightning, in honor of her prowess in hunting and on the battlefield.

Even the little, elderly tribal shaman, whose visions had driven him to the northern coast to seek out her help, had appeared awed by what she had done. Her axe drank from the blood of a dangerous predator that had savaged the tribe for years. Not long after, her sword imbibed the blood of a king, one whose warriors outnumbered that of the tribe she aided by more than five to one.

Now the time had come at last to return to the northern lands, across the Great Sea. She had a visit with a sorcerer on her mind, one who would experience her ire in a highly physical manner if she could lay her hands upon him.

"I would have to say it is most unfortunate that you need a tunic," Ammanus remarked, grinning with a look of mischief.

Rayden cast him a sharp glare. "Walk with caution, Ammanus. Your tongue can still get you in trouble."

"It is ill of me to fail to recognize a beautiful, amazing woman, even if she can slay me in an instant," Ammanus retorted, smiling wider.

Shaking her head, a grin came to her lips. For all his perversions, he never failed to amuse her. "What am I to do with you, Ammanus?"

Hearing panic-laden shouts, Rayden looked up to see a woman hurrying toward them. She made a great commotion, arms extended wide and looking toward the boy Rayden had just saved. Her face reflected a mix of fear and relief, announcing her identity at once.

"The mother returns … I shall handle this," Ammanus said, turning to face the incoming pair.

"Better you than me," Rayden said evenly. "My words to her would not be so measured. Foolish woman, allowing her own child to play unwatched at a river holding such monsters."

After clutching the boy fast to her, the woman looked

at Ammanus and Rayden with a mixture of anxiety and defensiveness. Ammanus spoke quickly with her in the regional tongue, gesturing back toward the river at one point in the conversation.

He then indicated Rayden with a nod. From his hand motions she could tell that he was describing the scaly river hunter and her rescue of the boy.

As Ammanus spoke, the woman's expression began to soften. Not long after, the mother walked toward Rayden. Clasping her right hand, the woman began speaking in a lower voice.

"She is thanking you, for what you did for her boy," Ammanus said in the way of translation. "She understands now."

"Tell her she is welcome," Rayden said, feeling awkward as the woman continued her expression of gratitude. "But tell her to heed the dangers in the water. One like me may not be around the next time."

Ammanus paused for a moment and then translated. The woman nodded her head emphatically and Rayden hoped she took the warning to heart. It only took one lowering of her guard for the mother to lose the boy to one of the river monsters in the future.

The woman then took the boy away and started for the village she had come from. Rayden watched them walking together for a few moments, remembering a time long ago when she felt the arm of a mother around her shoulders. Those days seemed so ephemeral and distant, little more than the fading mist of a dream.

Looking back to Ammanus, she said. "It is time to resume our journey."

Together, they continued on their way, shadowing the course of the river. When the day grew late, the river curved to the left, where it eventually merged with a much larger channel of water.

"Ah, the Queen's River, the city is not far away now," Ammanus stated, looking relieved at the sight of the confluence. "Before the next sun sets we will see its walls."

"It had better not be far," Rayden said. "I intend to have a hot meal and a roof over my head soon."

"Ah, that would be very welcome," Ammanus said. "Perhaps a few things more."

"I have had enough of all this dust and heat," Rayden replied, ignoring the second part of his statement.

"How long will we stay in the city?" Ammanus asked.

"I need to find passage to the west, to Kartajen," Rayden said. "From there we can find passage across the Great Sea ... if you would like to continue with me. I have not changed my mind. I am returning to the north."

She eyed her dark-skinned friend, who always seemed to have a smile shining through his thick black beard. She found in him a kindred spirit, in that he also sought to journey to distant lands.

They had been through so many trials already, sharing the kind of bond that could not be easily broken. It was one of the reasons she refrained from laying him out with a hard punch following some of his more lascivious remarks.

"I would like to see the lands of the north," he said, nodding. He then chuckled. "I could be the interesting one among your people, as you were the interesting one among mine. They have probably not witnessed one with dark skin where you are from."

"They would find you interesting, without a doubt," Rayden said. "Though I am afraid your tongue would get you in trouble fast."

"Or it would win me much affection, when it is known how good I am with it," he responded with a wink, causing her to roll her eyes.

"You may well get in trouble with me before you ever get

there," she admonished him.

"I like to live, is that so bad?" he asked, his broad face radiant with a big smile.

"No, it's not, and it's one reason I actually like you," Rayden said. "Consider yourself fortunate. I do not declare such things often."

"One day I will have many women gathered around me to hear my tales of traveling with the great Rayden Valkyrie," he said. "And I will always thank you when I am in their beds and between their thighs."

"I would hope you do not think of me then," Rayden said. She shook her head, looked at him for a moment and broke into laughter. "I will say you are good for me. In some strange way that I cannot define, you are good for me."

"I know I make you laugh," he said, winking again.

"We all need a little laughter in our lives, that is true," Rayden conceded.

"It makes the time pass faster, does it not?" Ammanus asked.

"Time does not pass fast enough when thoughts of a bed and a warm meal occupy the mind," Rayden said.

"Not much longer," Ammanus said. "The Divine City will come into sight soon enough. One more night under the stars, then you will have a roof over your head."

***

Though well past midday, the heat of the sun bathed the massive walls of great stone blocks surrounding the Divine City. The heart of the Mystic Kingdom sprawled along the banks of the Queen's River. The gleaming currents flowed on their course toward the great delta to the north, where crops thrived within an abundance of rich, black soil.

Great pyramidal tombs loomed in the distance, the final resting places of the land's greatest rulers. Looking as if poised to spear the underbelly of the sky, the giant constructs reflected the splendor of the longstanding, and often mysterious, realm.

As breathtaking as many of the sights were, Rayden never forgot for a moment that the veneer of awe-inspiring regality covered a pervasive brutality and indifference to most. The Divine City teemed with slaves and the poverty-laden conducting backbreaking labor at the whim of soft-skinned masters. Cruel overseers and guards drove with the lash what no man or woman would have consented to.

Seeking to placate one or more of the animal-headed gods of the Mystic Kingdom's sizeable pantheon, the elite class commanded the building of grand edifices and temples. Whips, toil, blood and death plagued the servile unfortunates compelled to raise the massive wonders.

Still, a few graces were afforded even the poorest. Under the rule of Mahu, a man who claimed deification, a time of relative peace transpired. Content to indulge in the opulence of his great palaces, he showed little inclination to war or placing additional burdens on the populace. Aside from skirmishes along the borders, little troubled the people of the Mystic Kingdom.

For the land's inhabitants, a time of thriving trade and stability endured. The river traffic thick, great barges, sailing vessels, and small fishing boats alike plied the waters. Mahu himself often traveled the Queen's River on one of his luxurious barges, visiting temples, oracles, and palaces in the kingdom's southern regions.

Trading caravans from the desert lands to the east, ships from across the great sea and merchants from the lands to the south flocked to the Divine City to sell their wares. A bustling, polyglot center of activity, the city harbored all sorts of dangers, pleasures, and opportunities.

A large, arched gateway flanked by two stout towers led into the city. A pair of spear-carrying men stood before the entrance, while several others could be seen atop the towers above. Bare of chest, with their medium-length hair cut even to each side of straight bangs, the guards wore only a white garment to cover their bodies from waist to knees.

The guards eyed those entering the city with dispassionate expressions. Their gazes lingered upon Rayden and Ammanus, but the pair gave the travelers no trouble in passing through the gate.

Inside the walls, the pulse of the Divine City resonated in the crowded streets and open-air markets. Wealthy buyers perused cages containing exotic wild animals, while clusters of olive-skinned women in opulent garb evaluated a wide assortment of perfumes.

Eyeing a lion in one of the cages, a pang of sympathy struck Rayden. Its golden eyes met hers for only a moment, but in that brief connection she sensed its fear and loneliness.

A part of her wanted to set her axe upon the cage's lock and free the trapped creature. It pained her to see such a proud and majestic beast confined for no reason other than the vanity of arrogant men and women.

She glared at one such individual, a small, balding man arguing with a merchant in strident tones. She had an inclination to grab the haughty figure and throw him against the lion's cage.

In her mind's eye she saw his petulance evaporating as he soiled his expensive clothes. The thought brought a grin to her lips.

She walked onward, shunning the temptation. She could not put reaching Kartajen in jeopardy, not when she could finally return to northern lands after the passing of almost three years.

Ammanus slowed when they passed stalls brimming with everything from rarer meats to wines. Hunger tugging inside, she cajoled him to continue forward.

Shadows beginning to lengthen, the day would come to an

end soon enough. She wanted nothing more than to have a bed and meal at hand when night fell across the city.

At last they came upon a suitable inn and tavern. It had a well-tended appearance and did not seem to be the kind of place serving as a den for a band of thieves, or the other kinds of rogues often congregating in populous cities.

After making arrangements for a room to serve as their quarters while in the city, Rayden wasted no time in attending to her sorely famished state. Ammanus keeping her company, she ordered up a couple platters of food from the young girl serving the taverns few occupants. Sharing little conversation, the two of them finished every last scrap and morsel.

When they were done, Ammanus showed an eagerness to indulge in another kind of appetite. Far from surprised, Rayden bid him well, the only thought on her mind attaining a sheltered night of sleep on a mattress.

Making her way up a wooden staircase to the room, she settled down onto the straw-stuffed mattress, keeping her weapons close. Shutting her eyes and taking slow, relaxing breaths, she endeavored to leave the waking world behind and sojourn into the realm of dreams.

***

Tossing and turning, Rayden found that restful slumber proved elusive. The night crawled on and only the weariness in her body showed any mercy to her sleepless condition.

When fatigue overcame her at last, fitful, vivid dreams followed in its wake. Heartbeat pounding, she gazed upon a terrible, stark vision.

Northern warriors lying broken and bleeding littered the ground before a village immersed in flames. Withering heat beating against her face, Rayden looked around for any sign of life, but nothing stirred among the corpses.

Abruptly, the scene shifted. She found herself in woodlands steeped in the dark of night.

Scant moonlight filtered through the trees, shrouding everything in a deep murk. All around her, bestial growls sounded. Hulking, inhuman forms moved among the trees to the left and right.

Reaching down on instinct, she discovered that she had no weapons at her side. Sounds of movement through the underbrush continued, as did the growling chorus.

A deadly menace moved to surround her, mustering beyond the edge of sight and raising the hackles on her neck. She knew that if she waited even a few moments longer she would find herself in the gravest of peril.

Turning, she sprang forward and hurried through the woods, hearing the sounds of pursuit rushing through the undergrowth. Breaking out from the trees, she found herself in a large stretch of open ground.

In her haste she came close to tripping over a form lying in her path. She did not stop, though her breath caught in her throat as she took in the view ahead of her.

A great multitude of bodies lay strewn all over the field. Their garb and features told her they were northerners.

The animalistic sounds fading behind, she cast a quick glance over her shoulder. Nothing had followed her beyond the tree line. Having put a considerable distance between her and the woods, she slowed, seeking to conserve her energy.

A full moon above illuminated the field of dead warriors. Coming to a halt, Rayden stood in silence, keeping a wary eye on the forest.

After a moment, she stepped over to the body lying closest to her. She recoiled the moment she set her eyes upon the figure beneath her. Face revealed in the moonlight, the dully, glassy eyes of Eigon, chieftain of the Gessa, stared lifelessly back to her.

At that moment, a growling cacophony erupted within the trees. Bringing her eyes up, she held hundreds of pairs of glowing eyes in the shadows beneath the trees.

The bestial chorus swelled louder and it appeared as if the entire forest surged forward. Towering, humanoid figures charged out of the trees all across the dark facing of the woods.

Sitting upright, Rayden found herself back among the shadows of the room at the inn. Her face caked with sweat and breathing rapidly, she took a few moments to steady herself.

Ammanus had not returned yet, likely having found the kind of bed and company he desired. She fingered the timber haft of her axe, glad to feel the familiar touch after the jolting dream.

She thought about the horrific visions of blood and fire, wondering what prompted them. No worse nightmare could greet her than to see those she deemed most dear in her life lying dead.

The entities in the forest were a mystery. She had not gained a clear look at even one of the things. Perhaps they had been the wolf-men known to rove the wilds of the northern mountains, but something inside told her the shadow-cloaked figures were another kind of threat entirely.

She could only hope the dreams were not premonitions of any kind. No seer or prophetess, Rayden could only take comfort in the fact that countless nightmares in the past had proven to be nothing more than dark visions with no tether to the waking world.

Part of her wondered about the sorcerer whose words and counsel had led to the three-year odyssey she had endured and somehow survived. The thought of him using his arts to violate her dreams and send such a terrifying vision kindled a flame of anger inside.

Regaining her full composure, she lay back and stared at

the rough-hewn timbers spanning the ceiling. Listening to the sounds of her breaths, she emptied her mind of the horrid dream images.

Falling unconscious a second time, she finally attained the state she sought, entering a restful slumber that lasted until morning's light.

***

Aside from a brief stroll through a market area close to the inn, Rayden kept to the tavern while Ammanus investigated their options for traveling westward. The patronage sparse, only a pair of older men, other than the serving girl and the tavern master, shared the dusky space with her.

She liked it better that way. There would be far less chance of others' stupidity inviting her fists.

Sipping on a tall cup of wine, she found herself missing the taste of northern ale. Rayden knew she had been in the south far too long. She longed for bounteous, mist-shrouded forests and great mountains, feeling the invigoration of crisp northern air within her lungs.

Inclined to spend all the coins remaining in her pouch if they could find a ship sailing to one of the northernmost ports, she knew she was not the one to negotiate terms of passage once they reached Kartajen. Ammanus knew her wishes well enough; that she wanted to cut short the journey by land as much as possible.

She reminded herself that they had not yet determined a path to Kartajen itself. Travel along the coast, even in lands under the authority of Kartajen or the Mystic Kingdom, could not be taken lightly.

Ammanus returned late in the afternoon, striding across the tavern floor with a bright grin on his face. He announced to Rayden before coming to a stop, "I bring you good news, Rayden

Valkyrie. Luck has shined upon us this day! Your wonderful and cherished friend's search has met with great success!"

"You have found a sorcerer who commands a roc that can fly us all the way to the tribal lands," she replied, smirking. "Now that is indeed good news."

He shook his head, laughing, but the smile he had entered with remained. "Nothing quite so good, my beautiful and dazzling blue-eyed friend, but you will be pleased. A large caravan departs in the morning for Kartajen. We arrived in the city just in time to join them."

"Large you say?" Rayden asked, intrigued.

"Yes, the size of a small army, from the looks of it," Ammanus said. "Many hundreds of camels to be used for riders, supplies, and goods are gathered outside the city walls. A strong force of guards will accompany them."

"That is good news," Rayden said, having feared they would endure a long tenure in the Divine City, awaiting precisely such a possibility.

Traveling along with the caravan would be worth the expense. Its large size warded strongly against most kinds of threats.

Only brigands attracted by the prospects of significant loot would seek to harass a caravan. From what Ammanus said, the one leaving in the morning sounded sizeable enough to fend off all but the largest bands of desert raiders.

"I have already agreed to the price asked," Ammanus stated. "It will take a few coins from our pouches to join them, but we will receive steeds to ride."

"Camels," Rayden said with little enthusiasm. "I've not found them the most pleasant creatures to be around or ride. The smell of them is bad enough. But they are well-suited for the terrain we will go through."

"Anything is better than walking all the way from here to

Kartajen," Ammanus remarked.

"I wouldn't be so sure of that," Rayden responded with a chuckle. "You may change your mind after a few days."

"At least we are leaving tomorrow," Ammanus said. "That is great news. No sitting around the city waiting days on end."

"Now that is something I will drink to," Rayden said, draining the last of her cup. Calling over the serving girl, she ordered another cup of wine for herself and one for Ammanus.

"Why thank you, Rayden, my news invokes welcome generosity," Ammanus said, watching the serving girl walk off to get their wine.

"Take your eyes off her. You've time to visit a brothel before we go," Rayden commented, grinning at the look in his eyes. "I know what's on your mind."

"Am I that easy to read?" Ammanus replied, laughing.

"When it comes to some things, most men are," Rayden said. "Then again, women are no strangers to desire. Who knows if one I deem worthy to share my bed might come to the tavern tonight. Then you will have to find another place to sleep, my friend."

"More likely the unworthy will end up with broken jaws, busted noses, missing teeth, or, if they are lucky, unconscious," Ammanus retorted, rumbling with laughter.

Rayden gave him a mock look of indignation. "Am I that harsh? And here I thought I was a sweet maiden, eager to swoon over the kind of men that frequent taverns." She laughed heartily. "Even so, a man has to earn the kind of treatment you describe from me."

"Something I never desire to achieve then," Ammanus said.

"I count you a friend, Ammanus, you would have to really go far to gain my ire," Rayden said, shaking her head and laughing again.

The serving girl returned with cups of wine filled to the brim.

Rayden paid her, adding a silver coin to the amount requested. The young girl's eyes went wide and she thanked Rayden with a jubilant smile before leaving them.

"You are indeed feeling generous," Ammanus said. "You just made her evening a great one, no matter how many louts she deals with."

"She doesn't get paid enough for having to endure what comes in here most nights," Rayden said.

"And yet you like taverns," Ammanus commented, shaking his head. "You perplex me at times."

"Taverns have their good sides too," Rayden said. "Food, drink, song, and ... once in a while, a man worth my interest."

"My way is much easier," Ammanus said. "I go to the brothel, look at many worth my interest, choose one, or maybe two, pay my coins, and all is good. Sometimes incredible!"

"Maybe it is better to have simpler ways," Rayden replied, chuckling as she took a swig of wine.

Raising his cup, Ammanus said, "Let our travel west be simple and smooth. Come morning, we will be on our way."

Rayden lifted her cup in response. "I'll drink to that and commend your triumph on our behalf today!"

Together, they took long draughts from their cups. Outside, the shadows grew longer as night approached. That evening, no dark dreams tormented Rayden and Ammanus remained content to sleep at the inn, on a mattress by himself.

***

Rayden stood to the side of the extensive caravan, hundreds of camels arrayed in a line snaking far into the desert. The great city walls rising behind her, an open desert wilderness beckoned under bright skies that appeared to go onward forever.

The signal had not yet been given to depart. She stood on the ground, preferring the feel of solid earth under her feet for as long as possible.

Rayden did not relish the thought of riding all day on a camel. Yet she knew she had the right mount for the journey about to be taken.

The animals were accustomed to austere conditions, capable of great endurance, and they were strong bearers of both people and goods. All that mattered was getting to Kartajen and the less pleasant qualities of the beasts could be suffered for awhile.

At last, the call to begin the march westward passed down the line. Rayden walked over to the camel assigned to her, a younger animal that looked to be in good condition. Mounting up, she acclimated to the feel of her steed as the beast took its first steps forward.

Glancing behind her, she watched Ammanus sway in his saddle. Her lips carried a trace of a grin, knowing what kind of day he would be having. Before nightfall he would be complaining of discomfort and aches.

Rayden settled into her own saddle and cleared her thoughts. Ahead, Kartajen beckoned and beyond the sea her homelands awaited. Her return to the north could not come a moment too soon.

She longed to watch a sunset in the mountains, the majestic peaks cradling a reddish jewel under skies draped in purple. Closing her eyes, she could almost feel the sweet kiss of northern winds.

She did not let the thoughts dwell long in her head, reminding herself to keep her focus. A long stretch of desert and journey of over forty days lay before her.

If all went well, enduring the merciless heat of day and the stench of camels would be the worst of it. She doubted things would go that smoothly, but each day would have to be taken one at a time, just as one step came before another.

Eventually, the journey would come to an end and the walls

of Kartajen would rise before her. Once there, she would have to turn her thoughts toward gaining a passage by sea.

Even so, having a firm destination at the end of it all, one that she looked forward to reaching, would be a boon in moments of weariness and hardship. It had been a long time since the end of a journey carried a chance of welcome and joyful reunion.

Bloodshed, wars, monsters, and sorcerers had driven far too much of her life. Long overdue, the time to go where she wanted to go had come.

CHAPTER 2

After several days of uneventful travel, Rayden began noticing some women in the caravan exhibiting sharp changes in behavior. Where they had conversed, laughed, and talked during the beginning of the journey, a few among them had become subdued and nervous in manner.

They quickly looked away whenever their eyes met Rayden's. She could sense their great agitation and knew something had gone amiss, suspecting that the women contended with a menace of a darker nature; one coming from inside the caravan.

Turning in her saddle, she motioned for Ammanus to come up alongside her. Spurring his mount and drawing a guttural response from the gangly creature, he brought the camel up on her right side.

"Trouble is afoot," Rayden told Ammanus when he rode next to her.

"What do you mean?" Ammanus said, looking puzzled. He glanced out toward the featureless landscape, squinting against the bright sun. "I see nothing out there. Just desert everywhere. What trouble?"

"No, not from out there," Rayden said. "Within. And I mean to settle this long before we reach Kartajen."

"I don't understand?" Ammanus said, looking more

confused. "What kind of trouble from within?"

"It is something I have seen before," Rayden said. "We have a predator, or maybe more than one, among us." Her gaze swept up the long column, wishing that the task of identifying a wicked heart were easier.

"Some blood is going to be spilled then," Ammanus said, a grim look on his face. "That is what you mean to say. I have traveled with you for long enough to know what you will do."

"I am giving you fair warning," Rayden told him. Her eyes narrowed as she thought of the women. "The nature of what I sense cannot be given leave to continue."

Ammanus took a deep breath and sighed. "When you have your heart set on something, Rayden, I do not think a god could stop you."

"I would fight a god over something like this, but I just wanted you to know, as a friend," Rayden said. "I accept the consequences of what I do. I do not wish to bring you into this."

"Thank you," Ammanus replied, though she could see he already feared her stirring up a tempest within the caravan. The smile that arose on his face a moment later looked forced, but his next words conveyed the kind of man she had come to know well. "I am willing to be brought into this, for you, whatever it is. There is nobody whose judgment I trust more than yours. If I am able to help you, please let me know. I know you do not confront things lightly."

"Thank you Ammanus," Rayden said. "Hopefully this can be taken care of quickly and in the shadows."

Looking behind her, she gazed upon one of the women whose change in mood had bothered her. The sadness evident on her face stoked a fire deep within Rayden.

Whoever had caused that change had to be found and brought to justice, as soon as possible. To delay meant to subject the woman and others to malevolence of a kind Rayden had encountered all too often before.

Knowing that something so malignant was happening and doing nothing about it would be little better than sanctioning it. Rayden, as so many in the past had discovered to their elation, rage, or terror, did not countenance the wicked.

***

At the break of dawn on the following day, Rayden espied one of the young women sitting by herself and crying while the caravan readied to set out. Downcast and heaving in sobs, the young woman bled painful emotions.

Wiping her tears away, she looked fearful and anxious when Rayden approached her. For a moment, it looked as if the young woman would try to run off.

"No need to be afraid," Rayden said in a gentle voice, holding her hands up, palms out, and seeking to calm the young woman. She then asked, "May I speak with you? Just for a moment. It is important."

The woman did not reply at first, simply staring at Rayden with eyes reddened from a cascade of tears. She then glanced about, appearing to be looking for anyone close enough to listen or see what was going on.

"Nobody's close enough to hear us, we're speaking in private," Rayden reassured her, keeping her tone soft and relaxed. "I just want to know something and only you can tell me. Something has happened to you in recent days ... and some of the others. I see the fear on your faces. I have seen this kind of fear before in my travels. I know the changes that I have seen come over you and some of the other women. I know what causes this. Just tell me. Who is he, or is there more than one preying upon you?"

The anxiety in the woman's face was replaced by a look of stunned amazement at Rayden's words. She looked around again with an air of anxiety, confirming Rayden's suspicions beyond doubt.

"I don't carry this sword and axe for decoration," Rayden said. "Even if this miscreant could hear us, you are safe. Just help me, and tell me about what has happened over the past few nights."

After a couple of attempts, the woman found her voice. Shaky and hesitant at first, she settled into a steadier cadence as her horrid tale took shape.

The woman told Rayden about the vile things that had been happening during the last few nights. What she heard set her blood to boiling. Her hands ached to reach for the weapons at her waist.

Everything was as Rayden had expected. A man in the caravan, who the woman identified as one of the guards, had taken to forcing himself upon a few select women.

The poor woman believed she had no redress, as she and the other female victims were low-level servants of a wealthy merchant's wife. It soon became clear that the wretch maintained caution in only preying upon those of the lowest status.

Rage filled Rayden to the brim by the time the woman completed her tale. Somehow, she managed to keep her voice calm and her expression somber, though inside she wanted to cry to the heavens and call for an open challenge to whoever had done such evil to the woman.

Yet she knew that she could not create a large disturbance or she would invite much more trouble to both herself and the victims. She had to stalk in the shadows, but to do that she had to know the identity of the predator.

"You must tell me who he is, so that I can be wary of him," Rayden said, looking the woman straight in the eyes.

She knew the woman would not fathom her ultimate intent. Being a lowly servant of a wealthy merchant, the woman would be unaccustomed to another taking up her cause or defending her. Enduring the evils of the world were the typical lot afforded to servants and slaves, but Rayden was neither.

Nodding slowly, the woman cast her gaze about once more. After a few moments her face tensed up, fear leaping to her eyes. She did not need to say a word as Rayden followed her eye line to the cause of the reaction.

Sitting astride a camel, a brute of a man laughed, talking with two other mounted guards. Rayden held back her initial urge to send her axe hurtling toward the man's broad, bearded head.

Loud and full of swagger, he carried himself with the kind of air that Rayden had seen of his kind before. He would not cross the merchants or his own superiors, but he would think nothing of inflicting harm upon the voiceless.

"You need say nothing more," Rayden told the woman. "I see him. I know who he is."

Calls were dispersed for everyone to mount up and begin the day's journey. The man who now held Rayden's ire barked out commands in a gruff voice, telling the people traveling in the caravan to get up and moving.

He saw the young woman and cast a mocking smile, failing to see the storm coalescing in the face of Rayden just a pace away from her. He rode onward, continuing down the length of the caravan. Rayden watched him go, her blue eyes staring daggers into his back.

"What you shared with me was not easy for you to do ... thank you," Rayden said, looking back to the woman. Her voice grew firmer and a promise carried on her next words. "I assure you, I will bring the nightmare to an end. I will be back when the caravan halts for the night. Do as I tell you when I return and this will be over."

The woman nodded back, though she had no way of knowing exactly what Rayden intended. For her part, Rayden could see the desperate wish in the woman's eyes that the torment would come to an end.

In that moment, the guard rode back up the side of the column accompanied by a couple of others. This time he did not even glance their way, looking engrossed in some jest with his comrades.

It was all she could do not to draw her weapons and spill the miscreant's blood on the sand. Hearing the man's bawdy laughter, Rayden seethed, needing every last shred of willpower to stay under control.

Getting up, she took a deep breath and put one foot in front of the other. Keeping her composure, she strode back toward Ammanus, who had already saddled up and waited for her.

Her own mount awaited and without a word she got up into the saddle. The beast rose to its feet, lifting her high from the ground.

Ammanus caught her eyes and from his response it was clear that he registered the simmering look coiling within them. "You found something out. You know what has happened and who is responsible. Am I right?"

She nodded curtly, keeping her eyes locked forward as the dreg and his two companions trotted by on their mounts again. He loudly berated and threatened a few people who were slow to fall in with the caravan. Her fingers tingled with an impulse to grab the hilt of her blade.

"Him, the big one?" Ammanus asked. "The charming one yelling at the two older women?"

She nodded again, and replied. "I mean to end this tonight. When the sun rises tomorrow, his terrorizing will be over, I swear it."

"Why not now?" Ammanus responded.

"I will spoil his next hunt," Rayden said. "Then, I will lay him to waste. It is what a monster like him deserves."

CHAPTER 3

Though Rayden anticipated that the low-life would seek to fill his hunger that night, it did not diminish her ire or disgust when he manifested. The reprobate worked his way into the young woman's tent, moving slow and purposeful. He likely thought himself quiet, but she had heard his approach well before he fumbled at the tent flap.

She knew the mentality of his type all too well. Coming alone, he relied on his large size, bearing the assumption that he could overpower and use a woman for his pleasure against her will.

Rayden had no tolerance for such vermin. This night he would find a woman that he could not dominate. He would know fear and accountability before the moon reached its zenith.

Safe and under the watchful eye of Ammanus, the young woman whose tent Rayden now occupied had nothing to fear. In a discreet manner, Rayden had taken her place, something that would come as a tremendous surprise to the would-be predator.

Posing as if she were fast asleep, she listened to the man crawling nearer. She wrinkled her nose at the first whiff of his noxious body odor, the only thing that would harm her senses that night.

He worked his way over her, breathing heavily as he moved

his bulk forward. A broad grin on his face, the man prepared to take his pleasure.

As he rolled Rayden over on her back and got between her legs, she wrapped the latter smoothly about him, with no sign of alarm or aggression. She could feel the rapid swell of his arousal, the man becoming excited in anticipation of another conquest by force.

His eyes bulged wide with astonishment when he found himself staring into ice blue eyes, alert and hardened. She knew he had been expecting fearful, dark eyes beneath him, but intimidation could be found nowhere within the wolfish gaze peering back.

"You chose the wrong tent to crawl into, scum," Rayden said in a low, cold voice. Locking her legs tight about him, all pretenses vanished. "But it is good for other women that you came here tonight. Your days of violation come to an end now."

The baffled expression on his face lasted only a moment longer. Fixing a hold on him with both arms and legs, Rayden executed a rolling move that changed their positions and had him on his back in an instant.

His eyes spread wide and he opened his mouth to say something. A sharp punch from Rayden stifled any utterances he might have made.

Straddling the thick-bearded figure, she unleashed a barrage of fists straight into his face. Crushing his large nose, she knocked most of his front teeth out by the time she stopped.

Teetering on the verge of unconsciousness, blood pouring from his mouth and nose, he moaned weakly. She shifted along his body and yanked his baggy trousers down, exposing the part of him that he had intended to make her suffer the most with.

Drawing forth the dagger she kept at her side during sleep, she made a concerted slice to the fleshy sack beneath his still-erect manhood. Continuing her onslaught, his testicles lay on the ground a few moments later.

Standing up, she stamped downward with great force twice in succession, crushing each of the severed parts underfoot. The only consolation to her disgust lay in that she wore sandals and did not sully her bare foot with the pulped flesh.

"I have removed the cause of your disease. Be glad you have your life ... if you can hold onto it," Rayden addressed the man in a low, angry tone, bordering on a growl. He offered no response, his face reflecting a delirium of pain. "Perhaps you can go serve in a palace with other eunuchs ... like the one you are now."

Gathering up her items, she left the violator bleeding and broken in the dark of the tent. She made her way back to the shelter where Ammanus slumbered, rousing both him and the young woman from sleep.

Seeing blood spattered on her, he looked up to her face in alarm. Gazing toward Rayden with sleepy eyes at first, the young woman snapped to alertness with a fearful expression.

"I removed one scourge from this caravan and a warning has been sent to any others who might wish to try something similar," she explained to both of them. To the woman, she added. "There is nothing more to fear from that snake. He has been defanged."

"A warning?" Amanus asked, looking nervous.

"Nothing you would like to hear me describe. I urge you to trust me," Rayden replied looking him in the eyes without any trace of humor in her gaze.

He nodded and heeded her advice, refusing to press her any further on the matter. The young woman looked relieved that something had been done to her tormentor, though she did not shed all of her anxiety.

Rayden told the woman to stay with them for the duration of the night. No argument forthcoming, the woman settled in and soon fell asleep.

It took a little while for Rayden's heated emotions to simmer down. Listening to the slow, relaxed breaths of the woman sleeping near helped her tempestuous mood ease bit by bit.

She suspected it was the first restful night for the woman since the first days of the desert journey. Somewhere in the darkness outside the woman's violator faced a struggle to live until the next morning. If the sun found him with breath in his lungs, he would serve Rayden's purpose.

He had been held to account and left with a severe reminder of his transgression that would last for the rest of his days. Not even the best sorcerer she had encountered on her travels could restore the brute.

She thought of what would transpire the following morning. Word of his mutilation would pass swiftly through the caravan, bringing with it an unspoken warning. When the next night arrived, Rayden doubted any further predations upon the women of the caravan.

The thought brought a smile to her face and peace to her heart. After a little more time passed, weariness finally came over her and she drifted off to sleep.

***

As expected, word of the grisly deed flowed quickly through the caravan when morning returned. She half-expected bluster from one or more of the brute's companions, but not one approached to confront her. If anything, they kept a wide distance and averted her gaze, though from their eyes she knew they were aware that she had been the one who had carried out the retribution.

Melisea, the woman Rayden had approached the previous day, was the first to express her gratitude. No words were necessary. Breaking into tears, she pressed her face into Rayden's shoulder and hugged her tight for several moments.

A few other women came up to Rayden when Melisea finally

released her embrace. Hesitant at first, they exhibited more confidence with Rayden as she received them one by one. She greeted each one of them warmly, after which their nervousness ebbed and they voiced their gratitude for what she had done.

Evidently, the man who received Rayden's justice had plagued the caravan every night since they had left the Divine City. He had availed himself of more women in the caravan than even Rayden had suspected.

Ammanus stood with her when the women came up, listening to the conversations and watching everything with both interest and a little unease. Finally, Rayden took leave of the women and started toward the front of the caravan.

"Is that?" Ammanus asked in a whisper, peering at a man whose face was bloated to a hideous degree, a motley array of fresh, swollen bruises covering his features.

The man limped in awkward fashion, as a couple of others worked to help him get astride a camel. Rayden could only imagine the ordeal he would go through riding that day.

Seeing his predicament, she felt no regret over what she had done to him. He still had his life, which was probably more than a monster like him deserved.

Rayden nodded to Ammanus. "Yes, that is the one."

"A warning indeed," Ammanus replied, wide-eyed. "One that nobody can miss."

They continued to the forefront of the long assembly, finding Barca off to the side. Rayden did not wish to start the day without speaking to the highest authority in the caravan.

"It seems you delivered justice last night," Barca said, a grim look on his face as she approached. "I see the women coming up to you and some of your victim's comrades came to me demanding that you to be dealt with or expelled."

"It was justice, for a man guilty of terrible crimes," Rayden said. "I will not apologize."

"Then why are you here?" he asked in a stern manner. "What do you want of me?"

"I wanted to speak with you, to know if I will have trouble with you. I know he was one of your men," Rayden said. "If you understand what has happened, I can more than make recompense for what you have lost in his service to you."

After a long pause Barca remarked with a dismissive air. "He brought it upon himself. I should have been told of what had been happening earlier. The dog's life should be put to an end. And I may yet."

"I still took a man from you," Rayden said. "Even if he deserved his fate, I will do my part to defend your caravan for the rest of this journey."

"I suspect you can wield a blade," Barca said, eyeing the axe and sword at her waist. "I can see in your eyes that you are not a woman tamed."

"And I never will be," Rayden replied evenly, staring into his dark eyes.

A smile broke his thick beard and his features softened. "Perhaps just the kind of warrior I need with us on this journey. Yes, you may help us in the guarding of the caravan. You will have no trouble from me."

Rayden gave him a nod of her head. "And should any trouble come to you, I will benefit you far more than the scum I took from you."

"You may yet have a chance to show your skill with a blade," Barca said. "Brigands roam this desert in large bands. Even a caravan of this size seldom deters them."

"If they come, they will regret it," Rayden said.

"You seek passage across the Great Sea, if I remember correctly what your companion said," he asked.

She nodded. "Yes, I am on my way to my homelands, in the far north across the Great Sea."

"Now that is a long journey," Barca stated. "Kartajen will give you some options for crossing the sea. No other city along this coast sees the number of vessels that Kartajen does."

"I'm counting on that," Rayden replied.

"Very well, I shall have my men place you where you can be useful," Barca said. His face shadowed over. "And I shall deal with the rabid dog you came across. You did me a favor."

Barca walked away from Rayden, calling over one of his guards of higher rank. The man hurried over and they exchanged a few words in private, before the guard indicated for Rayden to follow. Placed near the front of the caravan, Rayden judged Barca wanted to keep her within eyesight. In all likelihood he wanted to avoid disruptions from any seeking vengeance upon her.

He had nothing to worry about. She knew any such attempts would come in the shadows, when evening arrived. While daylight remained, none of the brute's companions would seek to threaten her.

Scanning the horizons, nothing but empty desert horizons met her eyes, all throughout the day. The terrain looked no different than had the previous day, and she doubted it would change the next.

While riding at the caravan's lead, she thought often about the brigands that Barca claimed were somewhere out there in the barren landscape. The dense forests of her homelands were much better suited to an ambush.

She wondered how any brigands could hope to draw near a large caravan without being detected. The movements of any large numbers would send up a dust haze that could be seen for leagues.

Perhaps they simply counted on overwhelming a caravan through sheer force and did not give much care to stealth. The thought did not bother her. Seeing them coming from far away simply gave her more time to ready herself to greet them. If it were not for the danger to the innocents in the caravan, she would have welcomed a good fight just to break the monotony.

Though every bit as long and hot as the others, the day did not wear on her as much as the last few had. She attributed the difference to taking up a more proper role for a warrior, in having a duty to attend to.

***

When evening fell, several men arrived as Rayden had expected. The companions of the newly-created eunuch, unfazed by what had been visited upon their comrade, converged on her shelter in the middle of the night.

Having already fashioned an exit at the back of the shelter, Rayden waited for the men to draw closer. Within her field of view, she counted five of them in all. They were spaced apart, the reflection of moonlight on their drawn weapons.

Her eyes narrowed upon one creeping nearer to where she crouched. Gripping a short blade, a terse look etched on his face, the man's intentions for her were clear enough.

The deep chill of the desert night could well have been the specter of death hovering over the shelter. A path leading to bloodshed well in motion, Rayden poised to unleash doom upon the bearded figure approaching ever closer. He crept forward, now only a couple paces from the tent.

With the explosive speed of a lioness, Rayden burst into the open and engulfed the creeping man. Moonlight glinted off her blades, both axe and sword.

Terror filled the face of the startled, would-be assassin. Agony swept it away. Blood leeching into the sands, his prone body lay face down.

Rayden did not pause for an instant, charging toward the second figure crouched a short distance from the first. Scrambling to his feet, he tried to give flight, but toppled over with her axe buried in the midst of his back.

Bounding over, Rayden took up the axe and stood with her back to the shelter. Hearing the cries of their companions, the remaining three had banded together and squared to face Rayden.

The bright moonlight showed their faces well enough. Hatred, anger, and more than a little fear reflected in their expressions.

Rayden strode toward the three figures, her eyes swirling with a feral hunger that only death could sate. Hesitancy took root in the men, followed by a surge of fright that saw them attempt to flee.

She spent the better part of the remaining night hunting the three men down. One by one, she found her quarry, bringing each of them the death they had intended for her.

One found his hiding place betrayed by one of the women who had suffered at the hands of his comrade, when he tried taking refuge in her shelter. Hearing her panicked cries, Rayden hurried to the tent and discovered the man inside. After sending him to the ground with one hard punch, she dragged him away from the woman by his hair.

Her nostrils filled with the stench of his voided bladder, right before she plunged her blade into the back of his neck. Pulling the weapon out, she shoved his corpse forward, where it fell face-first into the sand.

Rayden became alerted to another's location by camels, the beasts becoming agitated when the man tried in his desperation to hide among them. The creatures made further commotion when he cried out pitifully, Rayden's shadow falling over him. The cry ceased abruptly when her axe cleaved through skull and brain.

The last of the five men showed more backbone to his courage, trying to ambush Rayden when she came for him. She could only guess that in his fear he forgot that his tracks were simple to follow.

Having figured out his hiding location, Rayden curled around behind him on soundless steps, to where he crouched near the back of another shelter. He had no hint of his peril until she loomed over him. Far too late for the hapless man, Rayden severed his head from his body with one powerful stroke of her blade.

Shrouded in a cold, remorseless silence, Rayden made her way back to her shelter. Killers had come for her and she had done what had to be done.

Slipping inside, she cleared her thoughts, listening to Ammanus' muffled snores in the shadows. With no more disturbances expected that night, she availed herself of the night still remaining to her. The next day would be a long one and there would be the awkward matter of Barca losing five more of his guards.

***

Barca caught up to Rayden when the caravan set out at the break of dawn. His dark eyes carried a gleam of anger, not even a ghost of a smile resting on his lips.

"Five more taken from the guard of this caravan, their bodies found scattered all about the camp this morning, one of them headless," he announced tersely, offering no greeting. "All of them happened to be friends of the rabid dog you confronted. Nobody will tell me who killed these men. You and I both know it is no coincidence. Do not try to tell me you had nothing to do with this."

"Would you rather me allow five men to attack my tent and slit my throat in the dark?" Rayden asked Barca, her ice-blue gaze boring into his. "I did no different than you would have."

He held her stare for a moment. Finally, he nodded, though the anger still simmered in his eyes. "There is no argument I can give to that."

The pair rode together in silence near the head of the caravan. Rayden kept her eyes toward the horizons, while Barca brooded.

"You lost nothing," Rayden stated, cleaving the heavy tension.

"You count five men as nothing?" Barca asked with a tone of incredulity. "Out here in the middle of the desert with no prospects of hiring replacements?"

"Having me in your caravan guard is better than all six of them, including the new eunuch," Rayden responded.

"You will not see him again," Barca said. "I got rid of that dog before those men ever came for you."

Turning her head, she looked at Barca for a moment. She had not expected that announcement. "With me and without those animals, your guard is stronger than before. This I assure you."

"Let us hope we do not have to find out if your statement is true," Barca said. "There are still many days left to travel."

"We will get through them and see this caravan to Katarjen," Rayden told him.

"May it be so," he replied curtly.

Turning his steed, Barca made for the body of the caravan, leaving Rayden to her thoughts. She did not blame the man for worrying. He had not yet seen her fight, and he had lost six of the men he had hired to guard the caravan.

At the least, he had not let his emotions cloud his better judgment. He had recognized the truth of the matter; that Rayden had acted solely in defense of herself.

He also needed her. As he had stated, there were no possible replacements and every blade in his service now counted more than ever.

Shortly after midday, the outlines of many low, mud-brick huts appeared to the northwest. Accompanying the village were trees and green foliage, the mark of an oasis. The sight of something other than desolate terrain gave a lift to Rayden's dour mood.

She had endured all environments she had traveled, but the barren, dusty world around her stood in stark contrast to the vibrant forests and mountains of her homelands. The winters brought their own hardships in the far north, but she much preferred the snow to the parched conditions of the desert.

The caravan shifted direction to head directly for the village and oasis. It took a little longer than Rayden anticipated for the caravan to reach the place, but distances always seemed to take longer when traveling in an arid landscape.

Supported by the oasis, the small village consisted of about twenty huts scattered within a swathe of thicker foliage and trees. A number of children ran out at the caravan's approach, shouting to each other with eyes wide in excitement.

Rayden chuckled to herself, imagining the caravan to be the most interesting thing the children had encountered in a long time. She could not imagine living in such an isolated place, but imagined the small community survived well enough with the source of water they clung to.

The long procession slowed to a halt just outside the huts. Several of Barca's men spread the order to set up camp. Rayden lingered at the forefront, interested in their new hosts.

Barca appeared to know the elders of the village well, exhibiting familiarity with all of them as they emerged and clustered around him. Their smiles and relaxed tones told her that the men shared a longstanding relationship.

Caravans probably helped sustain the village in its needs, bringing needed and desired items in exchange for access to the village's water. She wondered how the village fared during times of war, or in its relations with the brigands. An oasis stood more valuable than piles of gold in the middle of a desert.

"Those men look like they've been around a few years. Must not have anything the brigands want to steal," Ammanus said, interrupting her thoughts, having walked up to join her. He looked toward the long-bearded elders surrounding Barca

Rayden cast him a sideways glance and a grin, glad to see her friend again. "Not much to steal here, not from what I can see."

"They cannot walk away with all the water," Ammanus said. His voice grew more serious in tone. "But I am sure they know the leaders of the brigands as well as they know him."

Ammanus inclined his head, indicating Barca, who laughed heartily at some jest made by one of the elders. For the village to survive in one of the more valuable pieces of land in all the desert, the elders would have to placate caravans and brigands alike.

"What are you thinking?" Rayden asked him.

"We must be wary," Ammanus said. "These people are survivors."

"We'll keep an eye out, you can be sure of that," Rayden said.

His face broke into a smile. "But it will be nice to wash this dust off and feel water on my skin again."

"You and me both," Rayden said. She saw several men and women from the caravan heading toward a thick line of foliage. "Looks like others share the same idea."

"I say we join them."

Rayden glanced back to Barca and the elders, nodding. "As good of a suggestion as any."

With Ammanus at her side, she started for the trees, offering the promise of cool shade and water.

***

On the edge of dusk, Rayden noticed Melisea returning to the shelters of the encampment with a worrisome look on her face. Seeing the distress, Rayden rose to her feet and walked toward the woman. She hoped there was nothing of the nature that the woman had endured before.

When she drew near, she asked her gently, "I see the look on your face. What troubles you?"

"These poor people," Melisea replied, her eyes glistening with sorrow. "Is there no place in the world where people do not prey upon each other?"

"If there is such a place, I have not found it," Rayden replied grimly.

After the nightmare Melisea had suffered early in the desert journey, Rayden felt a deep unease, seeing the woman exhibiting such a strong level of distress toward the villagers. She wondered what kind of plight could invoke such a reaction.

"What did you learn of the villagers?" Rayden asked.

Melisea paused, looking into Rayden's eyes. She then told her in a low, pensive voice, "I spoke with a woman ... a woman who just had a daughter taken from her. And another woman, who lost her son ... only three days ago."

"Taken?" Rayden replied, a scowl forming on her face. "The brigands?"

Melisea nodded, a tear escaping and running down her cheek.

Rayden had been wrong that the village had nothing the brigands wanted. But a further question remained.

"What do the brigands want with the sons and daughters of this village?" Rayden asked. "Children are of no value to desert raiders."

"To those who cross the seas they are of great value," Melisea replied. "It is rumored that the children are taken somewhere in Teveren lands."

The response perplexed Rayden for a moment. There were much easier ways of procuring children than bringing them across the Great Sea.

The hackles rose on the back of her neck as she thought of

the one possibility that made sense. Practitioners of dark sorcery would only invite retribution taking the children of Teveren families.

A few nameless children taken from the lands of an enemy would rouse no one to action. Voiceless, anonymous, and bereft of any to stand for them, captive children were doomed to any fate intended for them.

"You know something of this?" Melisea asked, evidently mistaking the darker look spreading across Rayden's face.

"Just a suspicion, born from years living in this cruel world," Rayden answered.

Several more tears fell from Melisea's eyes and her voice sounded thick with emotion. "I can't imagine what a mother or a father goes through. Having your children taken away like that? What must it be like for those who have not lost their children yet? Living each day not knowing if the brigands may come to take your daughter or son?"

Rayden's jaw grew taut listening to Melisea's sobs. Sorrow funneled through her own heart, transforming into a fiery anger that had no easy outlet at the present.

No brigands stood within the reach of her blade and a sea lay between her and the vile sorcerers she suspected were at the root of it all. The only thing she could promise herself was that any brigand who tried to come and take a child while she remained in the village would have to get past her first. A part of her regretted that the caravan would not tarry long before departing.

She would take the bitter knowledge to heart. She reminded herself that she sought to cross the Great Sea and while Teveren lands were not her destination, awareness always preceded the confrontation of evil.

"Living like that is a hell as horrid as any described by prophets," Rayden said after a long silence. "I share your sorrow for these people."

Melisea nodded. "I wish I didn't feel so helpless right now."

"I wish I didn't either," Rayden confessed, a wave of anguish passing through her.

The children were far away and nothing could be done, unless the brigands made an appearance at the oasis. Though Rayden had seen tremendous cruelties throughout her travels, she still could not reconcile how anyone could do such a thing and live with themselves.

That night, sleep proved difficult, her thoughts plagued by the story of the villagers' plight.

CHAPTER 4

Having replenished their water and allowed their mounts to partake of the oasis' bounty, the caravan moved out a day later. From what Rayden learned, well over half of the journey lay behind them and less than fifteen days remained to the walls of Kartajen.

Taking her place at the vanguard of the caravan, she peered toward the line where sky met land, finding herself wishing to see a sign of the brigands. At the moment, only empty desert met her eyes.

After listening to Melisea's tale, she hungered for the brigands to move upon the caravan. They would meet an axe and sword thirsting for their blood.

Her desire found no succor, the sun crossing the skies with no signs of brigands or anything else. The same transpired the following day. One day blending into the next, she fulfilled her promise to Barca in warding the caravan.

When not assisting with the watch at night, she joined Ammanus for food and conversation. She could tell he grew more restless and bored by the day, with so little to occupy his attention.

After the trials faced by the women in the caravan, he expressed having no desire to seek companionship of a physical kind. Rayden respected him all the more for that decision, but she reminded him that his famine would swiftly come to an end once they reached Kartajen.

Exotic beauties awaited him within the brothels of the great city, more than Ammanus could ever hope to handle. She promised that she would contribute some coins toward giving him a wonderful night when they arrived.

Seeing the spark of vigor in his eyes and the mischief in his expression, she laughed merrily, the first moment of levity she had experienced in days. It reminded her of the better things about life, including both friendship and the thrill of passion.

After dwelling in dark thoughts since the night in the village, she saw that she needed that kind of reminder from time to time. Life needed balancing when darkness stood so prevalent.

The next morning she took her place at the vanguard of the caravan again, as she had every dawn for the last several days. This time her heart rested in a better place. After the latest conversation with Ammanus, she had found a better equilibrium.

She still hoped the brigands made an attempt to take the caravan, so she could mete out justice, but she could not allow herself to be consumed with rage. A fire channeled could be the source of great strength, while one spreading out of control destroyed everything it crossed; innocent and guilty alike.

***

In nature, Kartajen proved to be like many cities Rayden had visited in the past. Behind towering walls and a massive gate flanked by great towers, a sprawling mass of humanity scraped out meager lives under the eyes of an elite steeped in luxuries and comforts.

Alleys choked with rickety market stalls offered an array of goods in the shadow of opulent palaces. Clusters of children ran through the streets to the curses of the elders they bumped into.

Heart of a Lion

Guards strolled at leisure, while women with harried expressions went about their daily tasks running households. Beggars and prophets vied for the attention of each passerby, both of them attracting the scowls of clean-shaven priests attired in garments of fine quality.

Rayden took all of it in, glad to be in the bustle of a city with all of its energy and activity. She welcomed the pools of shadow cast from buildings after so many days passed under a blazing sun. The monotony of caravan travel had finally come to an end, the city offering her a brief respite before a sea journey began.

Ammanus had already sought out his own form of relaxation. Once inside the city gates, he had wasted little time in seeking out a brothel, eager to indulge himself in carnal pleasures after enduring such a long period of restraint.

As she had promised, Rayden contributed a few silver coins toward his lustful foray, wishing him grand adventures while she explored the city for a little while. She smiled recalling the giddy eagerness in his face, like a child about to receive a favorite sweet food.

Her appearance attracted many gazes, some filled with curiosity and others with more prurient leanings. A northerner with flowing blonde locks and piercing blue eyes, she contrasted sharply with the darker hair and complexions predominate all around her. On the average, she stood a head taller than most, bringing further attention her way.

One glance at her axe and sword told many she was not one of the foreign beauties from a brothel. One glare from her proved enough to discourage other kinds of advances. Pickpockets thought otherwise of attempting to take the purse at her belt.

Walking deeper into the great city, Rayden passed down lines of market stalls. The air teemed with the sounds of merchants proclaiming the attributes of their wares and haggling with prospective buyers. Her nose wrinkled at some of the less pleasant odors of a city, from the excrement of animals to the pungency of sweaty bodies in close proximity.

A breeze would have been quite welcome, both for its cool touch and to drive away the less pleasant aromas. Yet the air remained stagnant, the heat carried within it seeming to weigh it down.

Looking ahead, she eyed a range of high tenements, the likes of which were only found in cities on the scale of Kartajen. Farther beyond spread the great harbor with its mass of sea-going vessels.

The waters glittering in the sunlight looked bejeweled, forming a welcome vision after staring at sand for days upon end. Rayden would be negotiating passage across the Great Sea soon enough and a tinge of eagerness to be on her way tugged inside.

The coins she carried with her would not see the pouches of merchants. Every last one remaining might prove necessary to get her aboard a vessel.

Once past the long-line of merchant stalls, she found herself at the edge of a large, open square. A dense crowd had gathered at the base of a high stone dais, accessed by a long flight of steps in the front. Sprouting from each side of the platform were curving, sculpted horns.

A deep unease filled her at the sight of an altar dedicated to Malech, the monstrous bull-god of the Kartajenians. To her eyes, the thing stood far more a demon than any sort of god. The statues depicting its bestial form always carried an air of malevolence, rather than any measure of beneficence.

She wondered how anyone could worship a god that took the visage of a dull-witted herd animal; much less a deity with a hunger for living sacrifices. Nevertheless, an elite priesthood maintained temples and altars of the god all over Kartajenian territory.

She noticed the midday sun had nearly reached the epicenter

between the two points of the great horns. A number of clean-shaven male figures garbed in crimson robes were gathered atop the dais, surrounding a tall, narrow-faced man clad in white robes, his shaved head circled by a golden headband.

Unlike the busy market area with its loquacious merchants, the area with the high altar harbored a reverend hush all throughout. Gazes filled with expectation, men and women both wealthy and poor looked toward the priests above them. In this single matter, they all stood together as equals.

A forest of billowing flames blazed from within some manner of cavity or pit set at the top of the steps. Snaking tongues of fire within the gaping maw licked hungrily, awaiting the next offering to the bull-god.

Horror filled Rayden a moment later, seeing another pair of figures surmounting the steps and pulling a young boy along with them. The boy flailed and struggled, but the robed figures were too strong for him to escape as they dragged their intended sacrifice steadily upward.

Only a small white cloth covered his loins, the rest of his olive-hued skin laid bare. His dark eyes reflected sheer terror as he looked about in a state of desperation.

Rayden's heart beat faster, taking everything in at once. The boy did not want to die in the fires of some bull-headed deity. He wanted a chance at life, no different than any other boy his age.

At the top of the steps, the priests held him firmly in place and the white-robed one began a loud, rhythmic chant. The boy started to tremble at the sound of the priest's voice. She could not imagine the kind of terror rippling through the boy, the heat of the inferno about to receive him beating against his skin from only a few paces away.

Another kind of fire sparked and spread fast within Rayden. Anger raw and furious swelled at the violation of everything she held sacred.

Slavery disgusted her enough, but watching an innocent boy being condemned to death offended every last fiber of her being. She stood witness to an outrage, a mockery of life itself.

Her greatest contempt fell upon the surrounding crowd. Standing like cattle, not a single one of them would speak out or seek to intervene on behalf of the boy. Unmoved by his plight, they would just stand idle when his agonized screams cut the air, his flesh given over to the ravenous fires.

To Rayden, all were guilty of a great offence, but she understood the motive that drove the priests. In their distorted vision, they were carrying out a duty to the god they had dedicated themselves to. The people filling the open ground were the ones who gave authority and power to the priests, to burn one of their own children alive.

Without the sanction of the crowd, the priests could never carry out what they were now doing. That immutable fact condemned all the onlookers in her eyes.

The boy looked back toward the crowd. The expression of despondent hopelessness on his face hit Rayden with the force of a thunderclap, as heavy as any physical blow she had ever suffered.

The look told her that he knew his fate had been sealed. Abandoned by everyone in his world, he believed nobody would stand for him.

Perhaps in other cities, at other altars to Malech, the boy's despair would be justified. But not on this day; not when one figure stood among the crowd bearing the will to act.

All thoughts of consequence fled Rayden's mind. She hurtled into motion, knocking bystanders aside and running for the base of the steps. Taking the first several at a leap, she propelled swiftly up the steep incline.

Gasps and cries of shock erupted in the crowd below at the audacity of someone daring to interrupt the sacred religious ceremony. Paying them no heed, Rayden's focus locked squarely upon the two men holding the boy in place between them. A lioness closing the gap with her prey, she only thought of bringing the priests down.

A few of the other robed figures tried to get in her way when she reached the top. Powered with fury, her fists smashed into their faces, crushing noses, breaking jaws, and sending one of the men tumbling hard down the steps behind her.

The two with the boy looked stunned and indecisive as her gaze fell upon them. She took up her axe and blade, striding toward the priests. Fear flooded their eyes. Letting go of the boy, they turned to flee.

Running them down, the blades of her weapons flashed in the sunlight, rising and falling in rapid succession. Her weapons coated in their blood, the two priests lay dead at her feet.

She harbored no pity for them. If they wanted to serve the bull-god, they could do so in another world.

The white-robed priest had withdrawn a knife and almost reached the fear-stricken boy when Rayden turned around. Reacting in a blur of movement, she hurled her axe toward the man. Whirling end over end the weapon rushed through the air.

His eyes snapped open, iron biting deep into the side of his skull. Toppling over, the priest rolled down the entire length of the steps to the cries and gasps of the astonished onlookers below.

From her vantage, Rayden could see several guardsmen running toward the base of the steps. The crowd parted way for them, allowing clear access to the altar.

"Follow me boy and stay close if you want to live!" she shouted, having no time to settle the frightened and bewildered youth.

Eyes resembling blue flames, she turned her rage toward the guards. Moving to meet their ascent, she gripped her weapon firm and kept a steady mind.

She met the first of the guards about midway down the

flight of steps. Her sword leapt to the fight. The body of the dead guard rolling down the steps gave the next one pause, but she fell upon him before he could change his course.

She descended the steps, one warrior after another falling to her blade and the death toll climbing rapidly. Only a couple of her opponents were able to stab at her with their spears. She batted aside their feeble attempts easily enough, unleashing doom in the wake.

Reaching the bottom, she retrieved her axe from the corpse of the high priest and squared her body in a balanced stance, staring at two guards who kept their distance. Gripping their spears tight, they eyed her warily but made no move toward her.

Casting a glance over her shoulder, she saw that the boy had followed after her. His face still reflected fear, but she also saw amazement in his features, his gaze darting among the dead bodies strewn all about.

She knew the square would be flooded with guards soon enough. Keeping her attention on the two remaining in view, she gestured for the boy to keep close with her.

Turning to the right, she charged forward, the entrance of a narrow alley beckoning from a short distance ahead. Passing from sunlight into shadow, she hurried down the confined channel.

High tenements loomed to either side. The danger of being trapped would rise once the alarm spread. Having no escape routes outweighed any advantage of having only a few enemies being able to come at her at any one time.

She slowed just long enough to make sure the boy continued to follow. Spared the maw of an inferno, he had obeyed his unexpected savior and stood a few paces away.

"We don't have time," Rayden said between heavy breaths. "You will have to listen to me and follow every command I give you without hesitating ... if you want to survive and not be burned alive. Do you understand?"

The boy said nothing, but mustered a nod in response.

"Good, then follow me closely. Guards will be swarming through this area very soon," Rayden said.

There was no time to ponder her greater predicament, of how to get out of the city either by land or sea. There was no chance of reaching Ammanus at the brothel. She had acted and now she could only react to manifesting threats.

A chase with deadly implications ensued as the pursuit began. There were not enough guards yet to fill every alley or street, but Rayden knew she did not have long before her adversaries enjoyed an overwhelming advantage.

More than once, she had to set a quick ambush, or spring into combat, coming into increasing contact with the city's guardsmen. To a man, they proved woefully ill-prepared to contend with a fighter of her skill and it took little to cut them down.

Every kill cleared a path or purchased a little more time, but she knew it could not go on forever. She was not a god, and there were limits in a body of flesh and blood.

Exertion took its own toll and every fight sapped a little more out of her. Her arms had begun growing heavier, draining speed from strikes and reactions. Before too long, weariness would become far more of an adversary than the guards themselves.

Hiding, running, and fighting when necessary, Rayden protected the boy and sought an escape from a worsening predicament. Afternoon grew late and before long dusk would drape the streets in shadow.

Night promised doom. Most of the city's residents would return to their homes, emptying the streets and exposing Rayden even further. With the deaths of the guards, the pursuit of her would not cease until she lay dead or in their captivity.

She had to find a way out of the section of the city she now roamed, but she began to suspect the city's guards had addressed that first. The few times she came to streets that appeared new, the ends teemed with shield-bearing warriors, living walls forcing her to double back.

Hurrying down another street she had been down before, Rayden stopped herself at the cusp of running out into the open. Dismay filled her as she eyed the steps, dais, and altar where everything had started.

Alert, with weapons in hand, over twenty guards milled about the spacious area. From their helms, armor and shields, Rayden could tell they were of a much tougher ilk than the ones she had been encountering.

Cursing her fortunes, she watched at least another twenty warriors march into sight, equipped like the others that they joined in the square. She knew they were all mustering to come after her. The fatigue accumulated after an afternoon of constant running and fighting had her at a severe disadvantage.

The hunt would come to an end soon. With all routes blocked and additional forces massing, the pursuers would close in for the final kill with overwhelming force.

Rayden glowered at them from the shadows. She intended to take as many of them as she could with her, every last one if she could find the strength.

Her mind knew the situation facing her, but her heart held no trace of surrender within it. The only lament she harbored concerned the boy, who would fall back into the hands of those who would see him burned alive. All she had done would be for naught.

Turning to the boy, she stared into his dark eyes. Fear and sadness teemed within his gaze.

She looked upon a boy who had been abandoned by his own family. She did not have to ask him to know that he came from a life that knew hardship and struggle all too well.

The children of the powerful were not the ones given over to sacrifice. Those in poverty had the expendable sons and daughters for the hungers of wicked gods.

Alone, with not a single coin in his possession, the boy crouched next to her as poor and powerless as one could be in the eyes of Kartajen. Her eyes viewed him in a much different manner.

Rayden's words flowed solemn and true. "I will defend you to my final breath, until you are safe and have a home free of those who would see you offered to a vile beast-god. By everything I am, this I promise you."

The look he gave in response told her that the words struck him deep. A whole square filled with people willing to watch him burn had been replaced with one choosing to guard his life. Eyes watering, a number of tears broke free and began trickling down his smooth cheeks.

"Why? Why did you protect me? I don't know you. I am nobody. Why did you risk your life?" the boy asked in a voice thick with emotion. "They will not let you leave here alive."

The questions drove deep into everything that Rayden had become over the years and there were no short answers. The only reply she could give the youth came like an embrace from her lips.

"Your life is worth defending."

Voices in the square rose in volume. Looking back, she saw the warriors being called into order. Poising for a final effort to root her out, they would march forward at any moment. She suspected similar scenes were taking place on all the streets around that section of the city.

Gripping her weapons, a fire surged throughout her spirit, girding her tired limbs with resolve. A sense of calm entered her mind, bringing clarity and a command of purpose.

She would earn a warrior's death, surrounded by the bodies

of her adversaries. A tempest of blood and fury coalesced, awaiting the enemy to make their move.

"Come! Come over here! Quickly!" a feminine voice called from the shadows in the alley behind.

Turning her head, Rayden espied a woman standing in an open doorway, gesturing to her with great urgency. Glancing back she eyed the warriors now assembled in a tight formation, presenting a wall of shields toward the alley. Bereft of any other viable options, Rayden sprung into motion.

Grabbing onto the boy's arm, she pulled him along with her and headed for the offered refuge. The youth almost tripped, her strength yanking him off his feet at the outset, but he kept upright and hustled along at her side.

The woman stood aside the doorway as they neared, waving Rayden and the boy inside as she kept her eyes toward the end of the alley. Once they passed into the tenement, the woman hurried after and shut the door behind her.

Outside, a handful of moments later, a number of angry voices sounded followed by the thumps of many footsteps. The noise swelled in volume, a contingent of warriors tromping past on the other side of the door.

When the commotion outside died down, the woman turned to Rayden. A nervous expression on her face, she remained silent and stared at her new guests.

Getting her first good look at their benefactor, Rayden saw that the woman was about the age her own mother would have been at the present time. Her face and hair showed the touches of age, lines about the eyes and traces of gray in her long dark locks, but the glow of youth had not faded entirely.

Wearing a simple tunic, sandals, and little adornment, her appearance announced that she held no high position in Kartajen. Yet her intervention carried the power of life and death in the balance, sparing Rayden and the boy.

"Thank you," Rayden told the woman, breaking the impasse. "You did not have to risk yourself for our sake."

Finding her voice at last, the woman replied in a hushed tone, "Word of what you did today has spread fast. They spoke of the she-lion running the streets. Some fear you, but others know the truth of what you did. At least one in this city will defy the priests and stand for the innocents."

"At least two, you meant," Rayden corrected her. "You just did by helping this boy and giving the two of us a chance."

The anxiety and fear in the woman's face crumbled as Rayden's words invoked a powerful reaction from her. Sobbing, tears streaming down her face in shimmering lines, the woman blinked rapidly. Taking several deep breaths, she tried to compose herself.

"I could not allow them to get to you, or the boy," the woman said in a voice choked with emotion. "What they do is evil. But you will need to flee the city. The wicked priests will not rest until they have you and the boy in their grasp."

"The gates will be locked and the walls watched closely," Rayden stated. "There will be no slipping by there."

The woman nodded. "And the vessels in the port will be watched over."

With the ocean offering the best chance of leaving the city, Rayden turned her thoughts toward the great harbor. Filled with merchant vessels, not everything could be warded closely.

She had come to the storied port city to find passage across the Great Sea. Stowing away on a vessel was not her initial intention to make the journey, but circumstances had changed and she would have to take her chances.

"How far is the port, from where we are now?" Rayden asked the woman.

"Not very far at all," the woman answered. "But what of the guards? The area by the harbor will be full of them by now."

"I could not simply walk up to one of the larger ships, but if I could approach them on water," Rayden said, thinking aloud. She looked toward the woman. "Do you know of anyone who might be a fisherman? Someone who might have a small boat that one person can use."

The woman's brow furrowed. She fell silent for a moment before replying and nodding to Rayden, "Yes. I know of more than one who has such a boat."

"Is there a way I can speak to them? Would they be willing to help? Maybe one that feels such as you do about the priests."

The woman nodded slowly. "I believe so. I will have to go to them and bring them to you. You must stay hidden. But you will have to wait. Even I cannot go into the streets now."

"No, not now," Rayden agreed.

"You must remain as guests in my home. My name is Asherah. You will receive food, drink and rest," the woman said. "I live by myself. My husband is no longer in this world. You will not be disturbed here, or be in any danger of discovery."

"My name is Rayden and I thank you for all of this," Rayden said, holding the other's gaze.

"Something must be done for one who would stand against a wicked god," Asherah said.

Her words sent a chill down Rayden's spine. She viewed her struggle against men of flesh and blood; not an attack on a god she did not believe existed. Nonetheless, the words rang sobering in her ears and for a moment she wondered what adversities could befall her by provoking the ire of a god.

No matter how fearsome in appearance, creatures that bled could be killed. How an adversary immune to blades or any other physical device could be overcome she did not know. Even the idea of contending against such an enemy left her with a sense of being adrift in waters she had no control over.

Yet even had the bull-god manifested that day before all

gathered at its altar, her choice would have been the same.

For the second time that day, she spoke aloud the reason she had acted. "The boy's life is worth defending."

CHAPTER 5

The night, morning and the following day crawled by in laborious fashion. Aside from conversation, little else could be done in the small dwelling space to pass the time. At least the interior provided relief from the relentless sun baking the streets outside.

Early in the day, Asherah prepared Rayden and the boy a meal including figs, bread, mutton, and a little wine, announcing that she would go into the city afterward to inquire about the use of a boat. Sharing the food and drink with them, she spoke at length about a number of things regarding Katarjen.

Over the past year, the sacrifices had increased in response to spreading conflict with Teveren. The rising power across the sea had seized many holdings of Kartajen and swayed a few prominent allies to switch allegiances.

The sharp downturn in fortunes had only increased the demands of the priests for Kartajenian children to hurl into the fires of Malech. To Asherah's knowledge, the bull-god had still not intervened to reverse Kartajen's losses.

The ruling Council of Elders had appointed new commanding generals in the hopes of stemming and reversing the course. Sent abroad to confront the Taverenians closer to their lands, the generals carried the hopes of all Kartajen with them.

Rayden valued the information. Having been in the south for quite some time, she did not know of the escalation of fighting between the rival powers.

Watching the door shut when Asherah departed to conduct her inquiry, she harbored little worry. In allowing Rayden and the boy refuge within her home, Asherah showed the kind of character that would not waver so easily.

Her eyes brimmed with contempt whenever she spoke about the sacrifices or the priests of the bull-god. She would not easily betray the two fugitives she now harbored.

Rayden found it strange that Asherah never mentioned having a child, though she referenced her dead husband many times. She did not press Asherah on the matter, sensing a dark, haunting tale lurking just under the surface. She caught a distinct sadness in the woman's eyes more than once, during moments when she thought nobody was looking and her gaze lingered upon the boy.

Rayden passed the time talking with the boy and trying to get some rest. She learned that his name was Hamilcar. He had a pair of older brothers and a younger sister. His father labored daily as a porter, loading or emptying the cargo from the ships in the harbor from dawn until dusk.

She found it hard to believe any father enduring such backbreaking work at a low rate of pay would cooperate with the desires of soft, wealthy priests. Yet Hamilcar's parents had readily given their own son over to the high priests, when the latter made their choices of sacrifices deemed suitable to Malech.

Her heart ached listening to Hamilcar's story, watching the boy break into tears more than once. He had evaded the fires of Malech, but a new and uncertain world awaited him.

Walking away from everything he had known would not be easy. Rayden had once taken that path and could understand the terrible ordeal the boy faced.

Later in the afternoon Asherah returned. A man with a head of gray hair and narrow features accompanied her. A fisherman, he stood willing to discuss the matter of his boat with Rayden. Like Asherah, he expressed a great resentment for the bloodthirsty priests of the bull-god.

He described the boat that he had and the general area where it was located. While willing to help in the matter of the boat, he would not take her there in person.

The port teemed with guards, looking out for Rayden and the boy. If she decided to use his boat, he wanted it to appear like theft to the eyes of others, with no trace of his involvement.

Rayden understood his position and did not argue. She dug out a couple of gold coins in the pouch she carried, easily enough for the man to purchase another similar boat. He accepted the coins and expressed his gratitude to her, wishing her and the boy well before departing Asherah's home.

The successful arrangement buoyed the spirits of their host as she set about fixing another meal. While they were eating together, she indicated that she would be leaving one more time, to help with the matter of reaching the port. Rayden wondered what Asherah intended to do but did not press her on the matter.

When evening approached, Asherah left the dwelling once more. She returned soon after with another man, one much younger than their previous visitor.

Harboring a fiery look in his eyes, he looked to Rayden and the boy while Asherah introduced him as Sibal. She described him as a guide who would see them to the harbor that night.

Like the fisherman, Sibal expressed his antipathy toward the priests of Malech and their child sacrifices. He had no qualms about guiding Rayden and the boy, indicating that he had an idea on how to get past all the guards unnoticed.

He left a short time later, indicating he would return at

midnight. Rayden found herself liking his spirit already, sensing a keen wit and determination.

After Sibal left, Rayden found her hands lifted up and cradled in those of Asherah. The sadness she had noticed earlier, when Asherah looked upon the boy, gleamed in her eyes.

"My part in this is coming to an end soon enough," Asherah said, her face somber. "I know that you do not worship Malech, but I know that whatever god you worship is one of light. I just ask that you pray to your god for me ... for mercy on my spirit when I must go into the next world."

Rayden did not have the heart to tell Asherah that she prayed to no gods. Nor could she find it within her to lie.

"If a god of light can hear the prayers of a woman who has spilled the amount of blood that I have, then I will offer that prayer," Rayden said.

The answer appeared to bring some peace to the other woman, the pained look in her eyes softening. "A god of light would listen to you. You stand against the darkness."

Rayden offered Asherah a smile and gently squeezed her hands before letting go of them. "I will not forget you, Asherah. You saved the boy, and me, from a terrible fate."

"I will not forget you," Asherah said, her eyes tearing up. "My only regret is that I did not witness such courage with my own eyes, when you intervened for the boy."

"I only acted as my heart told me," Rayden said. "It is the way I have always been, nothing more."

***

Laying a wooden plank down, spanning the narrow gaps between the six level structures, Sibal led Rayden and the boy from rooftop to rooftop toward the port area. Far below them, the streets crawled with search parties of armed warriors.

Once, they passed directly over a group that had just turned a corner, trudging down the tight confines of an alley with weapons and shields in hand. Rayden listened to their voices and grinned to herself, knowing they would never think of looking upward.

Watching their guide setting down the plank to span another pair of buildings, she admired his insight. Kartajenian warriors blocked all of the streets, but they never considered the possibility of their quarry passing right over them. Had any of the ten warriors below cast just one glance above, they would have seen the fugitives they sought outlined in silvery moonlight.

Reaching the final tenement at the edge of the harbor area, they descended several flights of stairs, taking them to the street level. Walking out of the tall structure, Rayden drew to a halt.

Peering outward, she took in the sight of the port. Moonlight glittered off the water and the looming, shadowy forms of larger vessels at rest could be seen all throughout the harbor. A considerable number of war galleys slumbered along the curving shoreline.

"There, to the right," Sibal said, pointing. "That one will leave at dawn. I made some inquiries earlier, before coming to Asherah's home."

Following the prompt, Rayden eyed a large merchant vessel tethered at the side of a stone quay. Its sail furled on a single, heavy mast, the ship had a raised, curved stern with a steering oar set on the starboard side.

Though she could not see anyone aboard the ship at the moment, she doubted it went unguarded. A merchant vessel with a loaded cargo hold offered tempting rewards to would-be thieves. No captain's reputation could endure the looting of a ship's cargo while in port.

"Come with me, let us go to the boat you will use ... the one sold to you," he said.

Sibal took Rayden and the boy down to where a small fishing

boat rested, pulled up snug on the sand. Robust in construct, it held a pair of oars within its belly.

He helped her drag the vessel down to where the water lapped the shoreline. When the boat bobbed lightly on the glimmering surface in water knee-deep to Rayden, Sibal looked to her.

"This is as far as I can take you," he announced.

"You have taken more than enough risk upon yourself," Rayden replied. "I thank you."

"It is my hope that one day altars to wicked gods will be a faded memory," Sibal responded. "I am glad to help you and the boy. Get him free from this city. May your journey be a safe one."

Rayden nodded to the man. "Whatever may come against us, I will see the boy to safety."

Sibal gave her a nod and headed away from the boat. Sloshing out of the water, he walked up the beach and strode back toward the tenements.

Holding the boat steady, she let the boy climb into it first before getting in herself. The boat rocked for a moment and then leveled out as she took a position at the midsection.

Taking up an oar, Rayden dipped it into the water and pulled the blade through. Repeating the motion on one side and then the other, she took control of the boat, slowly gliding out from the shore.

She did not have far to go in reaching the merchant vessel Sibal had identified. Using the bodies of other ships, she masked their approach until they reached the final stretch of water.

Eyeing the sizeable vessel aside the quay, she angled her boat toward an area closer to the bow. Careful not to collide with the hull of the larger vessel, Rayden slowed and pulled alongside as quietly as she could manage. Dense shadow helped conceal them, with the moon's light falling on the other side of the vessel.

Helping the boy upward, Rayden boosted him to where he

could grab the top of the large vessel's hull. With a low grunt of exertion, the boy hoisted himself up and over the side, climbing into the body of the ship.

Abandoning the small boat, Rayden followed right after, crouching low when her feet touched the rough-hewn planks of the ship's decking. Keeping still, she took in her surroundings for a moment, a hand resting on the hilt of her blade. Nothing stirred among the moon-cast shadows around her.

"Stay low, we must seek a place in the hold," Rayden whispered to the boy, her eyes falling upon a hatched opening leading down into the area of the vessel containing the ship's cargo. The hatch, to their luck, lay open.

Slow and silent, she led the boy over to the dark opening and the top of a short flight of wooden steps. She locked her gaze on a pair of the ship's crew standing sentry near a ramp spanning to the quay, but the two men had their backs turned and did not take notice of the new interlopers.

With the boy close at her side, she descended slowly, keeping the creak of the timber underfoot to a minimum. Enough moonlight leaked through the opening behind to outline the forms of the containers filling the hold.

Rayden paused, allowing her eyes to adjust further to the dusky environs. A cluster of large amphorae to the right would afford her and the boy ample concealment.

With no alarm raised, she took some time situating a space for the two of them at the back of the amphorae, by the outer hull. Careful to make as little disturbance as possible, she shifted a few of the clay containers about.

Forming an area large enough for the two of them to lay down in a curled up position, she told the boy to get some rest for the time being. Left to the darkness and sounds of creaking wood, the boy soon fell asleep while Rayden took up a steady vigil.

Having rested more than enough while taking shelter with Asherah, Rayden had no intentions of slumber herself. The delicate matter of meeting the captain loomed on the horizon, once the ship had taken to sea.

She had no way of knowing what kind of man captained the ship and she could only hope that fortune favored her. Without the blessing of the captain, she would find herself in a terrible quandary.

Further, there still remained the precise destination of the vessel, another answer she would discover soon enough. For all she knew, the vessel could be headed to the eastern reaches of the sea, where exotic cities teemed with dark sorcery, opulent palaces, and things steeped in shadowy mystery.

Nevertheless, the chances of both her and the boy surviving had increased. They had escaped the clutches of the city guards and priests of the bull-god. Passage across the sea had been found, even if not in the manner she had envisioned.

She simply had to wait for the morning to gain some answers. Settling with her back to the hull, listening to the creaking of the ship, she took a deep breath and maintained her calm.

**

The sounds of thumping footsteps above, mixed with a number of voices, indicated the approach of morning and the impending departure of the vessel. The commotion woke the boy, who looked to her quizzically as the activity above them increased.

Gesturing for him to remain silent, they continued to wait. A few men brought some additional cargo into the hold, but none of them drew close enough to bring any threat of discovery.

Golden rays of sun replaced silver moonlight, cascading into the opening of the hold. Above, members of the crew shouted to each other, preparing the vessel for departure.

After some more time passed, Rayden felt the ship's

movement when it left the side of the quay, beginning its journey through the harbor toward the open sea. Listening to the voices of the crew calling out to each other, she looked toward the boy.

Even in the shadows of the hold she could see the anxiety etched across his face. Smiling, she reached over and ruffled his thick, curly locks of hair.

"We are away from Kartajen, and I doubt the men on this ship are devout followers of Malech," she told Hamilcar in a low voice.

He mustered a smile, looking a little more relaxed at her words. The boy already impressed her with his courage. From the top of the sacrificial dais he had followed her instructions without fail, all the while leaving behind everything he had known.

Whatever ill-feelings he harbored about being given over for sacrifice, he was still being separated from his parents, brothers, sister, and all of his friends. She found the fortitude he displayed remarkable, especially for a boy with such little experience of the world. Much more would be asked of him in the days to come, but the early signs gave her confidence that he could endure future trials.

Before long the movements of the ship became more pronounced. The rising and falling of the vessel, climbing and descending a larger series of waves, resonated in the pit of her stomach.

She had little doubt they had left the harbor and reached the open sea, though she remained below deck for a while longer. She had to be certain that they were far out to sea, with no chance of turning back or being witnessed by other vessels.

Finally she got to her feet. Looking downward, she told the boy, "I think it's time for me to go up to the main deck and meet the captain. Wait here and do not come up until I call for you. Understand?"

The boy nodded. She gave him a pat on the shoulder and then edged her way through the amphorae. She girded her resolve, prepared to spill blood if necessary, but hoping that matters did not come to violence.

Everything rested upon the nature of the captain. She would have her answers in a few moments.

Rayden strode up the stairs, emerging into the open sunlight. Scattered across the heavens, the few clouds she saw carried no hint of storms. A light wind beat against the great sail and the creaks of ropes accompanied the splash of waves slapping against the outer hull.

Voices laced with surprise erupted a moment later, the crew members taking notice of the unexpected guest appearing within their midst. Rayden took a few steps forward, making no effort to subdue her presence.

Men began gathering around her, keeping a little distance. Among those approaching, her eyes settled on one man in particular. The air of authority surrounding him and confidence in his step identified his nature at once.

Weathered, leathery skin and streaks of gray in his ample beard indicated a veteran of the seas. A hard look rested within his eyes as he came to a halt and took in the sight of Rayden.

"It appears I have an uninvited guest," he said in a firm, humorless tone. "Not something I anticipated or welcome on my ship."

"Only out of necessity," Rayden replied. "I did not want it this way, but I had to leave Kartajen. I will pay for my passage and earn my place aboard your ship."

"Earn she says," remarked one of the men nearby, chuckling and exhibiting a lascivious grin. He flicked his tongue out in a crude expression. "Do all the men get rations or what?"

"You can earn your passage alright," chimed in another. "I can think of some duties for you aboard ship."

Heart of a Lion

More daring than his companion, he walked slowly toward her. The ship captain said nothing, watching the proceedings quietly as the man stepped closer.

Burly, with a rounded face and beard, the man conveyed an air of condescension. "Nothing original about you. Two legs. Two breasts. Three places for my cock. No, you are just another wench who should accept her place on this ship. A harlot for our pleasure."

Rayden gave him a smile, though the look carried no trace of welcome or invitation. Her eyes mirrored the ice of the far north, cold and dangerous to all life.

In a low, steady voice she said, "I will accept a place on this ship but it will not be in the way you desire. I might even save your sorry hides if trouble arises. The choice is yours. Make it a good one."

"The only thing arising will be me," the man replied, smiling, grabbing his groin area as many of the crew broke out in raucous laughter.

He took another step closer, bringing his hand up from his groin. He started to reach toward Rayden's breasts. A moment later he found himself crumpled on the decking, holding his groin for a much different reason, with blood pouring from a broken nose.

The surrounding laughter died instantly. Rayden heard the outraged curse from the man's comrade, the other one who had addressed her.

She let the brute charge at her, dodging his wild blows easily enough. A heavy fist to his mouth buckled his knees and dropped him to the deck.

He spit blood and a couple teeth out on the wood. Rayden stepped forward and pressed her right foot down on the back of his neck.

"Do you want more?" she said, ready to continue his beating

at the slightest provocation.

The man groaned, his eyes carrying a dazed, unfocused look.

"I didn't think so," she responded, grinding his face hard into the wood for a moment before lifting her foot off. The man stayed in place, making no move to get up.

She looked back to the captain, stating calmly, "Can we resume our discussion?"

The captain nodded and she recognized a newfound look of respect in his eyes. He spoke as if nothing unusual had just happened. "You were saying something about paying for passage and earning your keep aboard the ship, before my men interrupted us."

Rayden took up a pouch at her waist and tossed it over to the captain. Snapping up his hand, he caught it mid-air. Opening the pouch and turning it over, he watched his palm fill with silver coins.

"There's payment," Rayden said. "And your men have had a taste of what I can do should your vessel come under attack by pirates."

"I'm guessing you can use your axe and blade as well as you use your fists and knees," the captain replied, turning his gaze back to her, glancing toward the weapons at her waist.

"I would rather give that demonstration on pirates, not your crew," Rayden replied, staring into the captain's eyes and letting the implied threat coil within the air about them.

A moment later, he nodded to her. "I would agree. Best save that for sea rogues."

"I have a boy with me as well, who I have taken into my care," Rayden announced. She called aloud,"Hamilcar, come up here now!"

After a short delay, the boy came up the stairs, wide-eyed and fearful as he took in the hard-looking crew standing around.

He shuffled over to join Rayden at her side, keeping his eyes down.

"He is not yours, that is plain enough to my eyes," the captain remarked. "He is a Kartajenian boy. There is a story here."

"I spared his life from the fires of your bull-god," Rayden answered. "I disagreed with the priests' desire to sacrifice him."

The captain eyed the boy, then turned his gaze back to Rayden. His expression remained somber.

"So you are the ones we heard about last evening," the captain said. He paused for a moment. "I do not seek to offend gods, but Malech is not a god of the sea. The boy is in no danger of sacrifice aboard my ship."

Rayden stared into his eyes, discerning his meaning. Satisfied that the captain would not seek to harm the boy, she turned her attention to the rest of the crew.

"If any of you think of making sport with him, you'll meet death quickly. That I can promise you," Rayden declared, sweeping her gaze across the faces of the men around her.

Not a single one of them could hold her eyes for more than a moment. She knew none would challenge her openly, but she intended to keep a close watch upon the boy nonetheless.

The two men still lying on the deck testified to the presence of less than savory inclinations within the crew. Their battered condition also empowered her words, giving warning to what Rayden was capable of if provoked.

"I think we have reached an understanding," the captain stated, after a period of heavy silence. "You must earn your keep aboard the vessel."

"As I expected to," Rayden told him, nodding.

The captain eyed his men. "I command all of you to look upon these two as you would any member of our crew. If you seek to harm either of them, you will answer to me."

Rayden's expression remained unchanged but she welcomed

the open support of the captain. She knew she could protect the boy, but she did not want to spend her days spilling the blood of the captain's men.

"Is this understood?" the captain asked the men, glowering.

Scowls accompanied a few grudging affirmations, while others did not seem bothered at the captain's words. Rayden took note of the most disgruntled among the crew, knowing they would likely be the most problematic.

"That matter is resolved, then. Back to your duties, we have a sea to cross," the captain commanded.

Most of the crew began dispersing about the ship at once. The two lying injured on the deck remained, prompting the captain to bark out a few more orders to help them away. Beyond bruises and a few missing teeth, both would recover soon enough to return to their duties.

"May our passage go smooth and swift," the captain remarked in a lower voice, when they were alone. "I doubt any of my men will cross you, even the most thick-headed among them, but there are many other dangers on the open sea. I will not lower my guard until this ship is quayside."

Rayden could not have agreed with him more. Yet one question remained. "Where is this vessel headed?"

Her question evoked a short chuckle from the captain. He looked bemused, replying, "You must have been in a hurry to leave Kartajen."

"I did not have much of a choice," Rayden said.

"We are going to the port of Iellia," the captain told her. "With the shadow of Tevere creeping so close to them, I get a much greater price for the cargo I bring there. There is nothing to worry about. The Kartajenians keep a strong force of ships there."

The news dismissed her worries of being taken to the eastern edge of the sea. Iellia would put her and the boy farther south than she would have preferred, but it still kept them on the path to the northern lands she sought.

"Thank you captain," Rayden said. "Until we are ashore in Iellia, you have my blades if needed and our labor."

"Let us both hope that only your labor is necessary aboard this ship," the captain said with a grim edge.

"We are in full agreement," Rayden replied.

"An agreeable crew member is a welcome one aboard the ship of Medar," he said, offering a smile and extending his arm.

She clasped his forearm. "Then know that Rayden of the Gessa will stand with you, to the end of this journey."

CHAPTER 6

The next couple of days saw Rayden acclimating to a routine aboard the ship. The boy kept close to her at all times, showing no desire to stray too far.

Several men of the crew eyed her with lust, but none proved foolish enough to act on their feelings. Nor did any of them intrigue her in return.

Even if one of them had drawn her attention, she had set herself to avoid dalliances of a physical nature. The quickest way to sow discord in tight quarters would be to spark envy in favoring one of the crew.

A few of the men showed Rayden the main duties involved in tending to the sail and rigging. She also spent a little time with the pilot who operated the vessel's large steering oar, learning something of its function.

She passed along the things that she knew Hamilcar could handle, so he could do his part for the crew and have something to help pass the time. Being given a set of responsibilities evoked greater confidence in the boy. He took to his tasks with vigor and resolve, displaying a dedicated work ethic that gradually won him some good will from others in the crew.

By the end of the second day, Rayden and the boy found themselves invited to join some of the men for their meals. When she and the boy listened to their tales at night, they were included in the conversations and bawdy jests that ensued.

Even one of those she had fought with displayed a congenial manner, though his face remained bruised and swollen from their encounter. The comrade of his that had lost some teeth to Rayden's fist still glowered at her and kept to himself.

While not lowering her guard, she could not see any significant problems manifesting from the crew for the remaining part of the journey. Other dangers lurked in the depths of the sea, the weather, and in other vessels plying the ocean surface, but she welcomed the relative peace aboard ship.

At last she took leave of the others, taking the boy with her to the far side of the ship. Quiet and set apart from where most of the other crew members slept the night away, the place afforded her a chance to get some rest herself.

With the blessing of calm, clear skies, night brought a soothing atmosphere that made it easy to relax. With the boy soon lying fast asleep nearby, Rayden could allow herself a few moments to savor drifting off into slumber under a canopy of stars.

Pulling a cloak snug to warm her body, she let her cares dissipate. The caress of ocean breezes and flow of the ship over rolling waves lulled her ever deeper into a state of relaxation. Her eyelids growing heavy, the creaking of ropes and flapping of the sail serenaded her as she finally slipped into the embrace of dreams.

***

Morning brought death under clear blue skies. Under the newly-risen sun, a flash of movement, followed by a scream that sent ice through her veins, caught Rayden's eyes as she worked at a rope in the main sail's rigging.

Abandoning the rope she looked around just in time to

witness some manner of winged shape splashing down into the waves on the other side of the vessel. Every sense within her snapped to full alertness, her weapons in hand a moment later.

The thing did not enter the water alone. Ensnared in its clutches, the man who had cried out plunged beneath the waves and disappeared.

Seconds later, another similar ambush occurred just behind her. Her ears rang with the wretched cry of the second victim, the shriek cut off by the water sealing his doom.

Shouts filled with terror erupted on the deck as she gripped her blade and axe. Lowering down into a crouch, she looked for the boy, who she had last seen helping some of the crew at the opposite end of the ship.

Anxiety seized her, as the boy could not be seen in any direction she looked. Facing an unknown threat, she had little time to think with events unfolding rapidly all across the stricken vessel.

She watched one of the men running across the deck and finally gained a look at one of the assailants, if only for a few heartbeats. Larger than a man and winged, the creature moved at great speed through the air.

Multiple pairs of legs extended from underneath, the two in front ending in pincers that the creature used to snare the hapless man. The momentum carried both predator and prey out of sight. Rayden heard the man's desperate cry cut off as the creature bore him down into the sea.

The whirring from fast-beating wings brought Rayden's attention around in a rush. The clatter of several legs on wood accompanied the creature alighting on the decking.

Her eyes widened, staring at the gaping jaws of the monster containing more than one row of sharp, inward-curving teeth. The deadly maw beckoned to her with a promise of a grisly death.

The creature's small, black eyes were set just back from its jaws. Its segmented body ended in a broad tail fin, similar to that of a lobster.

Getting its balance, the creature lurched forward and scurried at her, extending its large front pincers. She deflected one of the pincers with her blade, darting to the side as the creature reached her.

The clacking of metal on the creature's outer surface gave her immediate appreciation for its natural armor. Strikes along most of its bodily surface would prove fruitless, making her desperate task even more daunting.

A predator of the ocean, its body found no hindrance from water on the deck. Moving fast, it whipped about and snapped a pincer in the space where Rayden stood just an instant before she tucked and rolled along the length of its body.

Her action confused the beast for a moment and it paused, giving her the moment she needed as she gained her feet and spun around. Rushing up behind the beast, she dived between its legs and hoped its underside proved to be more vulnerable.

Driving her blade upward, gore spattered her face and body as the metal drove deep into the monster's underside. The creature shuddered and stumbled, before collapsing to the deck with Rayden beneath it. Thankfully, its body, formed to fly and glide through water, proved far lighter than she expected.

Though not crushed underneath, Rayden still found herself pinned to the deck. She gagged, enveloped in the terrible stench wafting from the opened innards of the beast.

Straining and heaving, she tipped the body of the creature over to the side, pushing it off of her. Breathing heavily, she got to her feet at once and took assessment of the ongoing fracas. To her chagrin, she still did not see the boy.

Close to her, one of the beasts had trapped someone from the crew against the side of the ship. Whoever the person was loosed a shrill yell as the creature grabbed the individual with its right pincer.

Rayden took a deep breath and leaped forward, using the same method she had used to kill the other creature moments before. The beast never saw her coming, freezing in place as iron burrowed through its underbelly.

Coated in gore and smothered by a carcass once more, Rayden spit and gritted her teeth, heaving with all her strength to get the body off her. Rolling over, she pushed herself to her knees and got back up to her feet.

A few paces away, freed from the pincer, stood the man she had just saved. To her surprise, she found that he was the very one she had kicked in the groin, upon making her first introductions to the captain and crew.

"Be thankful I am with you," she told the rattled-looking man. He nodded back to her, glancing back and forth between the dead corpse of the beast and Rayden, looking to be in disbelief at the intervention.

Rayden had no time to await his response. Another emergency loomed a short distance away, where another of the creatures had ensnared the captain himself.

Medar's face a mask of agony, he struggled in the unforgiving grasp of the monster, to no avail. The creature lumbered toward the side of the vessel, only a few steps away from taking the captain into the watery depths.

Rayden lunged forward, springing across the deck and closing the gap between her and the monster swiftly. With no time to get behind it, she hurled herself toward the creature from its right side.

Eyeing the pincer grasping the helpless ship captain, she reared back with her axe. With all the power she could muster, Rayden brought her axe blade down at the base of the pincer, finding a narrow gap in its armor that exposed a vulnerable joint.

Sharp iron passing through cleanly, she severed the limb.

Without pausing, she straightened up and drove the tip of her sword into the fleshy black eye of the beast.

Putting her weight behind the blade and pushing forward with her legs, she shoved the weapon as far into its body as she possibly could. The honed iron barreled deeper, invading the monster's flesh.

Its movements came to a halt and a moment later it collapsed heavily on the decking. Gulping breaths of air, Rayden braced a foot on the creature's body and yanked her weapon free.

Turning, she went to the aid of Medar. While in considerable pain, life remained in him and did not look to be fading. To her eyes, he had not suffered any major injuries.

With a grunt of exertion she pried the pincer wide enough apart to free him. He flopped onto the deck, wincing and clutching the area where the thing had grabbed him.

"I said I would earn my keep," Rayden addressed the shaken-looking man.

She peered around, finding to her continued dismay that no sign of the boy could be found. At least the attack appeared to be over.

No other creatures could be seen and the men of the crew were regrouping. Weapons in hand, several had taken up positions at the sides of the ship and eyed the waves with great wariness.

"You...more than have," Medar replied, gritting his teeth and groaning from the pain. He continued, "I will be fine. I think some broken ribs. That is all. It did not break the skin."

"What ... were those ... things?" Rayden asked, looking about for the boy as she spoke with the captain.

"Makresia. Rarely encountered," Medar replied.

"Just our good luck," Rayden lamented. "Will these things come back?"

The captain shook his head. "Not likely. They strike and

move on. They do not stalk. They rove the sea."

"A fortunate thing," Rayden said, her breathing leveling out at a normal pace.

A high-pitched scream pierced the air. The men gathered near the entrance of the cargo hold scattered apart as Hamilcar burst into the open, followed close behind by one of the creatures.

Rayden's worst fears loomed nigh. The cries of the men who had been taken overboard echoed throughout her mind.

"To me!" she cried out to the boy, charging across the deck. "Run to me!"

Hearing her, the boy shifted course and ran straight toward Rayden. The creature altered direction and followed close behind, bearing down fast on its intended prey with a loud clattering.

Rayden ran past the boy and leaped upward. Soaring over the beast's maw, she landed behind its eyes, legs straddling the sides of the thing. Twisting to the left, she shifted her grip on her sword, orienting the blade straight downward.

She plunged the sword into an eye, the iron striking true and killing it instantly. The body of the creature thudded to the deck. Working her blade free, she slid off the side of the Makresia.

Hearing the pounding of footsteps, she turned to see the boy running over to her. A moment later, she found herself embraced by Hamilcar.

He hugged her tight, heaving with great sobs. Sliding an arm around him, she held him close. Tears flowed down his cheeks.

Around her, the men of the crew set about ridding the deck of the carcasses. Working together, they threw the remains of the dead creatures overboard, though many places remained slick from the gore left behind.

She remained in place as long as the boy needed, a mournful silence pervading a crew that had just lost several of its own.

"Thank you, Rayden," Medar said in a low voice, placing a

hand on her shoulder. He gave her a gentle pat and walked away.

"I owe you my life," another voice said, belonging to the man she had fought with the first day and saved on this one. "I wronged you once and for that I am sorry. I deserved what you did to me ... and more. Though it may mean nothing to you, you have my loyalty."

She looked into his face for a moment, seeing a different look in his eyes. She nodded to him. "I accept your apology. That requires its own kind of strength. We all grow in this world. Some for better and some for the worse. It is good to see you choose to grow for the better. Stay on that path and we shall never have conflict between us again."

"I would like that," he said, nodding to her before turning and walking away.

Others among the crew approached and spoke with her while she stood with Hamilcar. Like the captain, they offered their gratitude for what she had done to defend their lives against a deadly ocean peril.

That night the mood aboard the ship remained subdued and sorrowful. Rayden and Hamilcar ate a ration of bread and dates in silence by themselves.

When the time came to sleep, she took the boy down into the cargo hold for the night, taking an added precaution. Numerous breaths in the darkness told her that other members of the crew shared her wariness.

Slipping the bonds of consciousness came easily enough afterwards, fatigue of both physical and emotional kinds weighing down upon her. Consoled that the boy remained alive and unharmed, she drifted off into a dreamless slumber.

***

Taking assessment of their losses, it had been found that six men of the crew had fallen to the winged sea predators. The impact of the attack proved enough to require Rayden and the boy to help as best they could with every task involved with sailing the vessel.

A constant vigil maintained both night and day, the crew looked out for any sign of the Makresia. The levity that had been present before the attack vanished, a solemn atmosphere taking hold over the ship. The nerves of the men remained on edge and they spoke in low tones amongst each other.

Rayden knew the ship could ill-afford another such attack. Other monsters dwelled in the oceans and the specter of pirates loomed over any sea journey.

The only comfort came in the news that only one more day remained in the voyage. The sea journey could not end soon enough for Rayden. She hungered to feel solid land beneath her feet, having had quite enough of the seas for a long time to come.

When the time came for sleep that evening, she took the boy into the hold again. Shunning the open skies and continuing to maintain extra caution, they only had to survive until the next afternoon.

The following night they would enjoy a proper night's sleep in an inn, after consuming a bountiful meal. The pleasant thought helped to make enduring a sweat-filled night lying in a musty cargo hold a little easier to bear.

***

The large port city of Iellia drew into sight on the horizon about midday, instantly buoying the spirits of Rayden, Hamilcar, and all the crew. Seeing the end of the journey approaching and land before her eyes, a wave of relief flooded Rayden.

The threats of pirates and sea creatures alike would be coming to an end long before sunset. In truth, only the latter danger remained. No pirates of any sense would risk coming so close to a port harboring a large force of Kartajenian war galleys.

Rayden rested her hands on the top strake of the vessel,

watching the city grow larger as the winds pushed them steadily closer. A number of thoughts passed through her mind, a new set of circumstances looming near.

She knew that she would not be able to let down her guard when they went ashore. As in Kartajen, larger cities contained their own array of dangers and were no place for an inexperienced boy to wander about. She intended to keep Hamilcar close to her side until they reached open countryside and were heading north.

After a finding a good night's rest in a suitable inn, Rayden planned to start for the north and the tribal lands as soon as possible. The longer they tarried in Iellia, the more trouble they courted.

An attractive woman like Rayden lingering around an inn eventually brought the worst elements of humanity slithering from the shadows. Seeking no commotion, it would be best to pass through before she left an abundance of broken bones and blood in her wake.

All around her, the crew began yelling and pointing out toward the sea on the starboard side. Rayden turned away from her view of the city to see what had suddenly agitated them.

With grim observation, she took in the distinctive line of shapes breaking the horizon. She knew what they were, and her mind braced against the unwelcome surprise and everything it portended.

War galleys rode the waves in an oncoming multitude. They approached in a formation that told her at once they were not Kartajenian.

The vessels had bulkier appearances than the typical Kartajenian war galley. The larger, heavier ships reflected the sea fighting doctrine of the Teverens operating them, shedding a little maneuverability in exchange for sheer power.

The sight of a large Teveren fleet approaching Iellia presented a threat she had not anticipated. With calm scrutiny, she watched the galleys' progress and gauged their speed.

The enemy ships advanced on the port city at a steady pace, though the vessel carrying Rayden would reach the city long before being engulfed by the incoming fleet. That realization stood as the only consolation to be found in the face of the terrible development.

The decks of the enemy galleys bristled with warriors armed and prepared for battle. Wooden turrets had been erected at the bow and stern of the galleys, holding archers and slingers. The Teverens sought to take the clash of a land battle to the water, rather than focus upon ramming the vulnerable sides of an enemy vessel, in the manner of the Kartajenian's main naval tactic.

Rayden gazed all around the port, but saw no movement on the water. To her astonishment, no sign of a Kartajenian naval response could be found anywhere she looked. Heart sinking, she realized nothing stood between the Teveren fleet and the port.

Medar's crew worked with urgency to bring the merchant vessel into the port the rest of the way, maneuvering it over to the side of a long quay. An official from Iellia, accompanied by several nervous-looking guards, stood waiting to meet them when the ship drew to a halt.

"Captain, we saw your approach from afar," the official stated. "Your timing is unlucky. The Teverens assault the city at last, an attack we have long feared would come. Any of your men who would take up arms in its defense may stand with us."

"What is the meaning of this? A Teveren fleet approaching the harbor with nothing to challenge it?" asked Medar in a loud voice, looking and sounding incredulous. "Where are the warships of Kartajen? You shelter an entire fleet in this port!"

"Our fleet departed a day ago in pursuit of another group of Teveren vessels," the official replied, his face grim.

"Leaving the city unprotected?" erupted Medar, eyes

widening. "Your strongest defense sent out?"

Rayden saw the enemy strategy at once. The first group's diversion had cleared the port for an entire Teveren war fleet.

On its landward side, the port city had tall, thick walls to shield it. Without a fleet of war galleys to protect it, the city's seaward front presented a soft underbelly, vulnerable to a concerted enemy assault.

"There is no time to argue about what should have been done," the official countered in a hard tone. "We are being attacked now. Those who will stand can go with the guards to take up what they can find in the garrison's arsenal. I do not have to tell your men what will happen to this city should it fall to the Teverens."

"It might be well to flee it," the captain retorted. "That fleet will land here soon."

"Two Teveren legions are assembled outside the city walls," the official informed him. "There is nowhere to flee. We must defend the city."

Murmurs and curses broke out from the men on the vessel. Rayden kept silent, though the situation appeared to be turning increasingly dire, with every passing moment.

"So we are trapped? An entire fleet at your back and a pair of legions at your front!" shouted Medar, his words rife with exasperation. "What fools you were to let your fleet stray! How could you be so stupid?"

"Yelling will do no good. I have told you, your men who will fight can take whatever they require from our arsenal," the official replied. "Captain, there is no time to argue. We must defend the city or do nothing and allow it to be sacked, with everything that will come in the wake of the city's fall. You choose."

Rayden and the men of the crew needed no reminder of the attack's imminence. One glance showed the Teveren fleet drawing perilously close.

Even if Medar wished to try and escape the harbor, he could not. A war vessel with its multiple banks of oars and rowers could easily overtake a single-sail merchant vessel.

Several of Medar's crew agreed to join in the defense of Iellia at once. Taking up their own weapons, they gathered with the guards on the quay and waited to be led to the city's arsenal.

Rayden made her way over to the captain. Fuming at the side of his ship, he watched his crew disembarking while glancing back periodically to mark the progress of the incoming enemy fleet.

"You are a man who honors his word, Medar," she told him in a low, firm tone. "You have my gratitude ... and my respect."

"We escaped death on the open sea, only to find it again this soon," the captain replied with a sad look in his eyes. "I would rather we face those sea beasts again than be trapped in a Teveren siege. Will you stand in the city's defense?"

"I will cut any Teveren down in my path, but my oath is to ward this boy," Rayden said. "I must do what I can to see him to safety."

Medar nodded, looking at her for a moment before replying. "I understand. May good fortune walk with you always, Rayden Valkyrie. May death never have you in its clutches. It has been my honor to know you."

"May you slip death's grasp to see an abundance of better days ahead," Rayden told the captain, every word she said to him heartfelt. They grasped each other's forearms and looked one another in the eyes. "Goodbye, Medar. I hope our paths cross again."

"As do I," the captain responded, though the resigned tone of his voice told her that he did not think the possibility likely.

Releasing his arm, Rayden turned and ordered Hamilcar to follow her. Time had grown short and they needed to get away from the water.

As they started to walk away, the captain's voice called out to her. "Rayden!"

Turning, she raised her hand to catch the small brown object that Medar tossed to her. She heard metallic clinks as the pouch she had given the captain at the beginning of the sea journey hit her palm. She closed her fingers about the leather container.

"Take that with you," Medar said. "You more than earned your passage, and I believe you will find a way free of here. Maybe that will be of help to you."

She stared at the captain for a moment, moved by the gesture. "Thank you."

"May the gods protect you, Rayden Valkyrie," Medar said. "Now go, I have delayed you long enough."

Rayden nodded to him once more, before turning and gesturing for Hamilcar to come with her. At a brisk pace, they walked off the ship together, heading from the quay into a city huddling in the shadow of an impending attack.

Finding an inn out of the question, Rayden determined to get the boy away from the city as soon as possible. The Teverens had come with the strength to take the city and when it fell the streets would flow with blood.

CHAPTER 7

The problem of slipping past two entire legions loomed before her. Before she could envision any kind of plan, she needed to see the enemy positions with her own eyes. All armor had gaps to be found and exploited, if one looked for the openings.

Walking away from the harbor, she eyed the city with care. Numerous buildings within it, like those in Kartajen, soared to considerable heights, many reaching six stories of elevation. Not far from the city's outer walls, several such edifices rose. She knew where she had to go.

Rayden hurried down the street in the direction of the structures. She brushed past many frightened men and women running along the streets. Casting brief glances over her shoulder, she saw Hamilcar following close behind, keeping pace.

Panic and fear permeated the streets of Iellia. The expressions of the men and women Rayden passed testified that they were well aware of the terrible price a city's inhabitants paid when an enemy sacked it.

Fathers carried the horror of what would be done to wives and daughters, while children faced the specter of becoming orphaned before the sun set. Women harbored fears of having had the last sights of husbands, lovers or sons, among the men who had gone to defend the city. Grisly nightmares loomed before thousands upon thousands and hope faded swiftly within desperate hearts.

If the walls fell, a demonic orgy of lust and violence would sweep through the port city. Rayden could not assume the city would last even a day, not with the harbor undefended and an enemy fleet coming in. She had to get the boy out of Iellia and away from the enemy, before Teveren's warriors roved the streets with impunity and a spirit of cruel avarice.

The hike to the tenements took some time, especially with the feverish mood prevailing in the streets. On a few occasions she saw throngs of men carrying an array of various weapons rushing in the other direction, presumably to defend the harbor area.

Finally, she reached the cluster of high tenements that she had eyed. She continued until she reached the last of them, before heading inside the edifice and beginning the long ascent up several flights of wooden steps to the top.

Striding out onto the roof in terse silence, Rayden peered outward. The view meeting her eyes proved both clear and daunting.

Beyond the city's walls a great Teveren force had drawn up in orderly, rectangular formations, the sun glittering off the golden ornamentation crowning their standards. Numerous devices fitted with horizontal bows for the hurling of stones had been arrayed along the forefront of the massed warriors.

Several towers whose height surpassed the city walls stood idle for the moment. Rayden knew it would not be long before the towers rolled forward, filled with soldiers intent on storming the walls of Iellia.

Looking back in the other direction, Rayden espied the tops of the enemy ships' masts perched at the edge of the city. With the attack poised to fall upon the shoreline behind, she expected the assault from the front to be imminent.

Not long passed before the braying of horns signaled the beginning of a broad assault. A storm of arrows accompanied with a heavy stone bombardment preceded the advance of the towers.

The defenders on the walls did everything they could, including sending concentrated flights of fire arrows, but the hide covered towers failed to take flame and kept rolling forward. Stone throwing machines from the tops of towers along the wall managed to heavily damage a couple of the approaching siege towers, enough to take them out of the assault. The downed towers proved a minor wound, the attackers having constructed a great many of them and absorbing the losses with no significant impediment to their assault.

Smoke had begun to billow in many places near the harbor area, telling Rayden that the attackers were driving into the city itself. Down below, few people ran the streets. Those who were part of the city's defense had already reached the walls or harbor, and most others hunkered down within their homes.

No sense in denying the bitter truth, Rayden knew all of the city's inhabitants were trapped, including her and Hamilcar. She watched the fighting raging around the city walls, bracing for the inevitable conclusion.

The siege towers rolled onward, nearing the walls. Clouds of arrows soared from Teveren's ranks to fall upon the wall's defenders, while a long structure with a steep-pitched, hide-covered roof lumbered closer to the gateway. When the latter reached the city's main entrance, loud, rhythmic booms echoed as the head of the sheltered battering ram began striking the gates.

At last, a few of the towers reached the walls. The facings of their top sections opened and lowered using pulleys. Wooden platforms slammed down onto stone, followed by rushes of Teveren soldiers. Booms continued to thunder in the background and flocks of arrows arced toward the walls.

"They ... they are going to break through," Hamilcar stated at her side, his face filled with fear.

"Yes, they are. And soon," Rayden said, watching the Teveren soldiers spreading along the top of the walls from the siege towers that they had crossed from. The dark shapes of defenders being hurled from the walls told her enough about the course of the battle.

"How are we going to get out of here?" the boy asked.

"By keeping our focus during chaos," Rayden answered. "If we let our minds become frozen in fear, we will die."

"But ... to get through that?" the boy asked, pointing toward the several thousand soldiers on the ground poising to enter the city.

"They will not be so orderly when they storm Iellia," Rayden said. She looked over to Hamilcar and fixed a hard-eyed gaze upon him. "You have to heed my every word, without hesitation, without question."

"I will. I promise," the boy responded, nodding fast to her.

The booms of the great ram resonated across Iellia, and several more siege engines anchored to the walls up and down its long front. The rising columns of smoke behind had grown in number, with several rising much nearer than before.

At long last, the booms ceased. Horns erupted in a sonorous frenzy, filling the air with their proud call, followed by a swelling roar from the massed ranks of the legions. A dark tide with deadly intentions surged forward, funneling toward the gate of Iellia like the blade of a great spear.

Terror poured into the doomed city. Given leave to become savage beasts, Tevere's soldiers fell upon Iellia's inhabitants with a merciless fury.

Rayden's heart ached hearing the first of the screams and cries cutting the night air from the streets nearby. Not long after, the glow of new fires began appearing all across the city, a vision of hell sprouting right before her eyes.

"How are we going to escape this?" the boy asked again, sounding on the verge of panic.

She glanced toward Hamilcar. Looking out over the spreading chaos, his wide eyes reflected raw horror.

Not far from the building, a woman's desperate cries to her god turned into grating screams. Stomach-churning whoops of glee and laughter mixed with her frantic shrieks.

Turning her face away from the boy, she closed her eyes, wishing she could defend the poor woman. "We will find a way. Just do as I say. A path will be found through the chaos."

Instead of feeling trapped atop the building, Rayden judged it better to let the marauding Teverens disperse all throughout the city. Their expectations were a defenseless populace they could plunder, brutalize and, often in the cases of the city's younger women, indulge in their lusts. The invaders did not anticipate meeting a tempest of fury armed with sword and axe.

Rayden had to summon more willpower to temper the rage building inside her, hearing a growing number of female cries and screams. Dense throngs of Teveren troops moved through the streets immediately below her vantage, resembling serpents hunting trapped rats as they slithered about the buildings.

The cohesion began to break apart as the invaders began entering the lofty structures. The spread of chaos accelerating rapidly, Rayden knew chances to make a move toward escape would manifest soon.

She drew out her weapons, knowing they would be put to heavy use whether she got free of the city or not. The Teveren solders would not be making sport of her, nor would the chains of slavery be placed upon her.

A frantic scuffling brought Rayden whirling about. A young girl clambered onto the roof behind her. Thinking quickly, Rayden slipped her hands behind her body, concealing her weapons.

The girl scrambled up to her feet, almost tripping in her haste, followed a moment later by three Teveren soldiers. Her clothing torn, she gave a start when her eyes fell upon Rayden, silhouetted by the moon and red glow from the spreading fires far below.

"To me, girl," Rayden said in a firm, commanding tone. "Now! Behind me!"

The girl stumbled, hurrying in a state of panic to reach her unexpected benefactor. She fell to her knees when she reached Rayden, clutching tight onto her right leg.

"Two means plenty for all of us," one of the Teverens said, eyeing Rayden.

"This one doesn't run," added another. "Better lookin' too. I like this."

"I have no interest in boys though," the third said with a husky chuckle, taking notice of Hamilcar.

"He can be discarded," said the first, laughing. "Toss him over the side."

Rayden eyed them with cold intent, her axe and blade held at the ready behind her back. She wore no armor and carried no shield. For all the Teveren's knew, she was just another woman from the city, cornered and vulnerable to their whims.

The young girl kept her iron grip upon Rayden's legs. Sobbing and shutting her eyes tight, her fingers dug into Rayden's flesh.

"Let go of me girl, I need to move," Rayden said evenly, keeping her eyes on the soldiers.

"Yes, you do need to move ... into any position I desire," the first Teveren said, misunderstanding her intent as he laughed.

"To the victor, the spoils of war!" shouted the second in a boisterous air.

The girl did not let go of Rayden. "See to her, Hamilcar," Rayden told the boy, keeping her focus centered on the Teverens. "Do it now."

His body shaking, Hamilcar followed her directive and edged over to the girl. Gingerly at first, he reached out and pried her off Rayden, freeing the warrior's legs. He pulled the girl away with him, keeping behind Rayden.

The Teverens stepped closer, now only a few paces from her. Giddy looks in their eyes, the soldiers grinned, looking to be thoroughly enjoying the air of defiance she displayed.

"You are a bold one, I like that," the lead Teveren said, grinning wide.

"Got some spirit, this is going to be much more fun," his second comrade remarked.

They took a couple of steps forward.

"Won't do you no good to fight us," the first Teveren said. He clenched his hands into fists and opened them again. His eyes gleamed with a bestial sheen. "Will make it worse for you. Best to cooperate. Do that and you'll live."

Hearing the continued sobs of the girl just behind her, Rayden flashed the three men a smile. "Are you so sure of that? Wouldn't you like more of a challenge?"

"Feisty," commented the lead Teveren, his gaze brimming with lascivious intent. Spreading his legs, he reached down and fondled himself in a lewd manner, staring toward Rayden. "You are going to be a good one. I think I like you."

"Are you sure?" she asked him in a silken tone.

His eyes snapped wide an instant later, seeing Rayden spring toward him. Her right hand flashed by his head, holding a sword. He never saw her left hand coming or what it held.

Her sword blade barreled into the mouth of the second Teveren, the iron tip driving through the back of the man's head. Eyes filled with shock, the soldier gurgled and slumped down, blood streaming out of his mouth and down the blade impaling him.

The upward arc of her axe rushed into the area that the first Teveren had been fondling just a moment before. The haughty look on the man's face transformed instantly, becoming a mask of delirious agony.

She yanked the lodged axe backward with great force. Blood gushed from the mutilated remains of his manhood, spilling onto the roof. Somehow, in his momentary shock, he remained standing.

Rayden withheld the battle cry she wished to loose, not wanting to attract others of his ilk to the roof. With cat-like quickness she jerked her sword free from the mouth of the second man.

Slashing across the exposed throat of the Teveren before her, she finished him off, sending a spray of blood into the air. At last, he fell over face-first, hitting the surface hard.

The last Teveren fumbled clumsily for his weapon, but Rayden fell upon him before he could draw it free. When he toppled to the ground, joining his comrades in the maw of death, he bled from three mortal wounds.

Beyond the fallen Teveren, another person had just emerged onto the roof. Rayden lifted her weapons and stopped right on the verge of striking out. A woman of about middle-years, her face exhibiting signs of a severe beating, looked upon the scene in stunned silence.

"Mother!"

Rayden turned aside as the young girl she had protected rushed past her, throwing her arms around the older woman. The two hugged each other tightly, tears falling in abundance.

"Come, Hamilcar," Rayden said in a low voice to the boy.

She stepped carefully around the reunited mother and daughter and descended into the building. She heard Hamilcar following behind a moment later.

Before she had reached the bottom, six more Teveren soldiers saw their night of violence and debauchery come to a bloody end. Catching one Teveren in the act of violating a woman even older than the girl's mother, Rayden removed his head in one furious blow.

Rayden and Hamilcar stayed in the building until late in the night. A few occupants of the tenement, spared further terrors, thanked her and invoked the blessings and protection of gods on her behalf.

Rayden felt no joy, listening to the continued shrieks and cries filling the night outside. She took up a position near the door leading into the street.

Two more times during the night, Teveren soldiers entered the tenement, a pair of them on the first instance and three on the second. All five met their doom in swift fashion, unprepared for the blonde hellion ambushing them from the shadows. After the bloodletting, the people of the tenement pulled the dead bodies out of sight at Rayden's behest.

Talking to some of the building's occupants, Rayden told them they would need to get away from the tenement when daylight came. The worst urges of the invaders would be sated by then and they would be tired, but discovering many dead comrades would invite terrible retribution upon everyone in the building. Rayden did not wish to spare the people living in the tenement from the night's horrors just to see them become victims of Teveren brutality in the day.

The people assured her they would go elsewhere at dawn, the discussion interrupted when a Teveren soldier showing no effort at caution lumbered into the building. His face still held a surprised expression when he fell dead to the ground a moment later. Without a word from Rayden, the people she had been speaking with dragged the body away.

A few lengths of rope were gathered at Rayden's request, given to her with further expressions of gratitude for her intervention. The night growing old, she set about tying knots securing the lengths together.

Hamilcar sat by her side, quietly watching her work. The cacophony outside ebbed, the streets growing quiet with the approach of morning. Anything but peaceful, the atmosphere held a heavy, sorrowful air.

Carrying the coiled rope over one shoulder, she took the boy with her when the break of dawn loomed. She knew the gates would be heavily guarded, but much of the Teveren force in the city would be lethargic or fast asleep from a night of inflicting terror and slaking all manner of perversions.

Fires still burned all over the city, casting an eerie mix of light and shadows throughout the streets. Rayden kept to dark spaces as best she could, evading Teveren soldiers wherever possible.

Only once did she come across a pair of Teverens squarely in her way. They never saw her coming up from behind, both lying dead in growing pools of their own blood a few heartbeats later.

Keeping a low profile and instructing the boy to mirror her, she crept up a flight of steps to the wall walk at a point far down from the city gates. With the city taken, she doubted that she would find any Teverens that far along the wall and her hunch proved accurate.

With the sun rising in the east, the facing of the wall would remain cloaked in shadow for a while longer, providing a welcome boon if they needed to wait. Carefully, she peered beyond the rampart and did not see any sign of the enemy close by. To her eyes, they could proceed on course, without any delay.

Finding a place to secure one end of the rope, she lowered the other over the wall. Knowing fast movements to have a greater likelihood of attracting attention, she let its length reach the ground in a slow, controlled fashion. When finished, she tugged hard on the rope, measuring its tautness.

"Ever climbed a rope?" she asked the boy in a whisper.

The boy nodded.

"Good, then keep a firm grip on your descent and use your legs as you go," she told him. "I will go first. Follow me and go slow, with control. No fast movements."

Rayden made her way down the rope. Reaching the ground, she stood to the side of it, looking out for any enemy threats while the boy followed after her. Taking much longer than her in descending, Hamilcar finally made it to the bottom.

"Let's go now, while darkness cloaks us," Rayden said, leading the boy away from the wall and across open ground under the last shred of night.

CHAPTER 8

With Iellia fallen and much of the attacking force involved in the sacking of it, Rayden found it easier than she expected to work her way around the perimeter of the Teveren encampment. Sentries were easy enough to spot and avoid, their attention dulled in the aftermath of a huge victory.

Dawn unfurled, a bright sun rising in clear skies to the east. The radiance of the morning did not seem fitting, following a night brimming with blood and fire.

Far behind her, a forest of smoke columns spiraled from Iellia toward the upper skies. A desolate pall of silence hovered over the violated city.

Within her heart, Rayden mourned the fate of the hapless city occupants. An image of the ship captain Medras passed through her mind. She hoped against all odds that he and his men had survived the dreadful night, though the prospect stood unlikely.

Unable to afford any distractions, she pushed the rueful thoughts away, keeping her focus on the task of getting beyond the Teverens and into the open countryside. With the size of their camp, it would still require some luck for Rayden and Hamilcar to pass undetected. It only took one pair of eyes to catch a glimpse of them and sound an alarm.

In moments, she could find herself facing hundreds of Teverens, a force she could not overcome or escape from. Keeping low and moving carefully, she continued leading the boy around the outskirts of the camp.

After moving to another concealed position, her eyes fell upon a sight that inspired an idea to take root and grow. While daring, the notion offered a chance to get out of the camp before the Teverens could react in any significant fashion.

A number of horses milled about within a corral. All of them had saddles and were fitted with reins, spurring her thought process along. A few Teverens moved among the horses, preparing them for a coming ride.

Never would Rayden have claimed to be an adept horse rider, but she considered herself capable enough to mount and guide one. She weighed the decision of creeping past the rest of the camp or acting on the beckoning idea. With a deep breath, she made her choice.

"Stay here," Rayden told Hamilcar. "Keep low. Do not rise until I call for you."

He nodded and lay down flat in the high, swaying grasses. Satisfied that the boy would be well-concealed, she headed away from his position.

Making her way to the edge of the corral, she selected a steed for her purpose. With a nimble jump, she hurtled the barrier and set down lightly on the other side.

Speaking in soft tones, Rayden greeted the muscular brown stallion that she had chosen. Chiseled and tall, the horse had few, if any, matches within the corral.

She hoped the stallion's ability matched the creature's impressive appearance. A moment later, she sat astride its back, committed to her course of action.

Shouts and cries broke out everywhere as several camp servants and guards espied Rayden. Atop the horse, gripping onto its reins, she used her heels to spur the creature into motion.

A couple men in the corral made feeble attempts to grab at the reins of the horse, but she made it through the enclosure's opening and turned the horse sharply to the right. Bringing the stallion back around, she made for the place where the boy remained hidden in the grasses.

"Hamilcar, stand up now!" she called out.

The boy got to his feet, looking anxious. She adjusted her course, angling directly for him. Looking at her mounted on the horse, panic filled his face.

The outcry growing behind her, Teverens would soon be swarming over the area. Reaching down, she grabbed onto the boy and yanked him upward. Giving a little cry, he lifted off the ground and clutched onto Rayden about the waist, anchoring himself to the horse.

The horse neighed and Rayden braced herself, tightening her grasp on Hamilcar. She expected the creature to rear up, but to her relief it kept to its course, allowing her to finish helping the boy up behind her.

The horse picked up speed, racing at a full gallop as they bounded away from the camp and headed into the countryside. She could only hope the disposition of the Teverens after sacking a city would keep them from engaging in an overly strong pursuit.

Glancing over her shoulder, she noted four riders separating from the camp and heading in their direction. She pushed the horse harder, eyeing a broad line of trees in the distance.

The quartet of pursuers made no perceptible gain, unable to spur their mounts to any speed greater than her brawny stallion. She had chosen her mount well. A lengthy gap still remained between her and the Teverens when they neared the trees.

The horse showing signs of tiring, Rayden pulled up on the reins and slowed her mount down. At a walk they passed into the shadows of the woods.

Showing Hamilcar how to hold the reins, she slid down from the saddle. "Keep him walking forward. They will approach you, but don't worry. I shall be near," she told him. "You have to trust me."

Looking more than a little nervous, Hamilcar nodded to her. She gave him a firm pat on the leg before trotting off into the shadows. She did not go far, proceeding a little farther ahead of Hamilcar so that she could be in position for what came up from behind not long afterward.

Snorts, a neigh, and voluminous breaths heralded the approach of multiple horses. Remaining concealed at the base of a tree, she waited for the Teverens to close in on the bait she had set. She allowed Hamilcar to continue riding forward, harboring sympathy for the boy as she saw the raw fear in his countenance.

One of the pursuers passed right by her position, the slow clops of the horse's steps only a stride away from where she crouched with weapons in hand. The Teveren had not had time to don armor, but carried a spear in hand and had a blade resting in a sheath at his waist.

"Where is the woman? There were two!" one of the other Teverens exclaimed.

"Probably running through the woods," another answered. "Smarter than this boy."

"Don't move, young horse thief! Stay where you are, if you hope to live," the one nearest to Rayden said, addressing Hamilcar.

She could see the terror on the boy's face, but he had played his part to perfection. The Teverens, distracted, had no warning when she pounced.

One of the riders gasped, toppling from his mount with her axe deep in his back. Another, taking notice of the stricken man, did not get a single cry out from his mouth before blood gushed from his opened throat.

Rayden melted back into the shadows of the forest, blood

dripping from her blade. She crept over to the first Teveren she had downed and retrieved her axe. With lithe steps, she began circling around to come at the two remaining soldiers.

In the more confined space of the woods, neither one showed an interest in fighting or retaining the stallion. Eyes shifting toward every shadow and spears held at the ready, both turned their mounts about and began heading back the way they had come.

Neither man made it out of the forest alive. Rayden stalked them down in swift fashion, needing only one killing blow for each.

She made her way back to where the boy sat idle on the stallion. Two riderless horses meandered nearby, freed from duty for a time, though Rayden expected them to be recovered by the Teverens soon enough. A search party would be sent looking for the four men when they did not return to the camp in a reasonable time.

"None pursue us at the moment, but we need to leave this area," she told Hamilcar.

She took a few moments to have him dismount, allowing her to get back in the front position and take up the reins once more. When situated, she had him get back up behind her.

Guiding the horse back out of the woods, she made for the principle roadway that approached the port city. Consisting of hard-packed dirt cut through with wheel tracks in many places, the road held no signs of traffic.

Keeping her eyes out for any indication of movement, whether near or far, she traveled along the road in silence. The sun reached its zenith and then began its descent toward the western horizon. Coming across a narrow stream in the late afternoon, she diverted from the road long enough for the horse to get some water and graze for a short time.

Before they resumed, she and Hamilcar availed themselves

of the water, both for parched throats and washing the travel dust off their faces. The cool liquid cleansing her skin brought some welcome rejuvenation, and she paused to savor the kiss of a light breeze upon her face.

They rode for a while longer without incident. When the shadows lengthened and dusk's approach stood imminent, Rayden called for another halt.

"We go on foot from here," she announced to Hamilcar.

After helping the boy down from the saddle, she dismounted. Holding onto the horse's tether, she led the creature forward and watched the majestic sunset, the great reddish orb beginning its dip into the far horizon.

The horse ill-suited for the wilds, Rayden did not wish to abandon the animal to what would likely be a terrible fate. The hardy stallion had carried them to safety and exerted to the limit. While the creature had no particular loyalty to them, she wanted to give the dutiful animal an adequate chance to survive.

Taking the creature along with them, she looked for the earliest opportunity to leave the horse in a safer environment, rather than turning it loose in open wilderness. With the sunlight a fading glow lining the distance, she finally espied some open farmland set a modest distance from the road.

Leaving the road, she made for a small cluster of buildings set upon the cultivated land. Twilight draped across the land, the moon ascendant in a star-adorned, cloudless sky.

Under the cloak of darkness, she led the horse to a tree in plain view of the main residence building. Using the tether, she secured the horse to the tree, speaking soothing words to the animal. When morning arrived, the creature would be discovered.

With the horse taken care of, she returned to the road and set out for the north under the moonlight. Walking through the entire night, they sought shelter just after daybreak, using fallen branches and the area's foliage to create a place of concealment and shelter from both sun and rain.

Traveling by night and sheltering at day, the pair made their way steadily toward the north and west. Rayden fed herself and the boy with what she could find in the way of roots and berries, along with some fish caught in a stream during one of their halts, using a crude trap she fashioned from thin branches and reeds.

Having crossed into Teveren lands and heading ever deeper into them, Rayden maintained great caution. She knew how the Teverens felt about the 'barbarians' of the north, as the tribal people were called in the empire's lands.

She skirted great villas, the homesteads and estates of powerful Teverens, as well as a number of other smaller farms and landholdings. At last, they came across a rivertown, sprawled along the banks of a broad, silvery channel flowing with a steady current.

A rivertown offered possibilities of news and other opportunities. After a short deliberation, Rayden decided to go into the town to see she could learn.

She calculated that foreigners appeared often enough on the river and that her appearance in the town would not stir too much of a reaction. With Hamilcar's Kartajenian origin, she opted to leave him behind. The Teverens would not take kindly to someone from lands they currently warred with, even if just a youth.

Rayden entered the town by stealth, keeping to the shadows until she heard northern accents coming from what looked to be a small tavern. Moving closer to the structure, she eyed the front entrance, hesitating to continue inside as there remained one thing that she still needed.

Finding a solitary drunkard proved to be an easy enough task as those leaving the place swayed and staggered. All it took from Rayden was a broad smile, a slow lick of her lips, and a beckoning gesture to lure one of the inebriated figures to the side of the tavern.

She almost felt pity for the small, balding man, who stumbled toward her with an eager grin on his face. He reeked of ale and sweat, breathing heavily.

Once they both stood in darkness, she leaped upon him in a way he had never expected. Wrapping him up in a constricting hold, she cut off his air and subdued his futile attempts to struggle. In moments, she rendered the man unconscious.

Easing him to the ground, she searched the man until she found a small pouch containing a few Teveren coins. Judging as best she could, she replaced the ones she took with the Kartajenian ones she carried in her pouch. As if compensating the man for the trouble she had subjected him to, she left him a couple of extra coins.

"You'll be fine, sleep it off, but please get a bath soon," she whispered, chuckling as she gave him a light pat on his bare head and then stood back up.

Walking around to the front of the building and entering the tavern, she felt many sets of eyes fall upon her. Perceiving the lascivious thoughts behind most of the ale-glazed looks, she kept at the ready to reward any foolish enough to grope her with a fist to the jaw.

Those eyeing her either did not fail to see the sword and axe suspended from her waist, or they were too drink-sodden to be overly aggressive. Much to her preference, none gave her any trouble as she took up a place in the corner of the dusky establishment.

Setting her back to the wall, she could keep an eye on everything happening within the small room while listening to nearby conversations. A few looks were cast her way from time to time, but for the most part the patrons turned back to the conversations they had been engaged in. Other than the middle-aged serving woman who procured a cup of bitter ale for her, Rayden did not interact with anyone.

Most of the tavern occupants appeared to be locals, mixed with a few from other lands using the river for trade or pilgrimage. Over the course of a few more cups of ale, she learned quite enough about the current state of affairs in Teveren lands.

The war with the Kartajenians was not the only conflict the Teverens were engaged in. A recent slave uprising had swept across Teveren lands just to the north. From what she could glean, the slaves had fared well so far, beating back a few contingents of imperial soldiers sent to subdue them.

The tavern patrons mocked the young men of wealth who had been commissioned to put down the slave rebellion. What had been intended to be an easy military achievement to fatten their credentials had instead become a source of tremendous embarrassment for the would-be aristocratic heroes.

Things had evidently gotten serious enough that veteran legions had been brought in to confront the uprising. A few men remarked that the slaves had recently suffered their first significant defeat in battle, but most had been able to escape destruction.

From what Rayden could glean, the battle site lay not far from the rivertown. More than one local expressed relief that the slaves had been stopped at the cusp of reaching their province.

The men bemoaned the state of the Boreus Way, the main road leading from the Imperial City to the north. They indicated it would be quite some time before they would seek to travel along it, but the specific reason for their reticence went unspoken.

Whatever caused their shunning of the road had to be something horrific. Rayden could sense their deep revulsion by their faces and voices.

Learning nothing more new and with the night getting late, Rayden decided the time had come to leave. She finished off the cup of ale in her hands and set it down. Getting up, she walked through the room and exited.

A pair of men from the tavern decided to follow her outside, undoubtedly with ill-intent. Hearing their footsteps closing rapidly behind her, she grinned to herself and shook her head. So little surprised her anymore.

Both ended up unconscious, but unlike the man she had lured to the side of the building they ended up much the worse for wear. Broken noses, missing teeth, and a broken arm on one of the pair would serve as rude awakenings when they opened their swollen eyes, sometime the next day.

The brief, violent interlude restored some vigor to Rayden at the late hour, aiding her long trek back to where she had left Hamilcar for the night. She had gained what she needed from the excursion. She knew where they had to go next, even if the direction involved would be laden with risks.

After letting the boy know that she had returned, she settled down in the shelter they had prepared. Before allowing herself to nod off to sleep, she informed Hamilcar that she intended to head out in the morning, changing their pattern of travel from night to day. Despite all the thoughts swirling through her mind, she managed to drift into a deep sleep, gaining an extended, sorely-needed rest before sunrise.

***

A land abounding with chaos lay to the north and east. Walking through a land riddled with strife and war, Rayden expected an atmosphere of tension and hostility.

Nevertheless, the instability presented an opportunity to travel where the sight of a foreigner would not draw undue scrutiny. Traversing the lands containing a massive slave uprising would not be a simple task. But once they were on the other side it would not be far to the mountain pass that would see her and the boy to the lands of the northern people she called her own.

After rousing Hamilcar from slumber shortly after the break of dawn, Rayden started off to the north. They left the rivertown behind and headed across the open countryside, encountering no trouble along the way.

Their path finally crossed with the storied Boreus Way, after another day passed. She could not deny the roadway stood as a tremendous achievement on the part of the growing Empire. Running from north to south, it connected the Empire in a way that no other kingdoms or empires had been able to rival.

After a little thought, Rayden decided to take advantage of the roadway. The fitted stones forming the upper surface of the Boreus Way appeared as if they had grown together, with narrow ditches running to either side of the road.

Striding on the hard path, she wondered what the men in the tavern had been referring to, regarding the hindrance preventing them from traveling along it. She suspected she would recognize the cause clearly enough when they came across it.

For the time being, the road lay open and clear, easy to follow and heading directly where she intended to go. She imagined the road held much more traffic in the past than she observed as the day proceeded onward.

On a few occasions, lone carts pulled by horses rumbled by her. The occupants avoided eye contact, keeping to themselves. She imagined those passing by were not traveling far and their subdued manner girded her own sense of wariness.

The road afforded her an unobstructed view for a long distance, enabling ample warning if a larger force from either side in the ongoing conflict approached. As a northerner, she doubted she would have too much trouble were she and Hamilcar to encounter the rebels. The Teverens would pose a much more worrisome problem, especially with a Kartajenian boy at her side.

She deemed the likelihood of encountering Teverens

to be much greater. The road had been designed for speedier movements of soldiers during times of war.

With veteran legions on the prowl for the rebels, the roadway would be heavily used. She would have to be on her guard at all times.

With a little luck and the avoidance of any Teveren forts along the way, Rayden could reach the northern border in a few days. Though the road came to an end near there, she would have no difficulties crossing the remaining distance to Gessa territory.

***

Rayden's step grew slow and ponderous, a sinking feeling in her gut. She fought down the bile in her throat and the wave of nausea washing over her.

She had seen many horrors in her life, but the one she now witnessed rivaled the worst of them, if not surpassing it by a wide margin. She had found the reason why the men in the tavern refused to travel the Boreus Way.

CHAPTER 9

To either side of the road, rough-hewn timber beams had been erected. Suspended well above the ground, human bodies were affixed by ropes and iron nails to the wood.

Life had long since fled the bodies hanging on the crosses, likely for days judging from the decomposing states in evidence. Each and every form lining the road stood an icon of death.

Birds perched on the crosses, pecking hungrily at the putrefying flesh. A foul, rotting stench permeated the air, suffocating in the midday heat.

The men and women executed had been given no shred of dignity. Not a scrap of clothing could be seen on any of them; all had been hung upon the crosses completely naked.

From what Rayden could discern from her observations, a great many of the victims had suffered beatings or incurred other kinds of wounds. The display horrific and brutal, she knew it had not been done merely as punishment for those who hung upon the crosses.

The gruesome vision served as a dire warning for the slave populace within Teveren lands. The message from the empire's authorities sounded clearly enough. Those who took up arms against the Teverens and rebelled against their masters could expect similarly cruel fates.

Hamilcar vomited more than once, emptying the meager contents of his stomach until his heaves became dry. He kept close to Rayden's side, breathing through his mouth and keeping his eyes fixed downward.

Rayden hoped to reach the end of the macabre stretch of roadway before much longer passed, but it appeared that a tremendous number of slaves had been crucified. To her chagrin, even after walking amid the grisly visions for a long while, she could not yet see the end of the haunting array.

At the very least, they traveled along the roadway with little chance of encountering any kind of disturbance. Rayden kept her eyes fixed ahead, letting the parade of crucified figures become a blur on the periphery of her vision. Breathing through her mouth, like the boy, she did her best to avoid the noxious odors encompassing them.

No matter how tempting it might have been, she chose not to depart from the road. With the boy to look out for, she did not wish to risk the murky woods with its likely complement of outlaws and brigands.

The boy would be highly vulnerable in an ambush, even if Rayden could fend adequately for herself. On the road, she could see any potential threat coming from afar. That single advantage kept her striding along the stone path, though she hoped with all her heart that they would come to the end of it soon.

Keeping a rapid gait, she and Hamilcar continued onward, the sun reaching its peak overhead. Though hunger and thirst began tugging harder inside, Rayden opted to keep pressing forward, eager to reach the finish of the ghastly parade.

Hugging the base of one of the crosses ahead, obscuring much of his form, a man suddenly peered around at Rayden and Hamilcar. Loosing a shrill, depraved-sounding laugh, he broke the heavy silence.

Rayden whipped out her blade in a flash. Shifting to the

farther side of the road, she kept herself between the man and Hamilcar.

Listening and looking, she did not sense any other individuals within close proximity. The man ahead, unarmed, naked, and dirty, appeared to pose little threat, but Rayden had learned a long time ago to never lower her guard or underestimate any situation. The worst of dangers could appear harmless.

"Death triumphant!" the tall, lean figure shrieked with a giddy air, guffawing and looking about with a crazed expression. His gaze darted among the rotting bodies on the crosses. "This... an offering to the world's Master! An offering. In His Temple ... the entire world! On your knees, all kingdoms are the Master's to give!"

With greasy, matted hair and a scraggly beard, the man's unkempt appearance girded the wild, frenzied look shining from his eyes. From ribcage to shoulders, his bones protruded all over his emaciated body, giving him a starved, skeletal look.

His gaze snapping back to Rayden, his lips spread in a cruel mockery of a grin, exposing blackened teeth. An odd sound, somewhere between a low growl and a chuckle, came from the depths of his throat.

"The darkness is coming! It is spreading! This is our age!" the man cried out through frothing spittle, laughing maniacally as he leaped and scuttled along the side of the roadway in Rayden's direction. He kept behind the line of crosses, but he drew steadily closer to where she and Hamilcar stood their ground. "The Master guides the Imperator! The Master brings a storm to the east! The Master looses darkness in the north. The Master is everywhere!"

Whirling around in place, the man unleashed a torrent of whoops, cries and laughs. He waved his arms about in a frenzied manner, filthy hands clutching toward the sky.

"The world is His! He gives power to whoever He pleases!

The world is His to give!" the man shouted, coming nearer. "This age is His age! His will be done!"

"Get away from us!" Rayden retorted in a firm tone that brooked no argument, glaring at the gaunt figure. Her voice simmered with threat as she continued, "Or the iron I carry will swiftly bring the end to your age, right here."

"Kill me, you mortal creature of flesh and bones! I will find a new host! You cannot stop me or what is coming to this world!" the man countered in a defiant tone, one filled with anger and boastfulness.

"A new host? You will find the grave, madman," Rayden chided him, laughing. "There's your host. A dark, cold grave. Would you like that, you fool? Test my blade and discover this host for yourself."

Her reply evoked a peculiar response from the delirious man. He threw his head back, cackling hysterically and gnashing his teeth in a most bizarre display.

Abruptly, his eyes jerked back toward Rayden and his expression took on the appearance of a bestial snarl. For a brief instant, he held the appearance of a feral animal, enough that Rayden spared a glance away, checking to be sure that Hamilcar remained squarely behind her.

"Keep going. Keep behind me at all times," she told the boy, starting along the road.

She kept her weapons up and at the ready, not taking her eyes off the haggard figure for a moment. The boy heeded her, keeping pace.

The madman hopped and jumped in a crouching fashion, scurrying behind the crosses and shadowing them. He continued a short distance ahead of them, turned, and slammed his fists into the ground several times. His face a mask of rage, he bared his teeth at them in the manner of a rabid animal.

"The grave? You dare speak to me of the grave?" he called

out with great agitation, his tone changing in pitch to a growling level.

As he continued, a strange, disconcerting effect manifested within his voice. It sounded as if more and more voices joined in unison, speaking together through his mouth.

"We are the grave ... we are the destination for all," he continued. "All roads lead to us. This ... a road of death. Your life ... the boy's life ... the lives of all these men and women ... all roads to death. Death reigns over all life ... swallowing all! Everything ends ... in death!"

Whether an odd glint of sunlight or something more, his eyes appeared as burning embers when he uttered the final words. The thickening air of a threat gathering strength surrounded him.

Every sense within Rayden screamed aloud in warning. She had seen men and women alike gripped in the throes of madness, but she sensed something very different and worrisome about the figure stalking them along the side of the roadway.

The look in the man's eyes did not seem human anymore, to any degree. Malice and raw hunger brimmed within his gaze, of a kind that left Rayden unsettled to the core.

It appeared to her that something dangerous had come to the forefront within the man, roused to ire and filled with a burning desire to destroy her and the boy. She had the impression of a great, coiling serpent, poised to lash out and sink its venomous fangs deep into its prey.

"Come near ... fool ... and you will taste iron and the grave. Your flesh will rot in the sun, no less than the others here," Rayden told him in a steady, even tone. "Attack if you are daring enough. I have had enough of your foul mouth. Shut it and embrace your death."

The figure began making strange, hissing sounds, clenching his teeth and shaking all over. Rayden continued to step forward, continuing along the road. She made sure the boy stayed at her back while keeping a tight watch on the lunatic.

Using hands and feet, he hopped again in a crouching, frog-like fashion. He aligned himself with Rayden and the boy, beginning to shadow their movements once more. He continued to make the hissing noises, interspersed with guttural sounds and extended growls.

The demented figure jerked his gaze away from Rayden in abrupt fashion, staring up the road toward the north. Ceasing his wild ravings, the man grew rigidly still.

Without another word, appearing frightened, he leaped backward. Turning and using all four limbs to propel his body, he scampered off down the side of the roadway, heading fast toward the south.

Rayden looked back to the north, wondering what had startled him so powerfully, causing him to abandon his quarry and hurry away. He had not displayed any significant fear of her or the weapons in her hands. Rather, he had been on the verge of some kind of attack.

In the distance, she finally espied what had agitated him, though the sight looked to be anything but frightening. Far from invoking alarm, the vision meeting her eyes puzzled her.

A couple of elderly figures wearing simple woolen tunics and sandals stood out in the roadway, both of them facing one of the crosses. Their eyes closed, the pair seemed to be in a state of deep concentration. Finally, they raised their heads upright.

Unarmed, they had the distinctive air of priests, though Rayden had no doubt the men claimed a faith far different than the one that cast children alive into the fires of a bull-god. She could see nothing about them to be alarmed over and decided to continue along the road.

She cast a couple glances back in the other direction, making certain the madman had not turned back from his flight. A shrinking speck in the distance, it did not look like he would be returning to harass her and the boy anytime soon.

Opening their eyes and turning their heads, the two figures exhibited no surprise as Rayden neared, though they could easily see her weapons at hand. Keeping their gazes toward her, their somber expressions remained unchanged.

Not wishing to interrupt them, she edged over to one side of the road, opposite from the side where the pair stood. Despite perceiving no threats from the two men, Rayden still could not afford to lower her guard. Keeping her blade and axe in hand, she sought to pass quietly by them and continue on her way.

"There is no need for weapons with us. Peace to you, Traveler," one of the men greeted in a calm voice, a smile coming to his face. The taller of the two, standing to Rayden's left, he had a warm look to his eyes that mirrored the kind expression on his face.

"Well met," Rayden replied in acknowledgement. She slowed to a halt, though she kept her weapons at hand. "I cannot say the same for the man I encountered back there ... moments ago. A madman, I would say."

"Minions of the coming darkness," the tall priest responded, his countenance becoming serious once more. "They saw something in you. They wanted you. You are strong and a warrior, one of great skill I suspect. But that is not all they desired. The nature of your spirit invoked both anger and a hunger in them."

"A raving madman he was," Rayden commented, finding it strange that the priest used a plural term in describing the scraggly figure that had fled so suddenly.

"You were wise not to let them near you," the priest said. "What appears as a man to the eyes, may not be."

"One must always be alert when on a journey," Rayden said. "I take no chances."

"The others you seek have crossed the river," the other priest stated. "The Teverens marched through in great strength, not two days past. If they catch you on this side of the river, you will share the fate of these unfortunate souls."

Rayden looked toward the second priest, realizing that he had mistaken her for one of the rebelling slaves. She imagined that to be easy enough to do, seeing that she hailed from foreign lands and carried weapons in the heart of the Teveren Empire during a time of rebellious upheaval.

"And you?" Rayden asked. "What if they come upon you? You do not appear to be priests of their gods."

"Never would we serve their gods ... gods who are merely servants of a greater and darker Master ... we serve only the Creator, the One who brings life into being," the priest replied in a firm tone.

Rayden found the idea of a single god interesting and unusual, given the extensive pantheons of all the lands she had visited. She also found the idea that all the Teveren deities were nothing more than servants to a single dark god intriguing.

"The Teverens do not worry themselves over a couple of old men without weapons, who they deem to be senile fools," the first priest added. "I am grateful they do. It gives us the time to consecrate each and every one of these men and women to the Creator. Our work is not the work of this world. It is the work of another, one that is not sullied with death and sorrow."

Though not sharing their faith, or believing anyone could be consecrated to a god, Rayden had respect for the priests. She recognized their dedication and the goodwill within their intention toward the poor unfortunates who had died on the crosses.

In some ways, she wished she could share the kind of beliefs they held, which rendered the travails of the world impotent in light of a greater, wondrous realm yet to come. Yet only honed iron could she believe in, having seen that kind of faith justified many, many times over throughout the years. Iron never abandoned her and it always responded to her call.

She had heard the pleas of men and women to the gods they served when their lives stood in terrible danger. She had yet to see a deity respond to their servant's plight, at the time when they needed help the most.

The desperate cries to gods during Iellia's night of blood and fire echoed in her mind. Those supplicants had been brutalized at the hands of Teveren soldiers, while her iron had spared the young girl on the roof and many others in the tenemant. Rayden had no illusions about where to place her faith.

"You are men strong in your faith," she observed. "That you would honor those who suffered and died here speaks to the nature of your hearts."

The second man smiled. "Your words bear such irony. The more we learn of ourselves, the weaker we find ourselves to be."

"Knowing one's own weaknesses is a strength in itself," Rayden said.

"There is a deep wisdom in what you say," the first priest acknowledged, nodding. "Do you know of your weaknesses?"

"I know of some. I seek to know every one of them," Rayden answered the priest, looking him in the eyes. "Yet I always seek to grow stronger. If I discover a weakness, I know where I must gain strength."

"May the Creator give you strength and guide you always," the first priest commented.

Rayden nodded, unsure of what to say in response. While she respected what the men stood for, she still did not believe in their strange god. No amount of words from the priests would convince her otherwise.

"The Creator will speak to your heart, whether you believe or not," the second priest said, as if sensing the nature of her hesitation. "Not in the way we are speaking, but on a deeper level. Listen on that deeper level and you will hear."

Again she hesitated, not wishing to offend the man. All her life she had listened for the voice of a god, only to experience enduring silence. The things of darkness she had encountered in abundance, but her hunger and thirst for one ray of light from heavenly realms continued untended.

Thinking about how many grotesque entities of the dark she had confronted, a spark of anger took flame inside. If gods had no time for her, she had no time for them. If they wished to speak, then they could speak plainly without need for discernment.

"Do not tarry here with two old fools such as we are," the first priest interjected, in a more lighthearted air.

"You are anything but fools," Rayden replied, tamping down her own frustrations with the matter of religion. "To honor the dead along this terrible road, and seek their peace and existence beyond this world, is something I honor and respect in the core of my heart."

She meant every single word that came from her lips. The two priests embraced a noble vision, one she wished with all her heart could be true. The notion of the crucified slaves finding peace, joy, and restoration far outshone the idea of their paths ending in nothing more than rot and oblivion.

"In a world such as this, we are great fools," the first priest said with a gentle smile. "The new Imperator is a master of the ways of this world, wise in its arts, and dangerous to those such as yourself."

"No day spent in this world is safe or promised," Rayden countered. "I can only travel my road as best I can."

"It seems you are somewhat foolish yourself," the first priest replied in good humor, a grin showing on his lips.

"I have sometimes thought myself a fool for doing many of the things I have done, but I cannot be anything less than true to who I am," Rayden said, taking no umbrage at the priest's words. Oddly, she found his calling her foolish to be a compliment rather than an insult.

Many others had indeed regarded her as a fool, stating that she could have amassed great wealth using her exceptional skills as a warrior. Whether serving at the side of a king or plying the tools of the assassin within the shadows, Rayden could have filled coffers with gold and jewels many times over. There were many that said she could have become a chieftain or queen, if she wished.

Serving no gods, Rayden had never been inclined toward serving any human master, no matter how much wealth they wished to shower upon her. Neither did she wish to become a master of others. Rayden walked along her own road, facing each new day with iron in her hand and honor in her heart.

"Well stated, warrior of the north," the second priest said.

Rayden looked to the men, seeing a high level of respect in their eyes for her, one she had not been made to earn through the wielding of a blade. It stood clear that they valued her mind and the state of her heart more than the use of weapons.

The recognition took her a little by surprise, as it was not something she had been used to in her widespread travels. In a gesture of respect toward them, she returned her weapons back to their places of rest, at her waist.

"I am only stating what I am, nothing more than that," Rayden said.

"And what you are is a good and rare thing in this darkening age," the first priest said. His eyes shifted toward the boy as he continued. "You are a defender of life. You are a defender of those who would otherwise be defenseless. There is no greater calling a warrior can have."

Again, Rayden did not know what to say in reply. To her eyes, she had been surrounded and harried by death all her life, even when young. Death had taken so much from her and those who held places in her heart.

A fire burned inside to spare others what she had suffered. There had never been a specific calling, only a desire to live her days out in a state of honor.

"I can only travel my road," she said at last, following a lengthy pause. She looked to each of the men. "And for my part, I must now continue on my own journey. I bid the both of you both good fortune on your paths."

"Seek them on the other side of the river, to the east," the first said, continuing to mistake her and the boy for escaped slaves. "Its banks are no more than a league from here. You can reach the river before nightfall."

Rayden thanked the priests and started onward with Hamilcar at her side. After the encounter with the frenzied madman, the meeting with the priests brought her some much needed equilibrium.

Glad to leave the roadway and its grisly sights, Rayden followed the priest's directions and headed eastward, setting out for the river. The two men had given her valuable information, not only about the rebellious slaves in the area, but also regarding the Teveren forces on the hunt for them.

She held no enthusiasm toward encountering an entire Teveren army, especially not one brimming with a fire for vengeance. Having a Kartajenian boy with her would bring no favors from the soldiers of the rising Empire.

CHAPTER 10

Keeping to a steady pace, they reached the banks of the river late in the afternoon. A light wind tousled her blonde locks as she studied the breadth of the channel and strength of its current.

She knew at once that attempting to swim would only result in drowning. Looking up and down the great, glittering channel, her brow furrowed as she pondered the situation.

"How are we to cross this?" the boy asked, breaking the extended silence.

"We must find a place to ford ... or maybe a boat," Rayden said, with an air of jest on the last part of the statement.

"How far will that be?" he asked.

"For a place to ford? We had better get started walking," Rayden said, starting toward the north, the boy falling in behind her without complaint.

Rayden chose to walk among a line of trees set a little farther from the water's edge, keeping out of the open. The leafy branches provided some welcome shade from the sun. The footing sturdier, Rayden found it much better ground to fight on if something amiss should erupt.

They traveled about half a league when every instinct within Rayden cried out. Senses honed from years of perching on the edge of death told her not to take another step, even if she had yet to see or hear anything out of the ordinary.

Rayden froze in place, not about to take another stride. With a shuffling step, the boy came to a halt behind her.

"I know you are there," Rayden said with a calm demeanor, making no move to draw her weapons out. Nevertheless, her hand drifted to where she could draw her blade in an instant. "I am just a traveler. Nothing more. My business is to the north."

"You are no Teveren," a steady, feminine voice called from the left. "That is plain enough."

"I am not," Rayden said. "Nor do I wish to encounter any."

"We are in agreement on both counts," the voice stated. "But a traveler? In these times? Who would travel through these burning lands?"

"I am taking this boy north with me, to lands beyond Teveren territory," Rayden answered, matter-of-factly. "We have no other way than through these lands."

"You are not a slave," the voice declared.

"No, and as long as I breathe no master will have authority over me," Rayden said firmly.

"From now on, neither will I have a master, as long as I live," the voice replied with a tone of resolve and trace of anger. "And I see that you are a northerner, that also is plain enough."

Rayden's ears picked up the slightest scuff of a footstep, drawing her eyes toward some movement, though she kept her body in place. A woman stepped slowly into view by the trunk of a tree, just ahead to the left.

She held a fully-drawn bow with an arrow trained squarely upon Rayden's body. The posture of the woman told her at once that she had skill with the weapon.

Her face hinted at eastern origins, with higher-set cheekbones and a noticeable tilt to her eyes. Her long black hair tied into a pair of thick braids, she stood about a head shorter than Rayden. An extended tunic covered her upper body, with a set of trousers worn on the lower, ending in a pair of leather shoes.

"I am called Doros," the woman announced, relaxing the tension on the bowstring and lowering the weapon.

"I am Rayden, and the boy with me is called Hamilcar."

"A Kartajenian," Doros commented, looking at the boy. "By look and name."

Rayden nodded. "One I spared from their barbaric god. I eat the meat of bulls. I am not about to worship one."

The trace of a grin showed on Doros' face. "I think we are in agreement about their god."

"I have no masters. Neither do I have a god," Rayden said. "If a god wishes me to follow them, then they can make an introduction. I have been through the lands of many gods ... and none has come forth yet."

"I pray to gods that never hear me, so perhaps you are the wiser," Doros replied.

"Or I am more the fool, only time can tell," Rayden said. "But I place more trust in what I can see, hear, and feel. It is how I have survived this long."

"We both seek to survive and avoid Teverens, but if you remain on this side of the river you will surely encounter them before long," the woman said, her face growing more somber.

"I am looking for a place to ford this river, I do not have the skill to fashion a boat," Rayden said. She then added, as if an afterthought, "And I doubt I will find one lying about."

"Do not be so sure," Doros replied in a cryptic air.

"I would guess that you have a means of getting across then?" Rayden asked.

"I can take you across the river, I was on my way back myself," Doros said. "It is much safer in the lands to the other side. Those who were formerly slaves of the Empire are gathered in strength over there."

"I would rather take my chances across the river than remain on this side," Rayden said.

Doros slipped her bow and arrow into a case slung at her side. Rayden espied the hilt of a long dagger sheathed on the facing of the case.

Doros took a few steps toward them, her face coming into a patch of sunlight. Standing closer to the woman, and looking her in the eyes, Rayden marveled at the cat-like shape to Doros' pupils. Several questions bloomed in her mind at once, including a few that brought a heightened sense of caution.

"My eyes," Doros remarked, taking notice of Rayden's lingering stare. "You are not the first to look, and no, I am not one who can shift my form. I cannot turn into a beast. I was simply born this way."

"I have not seen the like … at least on a person," Rayden said.

"It is a rare trait, I am told," Doros said.

"Why are you here? Near such a terrible place?" Rayden asked, unable to stifle another curiosity. Recalling the road of horror that she had left behind, Rayden could not imagine any former slave wanting to be in close proximity to such a gruesome place.

"I came to see if my sister and brother were among those crucified on the road," Doros replied after a short pause, her tone and countenance grim. "I walked the entire length of that slaughter and I could not find them. They may yet live."

Seeing the look in Doros' eyes, Rayden could sense the woman burdened more by uncertainty than buoyed with hope. She could understand such a feeling.

Hope stood empty, an ephemeral thing of no true substance. Uncertainty loomed irrefutable, an intrinsic part of life each and every day.

Rayden already harbored great sympathy for Doros. She

did not envy the woman's ordeal, walking down the length of that terrible road.

She could envision the woman taking in the view of every single body, moving from one to another, not knowing if the next one she set her eyes upon might be that of her brother or sister. In Rayden's eyes, the woman possessed considerable inner strength to endure such a burdensome plight.

"May it be so ... may you find them alive and unharmed," Rayden said.

Doros nodded to Rayden, growing quiet for a few moments. Her chest swelled as she took in a long, deep breath, and then released it slowly. Straightening up, she looked to Rayden.

"There is no more to do here," she announced. "Come with me. We will cross the river and leave this evil place behind."

With Doros leading, they walked back along the path that Rayden had just traveled. Eventually, they arrived at a place where Doros came to a stop and began pulling away some brush. She revealed a small boat that had been carefully concealed.

"We passed right by it," Rayden observed, a compliment to the skill demonstrated in masking the water vessel.

"Then I may not be so inept after all," Doros said, a smile brightening her face. "I consider myself the least in skill among the friends that I grew up with, back in my own lands."

"And where are your own lands?" Rayden asked with genuine interest.

"My father came from the lands of the north, my mother from lands farther to the east," Doros answered. While speaking of them, her smile grew wider. "Both of them were warriors. I was raised among the Sytha, to the east of the tribal lands, north and east of where we stand now. I grew up on the vast steppes of those lands, seas of grass crossed with an abundance of rivers."

"What became of your mother and father?" Rayden asked.

Doros hesitated, a shadow passing across her face. "War

brought them together ... and war tore us apart. The Teverens came. For many years, they were held back, but they returned in greater strength each time. The last invasion could not be stopped.

"My brother and sister were taken with me into slavery. Of my mother and father, I do not know their fates. It is my hope to find all of them one day, but for all I know they may all be dead. For now, I am alone."

Rayden said nothing, understanding how difficult it had to be for Doros to contend with such uncertainty. She could only imagine the inner turmoil she would endure if she did not know if her mother and father yet lived.

"I am sorry to hear of what you have suffered," Rayden empathized. "The Teverens are a scourge to many people and many lands."

"I do not know the fate of those in my family, but I do know the Teverens must pay in blood for what they have done," Doros stated, her eyes narrowing and mouth growing taut. "Not just to me and my family, but to countless others."

"No man or woman should be made a slave," Rayden said. "Those who enslave others forfeit their own humanity. They are monsters ... monsters to be hunted down and slain."

"We share that feeling, Rayden," Doros said, looking into her eyes. "It is unfortunate that this world contains so many monsters."

Behind the simmering rage, Rayden saw great sadness and fear in the depths of the woman's gaze. She regretted that nothing she could say or do could bring comfort to her new friend.

"We will simply have to keep fighting them, until the day there are no more," Rayden said, offering the other woman a smile.

Rayden stepped forward and assisted Doros in dragging the boat down the bank toward the water's edge. Within the small vessel lay a pair of oars. Doros claimed one and gave the other to Rayden.

The three got into the boat with Hamilcar seated in the middle. Doros used her oar to push away from the bank. The boat glided out into deeper water, catching the current as Doros worked her oar to orient the vessel.

Doros demonstrated great skill with the use of an oar, attributing the ability to the period of her life spent on the great steppes to the east. The rougher current would have been a challenge to most, but Doros navigated the river with precision and decisiveness.

Rayden contributed wherever possible, following the other's instructions as they made their way down the river. At the cusp of darkness, they had worked their way across to the other side, far down river.

After helping Doros to pull the boat ashore, they set out for the rebel camp. The night had not aged much when the telltale array of campfires beckoned out of the darkness to the weary travelers.

Doros exchanged words with a quartet of armed men keeping a watch on the outskirts. They eyed Rayden and the boy with interest, their demeanors becoming less suspicious after Doros explained who they were.

Entering the encampment, Rayden looked around and took in the sights of the inhabitants. The rebels were of diverse origins. There were a few northerners like herself, people from the steppe, Kartajenians, Acharans, Hesperians, Thraikans, Teverens, and even a few with the darker skin and general characteristics of those living to the south of the Kartajenian lands.

Despite the different ethnic and cultural backgrounds, the looks in the eyes of the rebels held a lot in common. Passing through their midst, Rayden saw fierce determination shining within the gazes peering back at her. All had been brought together in common cause, the desire to break the chains of Teveren slavery.

Whether trained fighters or not, the rebels had the hardened look of veteran warriors. She was not surprised that they had already defeated several Teveren forces sent to subdue them. The Teveren Imperator would need to send overwhelming force and veteran legions to overcome the force Rayden saw all around her.

"You may stay with me, Rayden," Doros announced, slowing down as they neared a crackling fire surrounded by several men and women. "We will find some cloaks you can use to keep warm and cover the ground with."

Many around the fire rose to their feet at the sight of Doros, their expressions and voices warm in greeting at the return of their companion. The men and women no mere traveling companions of Doros, Rayden recognized at once the bonds forged among warriors who had fought, bled and suffered together.

A tall, broad-shouldered man with a thick, black beard and a large nose peered toward Rayden and Hamilcar. "What tidings from across the river? I see you have found two new friends."

"I have," Doros said, smiling and glancing in Rayden's direction. "Rayden and Hamilcar are no friends of the Teverens. I thought they would be safer among us instead of walking along the Boreus Way."

"A good judgment," the tall figure replied. He looked back to Doros and his voice lowered. "Did you find them?"

She shook her head. "I found no sign."

He put a hand to her shoulder. "Stay strong of heart. There is still hope that they live."

Doros looked downward for a moment, her face growing pensive. She answered the man in a voice just above a whisper. "That there is."

The man looked back toward Rayden and raised his voice. "Welcome to this rabble of a camp. I am Annocrates."

With the change in subject, Doros' expression eased as she turned toward Rayden and the boy. "A big, clumsy Acharan. Nothing to worry yourself over when it comes to this one."

Rayden laughed. "I have great affinity for the Acharans. I have been through their lands more than once. The most learned man I have ever known is an Acharan, a man named Archimenes who I call friend. Were his wit a blade, it would likely be the sharpest ever forged."

"There are Acharans with brains ... and there are Acharans who lack them," Doros said with an air of jest, grinning at Annocrates.

"I will not argue with you," Annocrates replied. "I am not the mightiest warrior. I am not a scholar. I am no sorcerer. I am not a priest favored by gods. But I am loyal to those I call friend."

"Aye, that you are," Doros said. Her softer tone of voice conveyed a sense of genuine affinity toward the man.

Annocrates smiled at her remark, before turning toward Rayden. "All this talking and I imagine you are hungry and thirsty after your journey. We have some fish, bread, and cheese to share with you. We also have a barrel of wine taken from the villa of one of the Teveren scum."

Casting a sideways glance, Rayden caught the look of eagerness in Hamilcar's eyes. She knew he had to be as famished as he was exhausted.

"A day's travel does build the appetite," Rayden said. "And some wine sounds good."

"Then come with me," Annocrates invited.

He led them over to the fire, where they took a seat on the ground while he procured all of the things he had described. While Rayden's hunger pangs had reached a high level, she consumed her meal in measured bites. Letting the food and drink ease into her body, she enjoyed the company of Doros, Annocrates, and the other men and women nearby.

For his part, Hamilcar abandoned all composure, devouring his food in a manner resembling a starved wolf. Rayden warned him about eating too fast, but his voracious hunger prevailed over her counsel. After he had finished, he suffered a precarious few moments when he almost vomited back up everything he had gulped down.

For an encampment that had so recently suffered a large setback and seen many of their number executed, the conversations and overall mood among the rebels proved lighthearted. Rayden found herself included in their banter and jests from the start, finding it easy to make their acquaintances no matter what land they had originally come from.

They also expressed curiosity regarding her story. Annocrates, Doros, and the others listened with great interest as Rayden described the escape from Kartajen and the ensuing sea journey. A couple of them had heard tales of the winged sea beasts that had assailed the merchant ship, but all eyes widened as Rayden gave them her personal eyewitness account.

The news of Iellia being attacked by land and sea brought the mood of the others down a little. Rayden learned that many hoped the Kartajenians would be able to challenge the growing empire of the Teverens, but the latter appeared ascendant while the former looked to be in decline.

Rayden found that she could not disagree with their assessment. She thought of the cities of the Kartajenian's subject allies, all of which had been made to tear their walls down to ensure their loyalty to Kartajen.

Those cities would be ripe for a bitter harvest when Teveren legions crossed the sea, one day in the near future. She could only hope that she did not find herself in those lands when that day of reckoning arrived.

Over the course of the evening, through several one on one conversations with the men and women around her, she learned much more about Doros and the former slaves. Putting all of it together, the tale of the rebellion's origins and events since took shape.

Annocrates had been a bodyguard to a wealthy Teveren of advancing years who had intended to make Doros a servant of his household and bed. Doros had refused to acquiesce to the latter desire.

Bound and unable to resist, she had begun to suffer a terrible lashing at the hands of the Teveren aristocrat when Annocrates could stand no more. The big Acharan had slain the two guards who had bound Doros and then strangled the old man with the whip that he had been beating Doros with.

Annocrates expressed no small amount of pleasure at his memory of the Teveren with eyes bulging out and the emptied contents of his bowels running down kicking legs. All his vast wealth and influence availed him nothing when lying dead in a pool of his own feces.

Listening to the story, Rayden could see that the two rebels shared a deep, abiding bond that had taken root the moment Annocrates had intervened. He had spared her life and put his own in peril, as nothing short of an agonizing death would be visited upon any slave who struck down their master.

Much more had sprouted and bloomed that day, far beyond what the two had intended. Seeing what Annocrates had done, other slaves in the villa became inspired to throw their yoke off. Before sunset, Teveren blood pooled on marble floors and a rebellion had sparked to life.

Spreading like a fire through dry grass, slaves rose up across the region and in days a nascent resistance had formed. The ranks grew in swift fashion, with slaves coming from all over as they abandoned their masters or rose up as Annocrates had done.

Many bodyguards and several who had been made to fight for sport brought experience and skill with weapons into the swelling rebel force. At the outset, those who knew how to wield weapons set to training those who did not. Every man and woman in the uprising knew that there was no turning back, only freedom or death lay ahead.

Early victories over a pair of smaller Teveren forces underestimating the numbers and strength of the rebels brought more weapons, shields, and armor into their hands. Sacking villas and sweeping through villages, the rebels supplied themselves further, their numbers growing daily.

Not long passed before they had become an army, capable of destroying a legion as they did before the Divine City understood just how serious and formidable the uprising had become. Soon afterward, two experienced legions marched north along the Boreus Way. The rebels, greater in number and buoyed with a string of victories, gathered to meet them in open battle.

The battle against veteran legions on the other side of the river had ended with the rebels' first setback. Maneuvering with discipline and precision, the Kittmins cut off a great portion of the rebel force, surrounding them and presenting a wall of shields to the rest.

Unable to break through and suffering too many casualties, the rebels outside the Teveren ranks had been forced to withdraw, crossing the river to regroup. The last to retreat witnessed the encircled rebels throwing down their arms in surrender to the Teverens.

At first, the leadership of the rebels began thinking about how they could help their comrades, knowing the Teveren tendency to parade the conquered in the Divine City. Many schemes were discussed, and it was determined that an attempt would be made to free the prisoners, everyone knowing they would eventually be put to death after the Teverens had celebrated their triumph.

A couple days afterward, scouts had been sent to learn the whereabouts of the rebel captives and enemy legions. They returned with the horrific report of what had transpired along the Boreus Way.

Even worse for the scouts, when they set their eyes upon the atrocity a greater portion of those hanging on the crosses yet clung to life. Struggling to breathe and weakening steadily, the men and women on the crosses could see the carrion birds circling in great numbers above, awaiting a grisly feast.

The Teveren legions did not withdraw from their encampment until the captives were beyond any hope of rescue. Doros had crossed many days later to search among the dead for her brother and sister, who had not been found among the rebels able to cross the river.

Even though the uprising had only been underway for a few months, Rayden found herself amazed at the courage and resilience in the hearts of those around her. Having endured a great tragedy, there was no lack of fight in the rebels.

Already harboring a deep sympathy to their cause, she found herself taking an immediate liking to them. Later that night, when Rayden sought sleep's refuge, she closed her eyes bearing a favorable impression of her new companions.

Tomorrow would bring new challenges and the problem of how to get safely to the north. But for the time being, she could find solidarity and a cause worth fighting for among the rebels.

***

At daybreak, after several groups of scouts and foragers had departed to glean what they could from the surrounding countryside, Rayden feared a long, idle day spent lingering around the encampment. Her trepidation proved unfounded, as Doros came to her late in the morning with a special task that she claimed would last the entire day. Glad to have something to occupy the time, Rayden agreed, though she insisted upon keeping Hamilcar with her.

Rayden set out with Doros, Hamilcar, and an elderly woman named Sagana toward the east, where an older expanse of woodland spread broad and far. As they walked, Doros explained the purpose of the excursion and the woman accompanying them.

Herbs and roots for the treatment of ailments were in thin supply. Very few among the rebels had the skill and knowledge to locate such items in the wilderness.

Rayden possessed a rudimentary knowledge of the things that grew in northern forests. She could also identify a few plants that grew in foreign lands, but she learned that Sagana carried a lifetime of experience in the arts of healing.

Most rebels had expressed reticence to accompany the old woman when Sagana had volunteered to go into the woods and gather up a store of herbs and roots. Rumored to be a witch, the old woman's presence in the camp was tolerated only because she shared the slave origin of all the others. Under other circumstances, she might well have been banished, or worse.

The group headed deep into the woods, with Rayden and Doros keeping close to Sagana. She could walk unassisted, but her movements were slow and required patience on the part of those escorting her.

"I cannot wield a spear or blade, but I can gather the roots and herbs that could save your lives," the crone remarked, with an edge of irritation. "It is foolish of the others to refuse my help."

"All manner of abilities are needed for an army to gain victory," Rayden replied to Sagana. "The skill you have is as valuable as any sword and more so to the one who takes ill from a wound, or the elements."

"You carry wisdom beyond your years, golden-haired warrior," the old woman stated approvingly. Her gray eyes shifted to stare at Doros for a few moments, before she continued. "And you have a rare gift, young one. One you do not claim. It is a power in your voice."

"I am not inclined to sorcery," Doros replied evenly, appearing uncomfortable with the remark.

The old woman sighed, looking resigned. "I suppose I should be grateful that you did not fear I would grow fangs and conjure up a storm when we were alone. Or maybe animate the bodies of those long dead."

"I do not share the feelings of many others," Doros said, looking toward the crone. "If I were afraid of you, why would I go into these woods in your company, far from the others? I am grateful that you are a friend to us. I would not let anyone harm you. It is just that the arts of sorcery are not skills I have a desire to possess. Nothing more."

"Each much choose their own way in life, none should be forced," the old woman replied, nodding her head. "It is the very reason why your uprising carries honor. It is a just cause."

"Our uprising," Doros replied. "You are with us and endured the bondage of slavery no different than any other. This is our fight."

The old woman smiled, exposing a few gaps among her remaining, yellowed teeth. "The future belongs to you. I have but a wisp of time left to me on this part of the journey. The Great Veil is close and I do not fear it. I merely desire to make what time is left to me in this world matter. Now, let us put our energy to gathering some herbs and roots that may be of help to you and the others."

Despite having an aversion to the things of sorcery, Rayden found herself taking a strong liking to the old woman. She wondered about the journey Sagana had taken over the long years of her life.

She hoped to have an opportunity to speak with her around a campfire on a future night, to learn what she could of Sagana's past. She imagined the old woman had much more to tell than an account of years spent in slavery.

Rayden always found herself the better for listening to the words of one nearing the end of life's journey. Wisdom gained from experience could never be purchased with gold. She always marveled how so many possessing such wisdom imparted it freely for those who would spend a moment to listen, yet so few among the young took advantage of the priceless treasure offered.

Voices faint in the air snapped Rayden to attention. The sounds drifted in from the east and she doubted they came from the lips of any scout who had ventured from the rebel camp.

Rayden held her hand up, bringing the others to silence. She then gestured in the direction of the voices. Doros nodded, quietly retrieving her bow and an arrow from the case slung at her side.

Rayden pointed toward the old woman and Hamilcar, then making another gesture for Doros to stay with them. Doros indicated her understanding with another nod.

Soft of step, Rayden started off in the direction of the voices, her blade grasped in one hand and axe in the other. Using the trees for cover, she drew closer to the source of the voices until the speakers finally came into view.

She took a few moments to study their look and attire. As she had expected, they were not from the rebel camp.

Hair short-cropped and faces devoid of beards, about twenty men in all comprised the group scattered about the area. Most of the men wore a type of sleeveless tunic, some worn in a manner that left the right shoulder exposed.

Leather belts adorned with dangling pendants girded their waists. Some carried hexagonal shields and their weapons included an assortment of short-hafted axes, pickaxes and a few spears.

Seafarers foraging inland, the men's presence and nature told Rayden a couple of things at once. A large Teveren force existed somewhere close, and it likely involved a fleet of vessels.

Neither revelation boded well for the rebel encampment. Their whole purpose for crossing the river to recover from losses and regroup, the rebels were not seeking any kind of contact with the Teverens for the time being.

She doubted the Teverens knew of the large rebel force, or twenty of them would not have chanced foraging within such close proximity of an encampment holding well over two thousand hostile, battle-hardened ex-slaves. The men before Rayden's eyes appeared disciplined and wary enough, but she could tell that they did not suspect any sort of imminent danger.

Moving back as noiselessly as she had come, Rayden departed the area and made her way back to where her three companions awaited her. The gathering of herbs and roots would have to wait until another day. Twenty armed Teverens posed enough of a threat, such that if fighting broke out the old woman and boy would be at great risk.

Before they could speak a word in greeting, she signaled for the three to keep silent and follow her. Without a moment's delay she guided them away from the Teverens and started back toward the rebel encampment.

The return hike proceeded far slower than she would have liked with the old woman among them, but Rayden would die before she abandoned Sagana to a cruel fate at Teveren hands. After they had put some further distance between themselves and the enemy, she broke the silence at last, telling Doros everything she had seen.

Doros' eyes narrowed and her jaw grew taut at the mention of Teverens nearby, but surprise and a little fear shone in her eyes at the discovery that an enemy force lurked on the same side of the river as the rebels. She listened to Rayden's assessment of the foraging party and then fell into silence for several ponderous moments.

"We must know if a larger force is now on this side of the river," Doros said at last, concern etched in her features. "And we need to discover where they are encamped. You think they were all seafarers?"

"I am certain of it," Rayden said. "These were sailors, foraging inland."

"Then we need to send scouts to the fishing villages on the coast not far from here, one a place called Liurni, the other Mauranium," Doros said. "If a fleet put in to shore, it is most likely to be one of those places. The bays are each large enough to shelter a fair number of vessels."

"I don't think they know of your camp yet," Rayden replied. "These men would not dare drift so close if they knew of it."

"It is a risk that must be taken," Doros said. "We must know their strength and see if we can learn why they are here. I do not wish to find us trapped, with legions on both sides of the river."

"Then send your best ... and as few as you can," Rayden cautioned Doros.

"Make no mistake, if it is a force we can take, we will spill Teveren blood," Doros said.

"We need to get out of these lands," Sagana interjected from behind them. "The longer we remain in Teveren lands, the more time we give them to prepare and overwhelm us. They will summon legion after legion until they have victory. Can we call upon more legions?"

Rayden glanced back to the old woman and then looked back to Doros. "Sagana speaks wisely. The Teverens can call upon more and more strength if given time. It is not something to underestimate."

"I am aware," Doros replied curtly.

They continued onward, falling into a lengthy silence. Sagana proved tough at heart, not voicing a single complaint though the sustained exertion left her exhausted by the time they reached the encampment. Rayden walked at her side, catching her from falling more than once in her growing weariness.

"A strong warrior like you showing compassion for a frail woman who cannot bear a spear," the old woman commented as they entered the outskirts of the encampment.

"Strength is measured in many ways," Rayden replied.

"All the same, I thank you for walking a path at odds with the ways of this world," the old woman said. "These old eyes have rarely seen such an individual."

"Your wisdom and your knowledge may be of great benefit to our force," Rayden said.

"I suspect there is more than that at work within you," the old woman said, voice heavy with fatigue. "But now that we are back, I must rest. This old body is not what it used to be."

Rayden helped the woman over to the first shelter they found. One hard glance from Rayden silenced the first look of protest from one of the men there.

After dispatching Hamilcar to gather up some food and drink, primarily for the old woman's benefit, Rayden turned toward Doros. "Go on ahead, I am going to stay with Sagana until I know she is safe and won't be harassed."

"I will organize a scouting party. We must have answers soon," Doros announced, before striding off into the depths of the camp.

With Rayden present, nobody gave Sagana any trouble. The men and women nearby went back to whatever they had been occupied with before, leaving Rayden and Sagana to themselves.

The boy returned shortly with some hard bread and wine. Softening the bread in the wine, Rayden broke off small chunks and gave them to the old woman one by one. She ate a few morsels, finding herself more famished than she had first thought.

"You need to counsel them to leave Teveren lands as soon as they can," the old woman said, showing signs of a little rejuvenation.

"I agree with you, entirely," Rayden replied. "They must go north, into the lands of my own people. It will be the best chance they have to survive."

"Staying here will see all of them lining the Boreus Way on crosses," Sagana observed, a grim look on her face.

"You'll find no argument from me on that either."

"Their hearts are filled with dreams of blood vengeance, it will be hard to overcome," Sagana replied.

"Vengeance for many good reasons," Rayden said. "It is a shame they are not strong enough to march on the Divine City itself and bring an end to this evil scourge."

"It is only a part of a much greater darkness," the old woman said. "The shadow this empire casts is but a reflection of something much larger ... something much, much worse."

"I cannot worry myself over such things, the gods will do as they will. I can only face what stands before me."

"You are a warrior," the old woman said, nodding. "But get them to see past the vengeance that clouds their sight."

"If I can, I will," Rayden said, knowing the challenge of achieving that to be great, if not insurmountable.

Rayden looked out over the camp as Sagana fell into an extended silence. Faces from all kinds of lands and places were mingled, brought together by a desperate hope and the will to survive.

Rayden had never known the scourge of slavery, but she sought the same kind of world as they all did. A life where a son could not be demanded for sacrifice to a god, or a woman could not be torn from her father, mother, brother, and sister, beckoned to everyone within the sprawling encampment.

Getting there would be an arduous task, but where some humans had created a dark world others could forge one imbued with light. The thought gave Rayden a little lift as she looked back to the youth sitting by her side. Reaching over, she smiled and tousled his curly black locks.

CHAPTER 11

"Mauranium, as I thought. At least eight ships," Annocrates told Doros and Rayden, who shared brief glances with each other.

The patter of rain sounded on the tent, the early phase of a building storm. The winds outside picking up faster, cooler air flowed throughout the rebel encampment and brought a chill inside the shelter.

"And you are sure these are slave ships?" Doros questioned him. "Not merchant vessels? Or even warships?"

Annocrates nodded. "We are positive. They have set up a camp on land, but have left the slaves in the hulls of the ships. We spoke to a fisherman who told us this group of ships is taking slaves out of the villas in this region. They belong to many who have sought the safety of the Divine City's great walls."

"To make sure we do not free them," Doros commented, anger creeping into her tone as her expression darkened.

"It is likely those hulls are tightly packed, a great number contained within," Annocrates said.

"We kill every last one of the Teverens from the ships," Crassor growled from the shadows. Adding potency to his words, thunder rolled through the skies outside.

Recalling the criss-crossing mass of scars filling the man's back, Rayden held no doubts that he meant every word. He knew the sting of the Teveren lash all too well and intended to repay them many times over.

"It is what they deserve," Doros said. "But we must not be reckless. First we must make certain to free those enslaved. Then the Teverens can pay in blood."

"Are you certain they do not know of us?" Rayden asked Annocrates.

He shook his head emphatically. "Nobody we have spoken with is aware of this encampment. The Teverens show no signs of knowing."

"How long will they remain?" Rayden questioned him.

"They are almost done with repairs to the vessels that suffered damage. They had been awaiting one more ship to join them before they departed," Annocrates answered. "That ship arrived earlier today, just before this latest storm rolled in."

"They don't intend to wait around long," Rayden observed.

"We must move with haste. When the weather clears, they will be taking up anchor and heading southward," Doros said. "We must strike."

"If they have good position, they can hold it despite your greater numbers," Rayden cautioned Doros.

Doros grinned. "I am not suggesting that we attack them on land."

Another wave of thunder unfurled outside as Doros proceeded to elaborate an idea she had in mind. Listening to the concept, Rayden came to admire both the ingenuity and boldness of it.

While drawing upon the skills she possessed, Doros showed that she had a mind for war. When she finished her description, all within the tent, including Rayden, agreed with the proposed plan.

Heart of a Lion

***

Low-profile structures huddled around the shore of a small bay, the village would have appeared an image of rustic tranquility were it not for the cluster of larger vessels dotting the moonlit water. With scant cloud cover, Rayden and the others enjoyed adequate visibility on their approach, a welcome boon to their mission.

Doros dipped her paddle into the water in a perfect rhythm, first on one side and then the other. Guiding one of the small boats they had commandeered from a village just up the coast, she headed directly toward one of the round ships bobbing in the water.

The vessel glided across the surface making nary a sound, the lapping of water at the sides and light splash of the paddle the only noises beyond the crisp, chilly breezes flowing over them. Thunder rippled to the east, marking the ongoing storm that kept the larger ships within the bay's safer environs.

At the late hour, with the inclement weather not far, little chance existed of the Teverens expecting an attack from the sea. In their minds, nobody of right mind would brave the open waters at night with a storm's fury hovering so close.

Fires visible beyond the shoreline showed where the Teverens had set up their temporary encampment. With most of their crews ashore, only a handful of guards would be left to tend to the bound slaves quartered within the hulls of the ships.

Nearing one of the slave vessels, Rayden eyed the shadowy forms visible just above the top strakes. Two guards leaned against the wood, their backs to the water.

The murmur of their voices carried through the night to her ears. Sounding relaxed, the men had no inlking of the lethal threat drifting near.

Doros glanced back to Rayden, ceasing her paddling and letting the boat slow its approach with the ship looming closer.

As planned before, the man seated in the center kept the boat moving in a controlled fashion, on a course bringing it alongside the larger ship.

Rayden patted her chest and then pointed to the enemy guard on the right. Doros nodded, tapped her chest, and pointed to the guard on the left. Rayden nodded as Doros set down her oar and took up her bow. She lifted her axe slowly above her head.

An arrow from Doros sped through the dark, reaching its target just a bit before Rayden's axe landed solid. The pair of Teverens standing at the edge of the vessel jerked upright, a grunt escaping the lips of one, before both slumped to the deck.

The man guiding the boat brought it parallel to the hull of the larger ship. Rayden reached up and grabbed the top of the enemy vessel, pulling herself up and over in a smooth motion.

Her feet touching the planks of the ship's deck, she took up her blade and got into a fighting stance. Behind her, Doros and three others climbed from the boat into the slave ship. They spread out around Rayden with weapons at the ready.

At the far end of the galley, three Teverens turned at the commotion and raised a cry of alarm. Yanking her axe free of the body it protruded from, Rayden bounded down the length of the galley to meet the enemy guards.

Ducking one's swipe with his blade, she brought her axe rushing into his side. Straightening up, she slashed down with her blade and finished the guard off.

Whipping the blade back up, she deflected the thrusting strike of the second man's spear and kicked out, catching him solid in the midsection. As he fell to the ground she unleashed an attack on the third man, finding an opening in an instant. Throat gushing blood and eyes bulging in shock, he toppled backward and crashed to the deck.

Turning back, she eyed the last of the three, scrambling to

get up to his feet. Wide-eyed and fearful, his face froze in place as an arrow barreled into the middle of his forehead. He fell forward, dead before his body sprawled upon the timber planks.

Doros stood a short distance to the left, bow gripped in her left hand. Reaching down with her right, she took up another arrow and looked about for other potential targets.

"Denying me my quarry?" Rayden asked, offering her a grin.

"If I didn't loose that arrow, you would have taken all of them for yourself," Doros replied, glancing back to Rayden. "Not feeling generous tonight, are you?"

Rayden chuckled. "In battle I cut my enemies down until there are no more and prevent them from killing me. That is about all I think of."

While speaking she glanced about, seeing no signs of any more guards aboard the ship. Cries and the clang of weapons sounded in the night from the other Teveren vessels.

Rayden eyed the closed hatch leading down into the belly of the ship. A feeling of apprehension took hold, not toward the guards of the vessels but rather the unfortunates she knew were huddled in the dark. She hoped the ill-treatment of the slaves did not extend too far beyond their dark, cramped confinement, but she anticipated the worst.

She cast a glance back to Doros, "If there are any more guards on this ship, they are hiding among the slaves, down there."

"They aren't going anywhere," Doros said. She looked to one of the men standing with them. "Keep a watch on that hatch."

The man nodded and took up a closer position to the hatch as Rayden strode toward the port side of the vessel. The spot afforded her an unobstructed view of the village and shoreline.

The rest of Doros' plan unfolded before her. Rayden watched several other boats landing ashore. Dark forms streamed outward as soon as the boats lodged into sand, the rebels moving fast to attack the encampment of the Teverens from behind them.

In a way of looking at it, the assault reminded her of Iellia where the Teverens had been the ones striking from the sea at the vulnerable underbelly of the Kartajenians. Rayden wondered for a moment if Doros had been inspired by the tale of Iellia's fall when envisioning the nighttime raid.

The clash of weapons, shouts and agonized cries filled the night air soon after, swelling rapidly in volume. Rayden knew the full trap had been sprung.

With the rear of the enemy beset, another rebel force that had been poised to attack from the front launched its assault. Jaws of vengeful fury closed from sea and land, crushing Teverens within iron teeth.

The other ships became quiet, the fighting aboard them coming to an end. Though the battle on the shore remained furious for a time, it was not much longer before the sounds of struggle died down there as well.

Rayden had no doubts as to the final outcome. The only question centered on how many Teverens had survived, if any had been spared in the blood frenzy. Doros had been adamant that not all of the Teverens be killed, as some would be useful in the more important matter of freeing the slaves kept aboard the ships.

Not much later, a few rebels began pushing boats back into the water from the shore. Heading toward the larger vessels, they brought news of the state of affairs on the land.

A fair number of Teverens had surrendered after the brief period of fighting. In the aftermath, the rebels had discovered several of the vessel captains among the vanquished. Taking up residence in the village, the captains had avoided much of the bloodshed, save for a couple whose blood had been spilled when they rushed to the area where the fighting had raged.

The surviving captains and their remaining crew members

were soon ferried back to the vessels that they had come from, to assist in addressing the matter of the slaves. Many among the rebels saw great justice in making the Teverens face those they kept enslaved, under a new set of circumstances.

With the Teverens overcome and subdued, there would be no danger in freeing the slaves and bringing them up from the holds. The only thing concerning Rayden involved the potential for violent retribution on the part of the rebels and newly-freed slaves. A tense atmosphere still clung to the air, and more than one rebel warrior cast the enemy captives glares filled with lethal intent.

Not many of the Teverens now under guard were the ones directly responsible for the slaves. They were just men employed to crew a sea-going vessel, with little other on their mind than attaining leisure, food, pay, and perhaps a woman if they were lucky.

Rayden did not object to the guilty being held accountable, but in her view those of a lesser offense should not be made to answer to the same degree as those who committed greater ones. The only things she could do involved keeping an eye on the proceedings and applying a discerning mind to everything that developed.

She accompanied the first of the rebels to walk toward the hatch opening into the hold below, wanting to help see to the matter of releasing the slaves. The stench wafting up from the dark when the hatch had been opened gave Rayden a moment's pause. Body odor and excrement, both at pungent levels, choked the air.

Shifting to breathing through her mouth, Rayden took the first steps down. Weapons at the ready, she remained poised should any Teverens be lingering in wait.

The lamp carried by the man coming down the steps just behind her shed light on a number of dirty, haggard faces. At first, their expressions appeared dull and weary. No Teverens crouched in the darkness as Rayden set foot in the hold, peering carefully at the faces around her.

A murmur broke out and rose from the slaves watching Rayden and the others coming down the stairs. The clinks of chains and shuffling of bodies on planks accompanied an air of rising excitement as word rippled throughout the congested hull. All those in bondage knew what loomed before a word had been spoken to them.

"We have come to free you," Annocrates announced in a loud voice, evoking an outburst of sobs and other emotive reactions from the ship's chained, battered occupants. "Whether you join us in our fight against the Teverens is your choice. You are to be free. Go wherever you choose. You do not trade one master for another this day."

Rayden found herself moved by the outpouring of gratitude coming from all around. Tears poured down the cheeks of man and woman alike.

She recognized that the rebels were the answer to desperate prayers for so many of the people that she gazed upon, crammed within that dark, stinking hold. Seeing the relief and pain in their expressions, she did not want to know the horrors that the poor men and women had been subjected to.

Keys retrieved from the body of one of the Teverens above unlocked the lengths of chain binding the men and women. The release of the slaves came as a reward greater than looting the wealth of a king after the sacking of a city.

Rayden committed to memory the looks on the faces of the men and women as the shackles clattered to the wood. In a dark world, each and every instance of liberation served as a ray of purest light.

It was not much longer before the freed slaves were trudging to the top deck. Sore and weakened, many stumbled and swayed, but those near assisted the haggard throng gathering under the stars.

A younger female, of an age where she was just coming into the bloom of womanhood, shrieked in dismay and fear. Rayden's focus snapped to the terrified girl, before following the line of her alarmed gaze.

It had fallen upon one of the newly-bound Teveren captives. As if in reflex, the girl clutched her tattered clothing about her, trying to cover up her body as much as she could. Rayden interpreted the stark reaction at once, a boiling anger rising within her.

An older woman walking near the panicked young woman moved immediately to embrace her, speaking in a low voice and stroking her long, matted hair gently. The sudden commotion drew the attention of the other liberators, some gathering around the agitated girl and others drifting near the Teveren whose presence had invoked the outburst.

Taking them out of earshot from the young woman, Doros questioned a few of the newly-freed slaves about the matter. Crassor, Rayden, and others listened attentively to the ensuing testimony. More than one of those who spoke had been an eyewitness to the reasons why the woman displayed such great fear toward the Teveren.

Everything was as Rayden suspected from the woman's raw, powerful reaction. Several of the men and women explained that the Teveren had been abusing the young woman on a regular basis, having his way with her whenever he wished to indulge his lusts during the journey down the coastline.

The black eye and swollen lip on the young woman's face told Rayden and the others all the rest they needed to know. Without saying a word, Crassor glared at the Teveren before striding away, disappearing into the emptied hull where the slaves had been quartered.

Rayden did not have long to wonder what the man was up to. Crassor returned shortly enough, dragging a substantial length of chain across the upper deck. Iron scraped against wood as Crassor made his way over to where the Teveren stood.

Unceremoniously, Crassor tore the clothes from the Teveren's body until the culprit stood naked before his victim, his remaining comrades, and all the former slaves. Fear brimmed within the man's eyes as Crassor improvised the means of his pending execution.

Seeing the method Crassor intended, Rayden judged it to be a suitable reward for the vile Teveren. She held no sympathy for him. She could not countenance the torture of those not guilty, but justice demanded the wicked be made to answer in full.

When finished, Crassor turned and flashed a cold smile, looking the Teveren straight in the eyes. Openly savoring the Teveren's terror, he paused for a moment before dropping the heavily-weighted end of the chain over the top strake of the vessel's hull.

The forefront of the chain pulled the rest of its length swiftly behind as it plunged into the water, the heavy iron plummeting into the dark depths below. The links remaining in the pile on the deck dwindled in a few heartbeats.

Using a piece of rope, the far end of the chain had been affixed crudely to the body part used to torment and violate the young woman. Hands and legs bound tightly, the offender could do nothing to stop his doom. Forced to witness the means of his demise approaching fast, his face filled with a delirium of terror.

The woman watched in silence with the eye not swollen shut. Countenance brimming with hatred, her gaze locked upon the hysterical Teveren, who had only a fleeting few moments left until meeting a terrible, well-deserved fate.

Trapped in a frenzy of pain and fright, the man jerked forward and toppled awkwardly over the side of the boat as the end of the chain pulled him along. With a loud splash, he vanished beneath the surface, dragged deep under and consigned to a watery death.

Rayden watched the conclusion of the justice meted out with a cold feeling inside, wishing all such predators of innocence were made to answer in such a way. The man's death had been swift and his suffering brief, but the same could not be said for the woman.

Her swollen eye and lip would heal in time, but a scar deep and invisible would remain within her in the years ahead. If true justice could be done, Rayden surmised, the violator could be resurrected and made to suffer again and again. Perhaps the priests speaking of a hell in the afterworld had something of merit to offer, after all.

A few other instances of retribution followed as the most abusive and brutal among the surviving Teverens were identified and made to answer for their crimes. No harm was done to the ones who had not committed grievous transgressions against the liberated slaves. Rayden doubted any of the remaining Teverens would forget the harsh lesson, if they ever happened to find themselves aboard a slave vessel again.

After everyone had disembarked for the shore, the vessels were set on fire, never to be used again to transport slaves or Teverens. From the land, Rayden watched the burning ships as the winds whipping the flames up higher tossed her flowing blonde locks about.

The victors gathered up all weapons that could be found, as well as anything else of value found on the surviving Teverens. The Teverens cooperated swiftly enough, after the first few to raise objections were met with busted lips or broken noses.

For her part, Rayden pocketed a fistful of silver coins taken from the chest of one of the wealthy slave owners, figuring it would not hurt to keep a few more Teveren coins with her. She also picked up an ivory comb she intended to give Hamilcar, to help him manage his thick, unkempt mass of hair.

As if an afterthought, she procured a well-crafted Teveren blade and sheath. She intended them for Hamilcar's eventual keeping, to wield when the time was right for him to begin training in the use of weapons.

There were plenty of spoils to go around, and the rebels appeared satisfied with the ample loot. With few losses incurred on their part, an influx of motivated, joyous men and women freed from the ships, and a prodigious bounty, the less savory energies that often arose following a battle were battened down.

While the villagers were just simple folk scraping out a living on the coast, they were still Teverens. Their possessions and lives spared, the villagers were given nothing from the abundance confiscated from the fleet.

Only a handful of Teverens, a group containing the most prominent of wealth and rank, would be taken along with the rebels. The rest were to be spared, much to their surprise.

Within nothing more than the clothes on their bodies and shoes on their feet, the remaining Teverens from the fleet were set free south of the village. Relief shone from their eyes, but Rayden knew better than to think that the same men would not desire to return with a large Teveren force and see the upstart rebels conquered and put in chains.

Nevertheless, the rebels had done the right thing. They were not in the business of slavery nor could they take it upon themselves to feed around a hundred more mouths, especially when it was challenging enough to find sustenance for the rebel force.

Rayden could not have stopped them from killing the Teverens outright, but she found herself with a stronger affinity for the rebels in the aftermath of the slaves' liberation. It took another kind of strength sparing the Teverens' lives when the grisly crucifixions lining the Boreus Way testified that the same mercy would not have been shown to the rebels had the circumstances been reversed.

The rebels had proven themselves worthy of her loyalty and they deserved to find a home free of the Teveren shadow. Staring out at the billowing flames reflecting off the water's surface, Rayden made a promise in her heart to do everything that she could to help the rebels attain a haven.

She had committed to safeguarding Hamilcar, but she knew that the goals had common cause. If the rebels found their way to a refuge, the boy would find one too.

CHAPTER 12

The haughty boasting of a Teveren citizen of high-rank, one who had owned a large number of the slaves being taken southward, proved fortuitous. Everything he blurted from his fat mouth loomed valuable to Rayden and the rebels standing in the tent with her.

"Three veteran legions are being assembled in the Divine City ... as we speak," the portly, middle-aged figure said, glaring at Doros, Rayden, and the others. His eyes glittered with the sheen of crystalline ice as he continued, "Peronnius will crush your treason soon enough. Every one of you will fall to him."

"More Teverens for us to kill, that is welcome news," Crassor replied in a low voice, adding a dismissive shrug that spurred a redder hue on the enraged Teveren's face.

Though she left her thoughts unspoken, the news came as anything but welcome to Rayden's ears. She knew the name spoken by the Teveren well. Peronnius represented ill-tidings for the prospects of the motley force of ex-slaves.

Several victories over the Kartajenians had spread the man's name far and wide. At the center of the growing Teveren empire, Peronnius possessed an unrivaled aptitude for war.

If the rumors about him could be believed, he also had great skill at combat and would not be an easy opponent were Rayden to meet him on a battlefield. A commander with honed fighting skills demanded respect from all but the most foolish.

Three veteran legions would have the rebel force badly outnumbered. Commanded in person by Peronnius, the legions represented near-certain doom for the upstarts.

No matter how tough their hearts might be, the former slaves remained an undisciplined rabble, and the warriors of Peronnius would fight as a unified body. A cohesive force under the storied Teveren could prevail against one several times their number. In this instance, the situation loomed even worse as Peronnius would also hold the advantage of numbers.

"Say what you will, slave, that is not all," the man began once more, with an air of disdain. He grinned icily at Crassor. Rayden raised her hand up to halt the big warrior from striking the levity from the Teveren's puffy lips.

"What's not all?" Rayden pressed, casting Crassor a hardened, sideways glance and shaking her head. The latter's face clouded over with ire, though the brawny man managed to restrain himself.

"Marus is bringing two more legions, the very ones used to ornament the Boreus Way with the bodies of you scum," the Teveren lashed out, a look of malice rising in his eyes. The cold smile spread wider across his face. "How long can you hang on a cross in the hot sun before you rot? I'm thinking you will find out very soon. I would love to see all of you scum rotting. I would stand there and enjoy every last moment watching the carrion birds feast upon your carcasses...I would..."

The man became silent and his eyes grew wide as a large shadow engulfed him. The arrogance in his expression fled in an instant, replaced with shock and panic.

This time, Rayden did nothing to halt Crassor when his fist exploded into the man's face, crumpling the Teveren's nose and eliciting a high-pitched sound resembling a pig's squeal. Several more heavy blows rained down upon the Teveren, rendering his face into a bloody mess and removing all traces of smugness.

When Crassor pulled back, life still clung faintly to the battered, unconscious man, but his arrogance had reaped a bitter harvest. Thick splotches of blood, a few containing broken teeth, littered the floor in front of him as he was dragged away by a couple of men.

"I would say the questioning is now at an end," Annocrates remarked, matter-of-factly.

"We got what we needed," Rayden said evenly. "Enough to inform our decisions."

"Our decision is easy. We fight them," Crassor growled. "What is there to discuss?"

"You would confront five legions. And these are no average legions," Rayden told him. "You have already faced those under Marus. None of these legions are led by those whose minds are fixated on wine, sweet meats, and getting in between the thighs of women. These legions are commanded by men of war."

"They are still men, not gods," Crassor said. "All men can be slain."

Rayden glared at Crassor, astounded at his thick-headedness. The military acumen of Peronnius combined with the cruel ferocity of Marus stood as a sentence of death upon each and every man, woman, and child within the rebel horde.

The righteousness of the rebel cause would not determine the battle. Overwhelming power guided by merciless spirits would prevail no matter how many Teverens she could kill on a battlefield.

"I am not questioning your courage," Crassor said. "I want blood for what they have done across the river."

"If we were driven across the river by one of these commanders, what will happen if we meet the legions of both of these Teverens in open battle?" Annocrates questioned, looking to Crassor. "The enemy against us would be well over twice as large as the force we already could not overcome."

"I will not run. There will be no cross for me. I wish to make my stand," Crassor stated firmly. "I will prevail, or I will die."

A few others within the tent met his declaration with nods or voiced affirmations. Rayden understood what burned within them, but following a path of reason did not mean a warrior lacked courage.

"I would stand with you and fight them all to the end," Doros stated. "But the decision made by the leaders of this group will guide the fates of many who trust us to seek the best path of wisdom."

Crassor's jaw tightened and Rayden knew he harbored a death-wish. His hatred for the Teverens flooded any attempt at reason. Anyone would have to tread carefully to get past the man's storm of emotions.

"We should take some time to think upon what we have heard," Rayden said, interjecting to defuse the rising tension. "And then we should meet together, once we have each had this time to ourselves. It is not an easy choice we are faced with."

One by one, the others agreed, including Crassor, which gave Rayden a shred of hope concerning the strong-willed man. The questioning of the high-ranking Teveren prisoners came to an end.

The only relief that could be found within the tent rested upon the faces of two Teveren prisoners awaiting interrogation. For the others gathered in the shadowy interior, powerful emotions to be wrestled with and momentous decisions to ponder loomed nigh.

***

Rayden left the others and strode into the night by herself. She continued out toward the edge of the encampment and made her way over to the edge of a campfire, where only two older men sat quietly together on the opposite side.

Feeling the heat on her face, she gazed into the crackling depths of wood and flame. Many thoughts occupied her mind.

A terrible dilemma loomed. She could see the stark, inevitable consequences that would come with one of the choices available to the rebels. The other choice held no promises, filled with uncertainty and further hardship. But a chance, no matter how slim it might be, stood far better than having no chance at all.

Yet even Doros had shown an inclination toward Crassor's desire to charge headlong into certain death. Though admiring the heart of the rebels, Rayden had not come as far as she had to see her life and that of Hamilcar hurled away so recklessly.

Frustration welled inside of her. She possessed a gift for fighting, not giving speeches. How she could sway Crassor and the other rebel leaders to see the truth of it all eluded her. She let loose an extended breath and then heard footsteps.

She knew the softer step coming up from behind. Without looking, she said in a terse manner, "Doros, I am in no mood to discuss anything. It is best I be alone right now."

The footsteps slowed, drawing closer. "I wanted to see how you were. I could see the anger on your face."

"Anger for good reason," Rayden said, the fire hissing before her. "Are you all that blind? Can you not see the obvious? Do you wish for death that badly?"

"We are not blind," Doros responded. "We have been through hell, and they have not answered for what they have done to us."

"So you seek certain death, instead of living ... and living free of Teveren rule," Rayden said, casting a quick glance toward Doros. "Would not living free be a better triumph?"

"What choice is there?" Doros asked.

"You are that blind," Rayden declared, eyes narrowing.

"Then tell me, Rayden," Doros said.

Rayden said nothing at first. The tension between them coalesced until finally she broke the silence.

"Only one path holds any chance for you and the others," Rayden said, looking toward Doros, who stood brooding near the firelight.

"And what path is that?" Doros asked with an indignant flare. "Tell me what great path beckons to us?"

"It holds dangers of its own, but the north is the only chance that you and the others have," Rayden answered. "Only in the north can you live, and live free."

"The north?"

"You cannot go south. Even were you to cross the seas, the Kartajenians will not look kindly upon a mass of former slaves who took up arms against their masters. The Kartajenians have slaves of their own. They will not like the idea of slaves being able to rise up spreading throughout their lands. Especially at a time when their power is waning."

Doros nodded slowly, a somber expression on her face as she listened to Rayden's words. "But the north is filled with ... tribes."

Rayden caught the hesitation in the other's words. "Barbarian tribes ... I believe you were about to say."

Doros looked downward, saying nothing and confirming Rayden's suspicion at once. The aspersion anything but unfamiliar, she chuckled.

"It is what we are called," Rayden said with an air of good humor. "I have heard my people called barbarians more times than I can count. If I had a silver coin for each instance, I would possess the wealth of a great queen. But whether you call us barbarians or not, the tribal lands are the only hope for these men and women."

"Crossing the mountains will be perilous."

"There is a great pass that leads into lands I know well enough," Rayden told her. "The journey will not be easy. But it is the only way."

"Or we could stay and kill Teverens," Doros said with a hunger in her eyes.

"If you stay and do not fall to Teveren blades on a battlefield, you will hang from a cross until you cannot hold yourself up to breathe," Rayden said, staring into the other woman's eyes, seeking to convey the enormity of the situation facing the former slaves. "Then you will suffocate and die after a long agony, and your body will be meat for scavengers."

The image grisly and terrible, Rayden could not afford to soften the magnitude of the threat. Death or a danger-filled, slim chance at survival stood as the only options for the polyglot rabble. She had to make Doros understand that.

"What will you do?" Doros asked, voice lowering.

Rayden knew she could quietly slip away and take the boy with her. But that would not be an option unless the rebels were foolish enough to choose to stay and await the arrival of Peronnius' and Marus' legions.

"I will not see Hamilcar's life thrown away," Rayden stated. "I will fight alongside you if the path of reason is taken."

"So you will leave us?" Doros said.

"I will see if there is any wisdom left among you first," Rayden said. "Then I will decide. Or rather, you will decide."

CHAPTER 13

Rayden's gaze swept across the faces of the rebel leaders. A day had passed, and the time of decision had arrived.

She thought of Hamilcar and felt unwavering conviction. In her heart, she had come to terms with the decision to leave the rebels immediately if they chose to meet the legions of Peronnius and Marus in open battle.

Doros and Annocrates arrived together, taking up positions near her. Across the small circle, Crassor had gathered with several loyal to him.

Though a council of leaders, there were no formalities to be heeded. As soon as all were gathered, the deliberation could begin.

"We must come to a decision," Annocrates began. "We have all taken time to think upon the choices we have before us. Now speak freely, and openly, and we will choose our fate."

"I have thought further on Rayden's words," Crassor said, casting a look in her direction as he paused. "I cannot dispute her wisdom."

A hush fell over the gathering. The words sounded more like capitulation than agreement. The hard look in his eyes and dour expression on his face told Rayden that he wished he could advocate anything other than avoiding battle.

"I am not afraid to die, but I must seek life for all who have escaped Teveren chains," Crassor said. He turned his attention toward a couple of men who had been freed from the ships in the bay. "To have their chains lifted and then be taken to their deaths is not the right path, even if I wish to fight to my last breath spilling Teveren blood."

There was no doubt in Rayden's mind that Crassor hated speaking for anything less than fighting the enemy. His strength in overcoming his inner rage and passions surprised her, as she had not thought him capable of overcoming his fury.

Murmurs broke out among several near to Crassor. Looks of surprise were displayed on many faces, but none of those loyal to him offered any objections to his statement.

"So, what is our other path?" Crassor asked, looking to Rayden and Annocrates. "Tell us of the hope within it, if there truly is any."

"Rayden speaks of the north," Doros stated. "Lands beyond Teveren control. Lands not controlled by empires."

"Lands that still have others living in them," one of Crassor's loyalists said. "The north is the land of the barbarians. I would not think we would get a kind welcome there."

Doros looked to Rayden and nodded. She stepped forward so that all could see her.

"The tribes of the north live within large territories, much of which is wild and unsettled," Rayden told them. "I know the people of the northern lands and I believe we can find our way to land that all of you can make your own. It will not be an easy life at first, but it will be one gained without bloodshed, and no Teveren shadow will fall upon you."

"In this age, the Teverens turn their eyes everywhere in this world," Crassor said.

"And then a sea of Teveren blood can be spilled, if they dare come north," Rayden said. "That will be the time to fight them, and you would not be standing alone if they dare to tread on northern ground."

The thought appeared to placate Crassor. He grew silent and gave her a curt nod.

"Where must we go, to enter these lands?" one of Crassor's companions asked.

"A great mountain pass leads from Teveren lands," Rayden said. "We head north from here, and then take a western route through the mountains to the pass. A few days steady march will be needed. The strength of the Teverens resides in the five legions under Marus and Peronnius. I do not think they can overtake us if we depart from here soon."

A flurry of low voices sounded as the rebel leaders conversed among each other. Rayden remained in the center, awaiting the end of their private deliberations.

After some time had passed, Doros and Annocrates stepped forward, taking places to either side of Rayden. Annocrates looked around at the rebel leaders, their voices dying down as they gave him their attention.

"Time is not our ally," he addressed those gathered. "What path are we to take? Do we have a consensus?"

One after another, the various leaders voiced their support for seeking out the mountain pass to the north. Relief filled Rayden at each of the pronouncements.

She had wanted to stay among the rebels. In choosing to take the mountain pass, the rebels made it possible for her path to remain joined with theirs.

***

The rebels began the long march to the mountain pass only a day later. A nervous energy rippled throughout the encampment as everyone prepared to leave. No solid destination beckoned to them, only a journey into an unknown future.

Rayden and Hamilcar kept close to Doros, who walked near

the front of the loose, lengthy column. On the first days of the march, they headed through woodlands along more level terrain. The skies remained clear and the temperature stayed mild, bringing no additional hardship to their travel.

Scouts ranged farther ahead, keeping an eye out for any Teveren threat. Reports came back to the column periodically. As Rayden expected, nothing stood in their way, and they were able to reach a series of low hills within a few days.

The hills slowed their progress as the rebels found their route through them, but the goal had drawn into sight, great mountains lining the horizon. Mountains presented a much more difficult task than hills, and Rayden knew they would soon have to pick their course carefully.

As the column reached the base of the mountains, Rayden and several others met as camp was struck. They agreed to form a vanguard through a narrow ravine leading westward, heading toward the pass they sought. In order to make certain no time was lost with the main body of the column, the group decided to sweep through the ravine at night.

If no Teverens or other large groups were detected, the primary mass of rebels could travel from the outbreak of dawn and make use of every moment of daylight. Gladdened at the news that she would be escaping the monotony of a slow march, Rayden returned from the meeting and met with Hamilcar.

She told him to stay with a young brother and sister, both a few years younger than he, who had taken to walking along with Rayden and Hamilcar during the march. She sensed that the two youths needed some guidance and company, while Hamilcar would benefit from having a duty.

She told him to watch out for the younger ones until she returned. His mood perked up considerably at being given the task, allowing Rayden some peace of mind. With Hamilcar taken care of, she could turn her full focus to the approaching night.

Heart of a Lion

***

Navigating the ravine proved a difficult challenge on a night when thicker cloud cover obscured much of the moon's silvery light. Progress came in a tedious manner when darkness cloaked treacherous footing and perhaps other, unsavory things.

From time to time, cool breezes coursed down the channel hemmed with lofty rock formations, but for the most part the air remained calm. Yet instead of finding comfort in the stillness, Rayden's nerves remained on edge. A heavy disquiet permeated the atmosphere, an unsettling feeling she could detect after years spent living amid all manner of threats and dangers.

Ears and eyes poised for any hint of disturbance, she maintained a disciplined, soft step as the group continued along the bottom of the ravine. She looked out for any sign that might justify the queasy feeling in her gut, but after covering a considerable distance she still saw nothing out of the ordinary.

Near to her, Doros proved to have good skill at walking in silence. A couple of brief glances toward the woman told Rayden that she also sensed something amiss. Tension reflected in her face, while her eyes shifted about, peering intently at their murky surroundings.

Proceeding far into the ravine, Rayden's senses did not recede from the edge that they had been on from the time they entered it. If anything, the unease within her deepened further. Every pool of shadow they passed left her with a heavier inner weight. Something about the ravine was very wrong.

She wished the clouds would break and allow the full light of the moon through. Uncooperative, the overhead mass drifted through the night skies unabated, leaving everything draped in a concealing murk.

Rayden snapped to a rigid position, hearing a light buzzing in the air above. The sound rose with each passing moment. The noise resembled the beating of insect wings, though it came to her ears far too loud to be anything of the sort.

She raised her head to search the sky when a terrible scream cut through the darkness behind her. Shrill and desperate, the cry sent ice through her veins. Drawing her gaze downward, she stared into the gloom but could see nothing.

At that moment, a small break in the clouds freed the moon for a moment, allowing more light into the ravine. Looking back toward the buzzing sound, Rayden saw an elongated, winged shape crossing overhead.

The sight confused her. To her eyes, the thing looked to be segmented in form, unlike any bird, bat, or other flying creature she had ever seen. She tracked it with her eyes, trying to make sense of its odd form.

Rife with fear, another cry erupted in the darkness, much closer to where Rayden stood. Blade and axe in her hands, she took up a defensive posture, as did Doros with her bow and a spear-armed man a few strides away.

A bizarre and shocking scene unfolded as the man yelled suddenly in alarm, his spear dropping to the ground as he began clutching at himself. At first it seemed that he moved ponderously, but Rayden realized his movements were being hindered by something else entirely.

Looking up and to the right, she espied an extensive form clinging to the rocks. Eyes adjusting, she perceived a series of ghostly white tendrils running from the dark body of the creature toward the increasingly immobilized man. Drifting in milky layers, the secretions clung to the man's body, his movements finally ceasing as he toppled to the ground.

Larger of body than Rayden, the elongated shape perched on the rock facing scuttled downward, heading swiftly toward the inert man. Several narrow, extended legs propelled the creature, attached to a body covered with a layer of fine hairs. Multiple dark eyes glistened in the moonlight, perched above a prominent set of fang-like extensions.

Its immense size not the only difference from other spiders, the creature possessed a distinctive and troubling feature. The characteristic added an entirely different dimension to the situation at hand, one that contrasted sharply with its much tinier brethren; the monstrosity had wings.

Hearing a buzzing sound growing overhead, Rayden had a sinking feeling, realizing that the things flying above were the same as the menace before her. She glanced up just in time to see one of the spider-beasts drawing into a hovering position over Doros. Thin webbing filaments had just started to fall downward when Rayden sent her axe hurtling toward the dark shape.

The beast jerked in the air for a moment, before plummeting toward the ground below. Rayden leaped past the wide-eyed Doros as the winged hunter slammed into the rocky ground. She hacked furiously at the creature with her blade before it could gain full equilibrium.

Gore spattered Rayden as her blade chopped into the creature's innards. A few of its legs twitched as its insides oozed and spread along the ground.

Retrieving her axe and turning away from the dead thing, Rayden saw that Doros had regained her focus. Loosing two arrows in rapid succession, she attacked the one that had come down from the rocks to beset the spear-carrying man. The creature toppled backwards, both arrows protruding from its body. Its legs constricted, folding into its body as the creature grew still and expired.

"Rayden!" Doros cried out in alarm, eyes jolting wide and looking above her.

Rayden dived to the side just in time. Another winged spider swooped in, gliding without sound and attempting to take her unawares.

The creature alighted on the ground where she had been

standing in perfect balance, whipping about to face her with astonishing speed. She stared into an array of dark pitiless eyes, all of them filled with her reflection.

Reacting in an instant, Rayden cried out and drove her blade forward in a powerful thrust. She took the creature squarely in its face, driving the honed iron between the fangs and cluster of black eyes. An arrow streaked in from the side a moment later, burrowing deep into the rear segment of the creature's body.

Rayden yanked her sword free and landed several extra blows, hacking the spider's visage into an unrecognizable, gory mass. She did not take a single step away or turn her back on the thing until she was certain it lay dead.

Rayden scanned the nearby rocks and looked above, but did not see any more of the spider creatures in the vicinity. Blood sped through her veins, every last part of her focused in combat mode.

"Follow me," she called to Doros, heading back the way they had come.

A couple of men emerged from where they had sought hiding places during the tumult. Taking courage from Rayden's lead, they hurried to follow in her wake as she and Doros bounded along the narrow trail. After about a hundred paces, the four came upon the first victim of the attack.

Wrapped thoroughly in silken webbing, the body could not be identified at first sight. The winged spider, with fangs buried deep into its hapless victim and gorging itself, paid little heed to the new arrivals.

A moment later, an arrow tore into the area just in back of its eyes. Rayden charged in behind the arrow and severed two of the creature's legs off with one sweeping blow, causing the thing to stagger and struggle to gain balance.

The creature flopped awkwardly to the ground, losing two more of its legs as it suffered blows from the two men who had followed Rayden and Doros. Blades rising and falling in rapid succession, Rayden and the men reduced the spider to a pulpy, mutilated carcass.

Breathing heavily, Rayden turned toward the victim wrapped in the webbing. The face of the young man she discovered when she cut away the binding filaments held no signs of life. His dull eyes stared upward, without the faintest spark or sign of response.

Nothing could be done for him. Closing his eyes with her hand, she could only hope he had died swiftly.

Carefully, those who had survived the attack began to regroup. Only the young man in the webbing had died in the horrific assault, but no chances were taken as the rest stayed together and remained in place for awhile longer.

No buzzing sounds broke the heavy silence, and no further signs of the flying predators manifested as the night dragged onward. After becoming satisfied that the immediate threat had passed, Rayden and the others started back for the main body of the column. Moving together with weapons out, they maintained a guarded wariness through the entire distance.

Reaching the encampment, they spread warning of the winged spiders, raising the state of alertness everywhere they went. Few in the camp slept well for the remainder of the night.

Despite the discovery of the creatures, it was decided that the column would still proceed through the ravine at daylight. Most who had scouted during the night, including Rayden, believed the predators would remain hidden with the light of the sun above. The full numbers and strength of the entire column would also stand a powerful deterrent.

When dawn arrived and the column moved into the ravine, hands gripped weapons tightly. A host of eyes and ears kept watch for anything scuttling or flying.

With only one trail suitable for such a large body of people, the rebels pressed steadily forward. They took the risk of pulling back their scouts for the time being, in exchange for keeping everyone together.

Though she knew little about their natures, Rayden doubted the winged spiders would chance attacking such a large and concentrated group. With the sun bathing the floor of the ravine, the things would probably scurry back to the dark crevices or holes that they had initially come from.

Having witnessed the incredible speed of the creatures, she still kept her weapons at hand and urged the warriors in the column to do the same. Her gaze locked to any small cave or pool of shadow that they came across on the march, relinquishing its hold only when they were well past the spot in question.

The column remained quiet, such that a single shout of alarm would carry fast. She kept Hamilcar to her right, putting herself between him and any potential ambush on their side of the ravine. She could tell the boy wanted to ask many questions, but he heeded her insistence on silence.

When they finally reached the end of the ravine and no longer were flanked by towering heights of craggy rock, the rebels exhibited a sense of relief and joy. Rayden, Doros, and many of the other warriors turned back and remained at the exit of the ravine until the last part of the column finished its trek.

She stared into the sunlit ravine, recalling the horrors that stalked the rocks and soared through the heights in the darkness. She committed everything she had experienced about the winged spiders to memory, making another addition to her knowledge of the dangerous and rare things lurking within the shadows of her world.

The night encounter stood as yet another testament that no such thing as certainty existed in the world, only probability. The unknown could arise in any place, at any time and in all kinds of appearances; even in the form of a giant spider capable of taking flight.

CHAPTER 14

After passing through the ravine the rebels continued onward. They maintained a brisk pace until nightfall, before setting camp.

Despite a healthy distance from the ravine, none of the rebels objected to maintaining an extensive, sizeable watch throughout the night. Additional fires were lit all around the perimeter and eyes kept a lookout on the skies as well as the ground.

The night passed without incident, dawn breaking clear on the eastern horizon. The column formed up and set out westward, the morning beginning the final approach to the entrance of the great mountain pass that would take them north.

Less than a day's march remained in the journey. A chance at freedom beckoning, the mood of the men and women began to lighten. Laughter began filtering through the extended ranks, reflecting a buoyant energy flowing from the anticipation of reaching the pass that would see the Teveren Empire's lands left far behind.

About midday, a group of forward scouts returned to the column with terrible news. The dark tidings rippled through the rebel mass, dampening their spirits at once.

A large Teveren force occupied the heart of the pass. The far-ranging scouts related the daunting account of a palisade-surrounded camp, filled with the empire's soldiers.

The enemy camp lay squarely in their path. There were no routes for the column to go around the obstacle. From the estimate of the scouts, the Teverens outnumbered the rebels by a wide margin, causing further distress within the column's ranks.

Having drawn to a halt, the column reversed course for a short while until the rebels set camp about a day's march from the pass entrance. With the camp situated near a small river that could provide ample water, the rebels claimed an advantageous site, but there was nothing to celebrate.

Unable to go forward, with nothing but death at their back, the rebels entered a restless period of inaction that crept from one day into the next. No clear answers loomed before them. A stronger enemy force blocked the pass, and the ranks of the former slaves would not be growing stronger anytime soon.

Foraging and hunting parties were organized and dispatched to the surrounding land. Those skilled in fishing took to plying the river for whatever could be harvested from it. Feeding over two thousand people presented a grave dilemma, one that would soon become a greater adversary than the Teverens.

A close watch was kept on the Teveren position. After the rebels had settled into their camp, Rayden accompanied a scouting group to get her own look at the fortified enemy. Everything that she witnessed was as the first scouts had indicated.

A palisade of sharpened timber stakes fronted by a trench protected a force that numbered much larger than the rebel horde. Attacking the camp directly was out of the question, the only option would be for the rebels to draw the Teverens out of the camp for an open battle.

Observing the enemy carefully over the course of the next day, Rayden became convinced that drawing the Teverens into open battle would be folly. The high discipline she saw displayed everywhere reflected a camp brimming with veteran soldiers.

Her suspicions about their capability were confirmed soon enough, when a small number of rebel scouts engaged in a skirmish with a Teveren patrol. Only a couple of the scouts escaped with their lives.

The two rebel scouts still breathed only because Rayden had reached them in time, cutting down the five Teverens pursuing them. Spared from a death they believed certain, the elated men hugged her tightly, one of them weeping openly.

With advantages in both numbers and experience, the Teverens would not fear meeting the rebels in open battle. Rayden knew the enemy could not be drawn too far away from their main encampment, but were the rebels to offer battle in closer proximity to the Teveren position, the enemy would undoubtedly oblige.

Even so, the scenario echoed the one that had driven them north, offering almost certain defeat for the rebels. A disciplined Teveren force that significantly outnumbered the rebels would prove an adversary far too much to overcome.

The situation presented a vexing dilemma. Caught in what looked to be an endless limbo, the rebels could not go forward or back without meeting destruction.

All the while, time would become an increasing adversary. The situation could not remain in stasis forever. Strains within a camp dwindling in food and supplies were certain to break into a destructive storm of the kind that would divide the camp and pit rebel against rebel. Rayden had seen those fracturing dynamics happen more than once before, in sieges and on campaigns.

As the days passed, Rayden could see the agitation rising in the moods of the idle rebels. Crassor and some of the other rebel leaders started to advocate for drawing the Teverens out in open battle, surmising that the rebels stood a better chance of prevailing if a battle was fought imminently. Rayden could not dispute Crassor's argument that waiting only degraded the rebels' strength and did nothing averse to the enemy.

Something had to give eventually. Rayden could only hope reckless decisions were avoided. One way or another, she knew the current circumstances would not last much longer and she had to be prepared for the worst.

***

No more than a day later, Rayden made an unpleasant discovery that struck much closer to her heart. Hamilcar could not be found anywhere, having gone missing since the early morning.

At first, Rayden thought he might have wandered off with one of the foraging groups. But when midday crossed into afternoon, and then evening, with no sign of the boy, she began to worry. Dread took root with the fall of darkness, the worst possibilities occupying her thoughts.

Later that night, Rayden searched throughout the sprawling camp, asking everywhere she went after the boy. A fixture around the campfires, he loved listening to the tales spun deep into the night, and she knew his extended absence unusual. Passing campfire after campfire, her search continued to turn up empty.

She could not rest until she knew he had not run afoul of someone in the camp. With a couple thousand people in the rebel multitude, a young boy with little experience of the world at large provided an inviting target for those of ill intent. The fact that most in the camp had so little to occupy their time with on a daily basis only worsened the possibility of grave harm coming to the boy.

At last, an older woman sitting by herself at a fire near the camp's outer edge nodded at Rayden's inquiry. She pointed off into the darkness beyond and told Rayden that the boy had gone that way. Though the woman insisted he had been alone, Rayden took her leave without delay and hurried off into the night.

Thankfully, the boy left a trail easy enough for her to pick up and follow. The moonlight revealed the telltale impressions in the dirt, bringing Rayden some comfort in the fact that no other footprints, human or otherwise, shared the same pathway.

At last, she came upon Hamilcar, a fair distance from the camp. As the old woman had said, he was alone, arms wrapped about his knees and staring up into the starry night skies.

Steps making no sound, she came up behind him. She drew to a stop about five paces away.

"Hamilcar," she said gently.

Her voice could have been a thunderclap, startling the boy as he scrambled about to face her. The night could not mask the glisten of tears along his cheeks, nor the moist sheen coating his eyes.

"Rayden," he muttered in a voice thick with emotion. "I ... I did not expect to see you out here."

"Leaving the camp alone in the night is a sure way to bring me to you," Rayden stated, a tone of admonishment girding her words. "If Teveren scouts roam the night, you are far enough out to be within their reach. If some beast prowls the darkness, you would be easy prey. What you have done is foolish."

"I ... I did not mean to worry you. I ... just needed to be alone," the boy replied nervously, with an air of apology.

Rayden walked closer to the boy and took a seat on the ground by the spot that he had just gotten up from. Her voice softened, and she patted the ground at her side, "Sit back down with me, for a few moments."

The boy sat on the ground next to Rayden, looking toward her with a curious expression.

"I never said we have to go back right now. I just do not want you wandering away alone while we are on the march or in camp," Rayden told him. Looking into the boy's eyes, she took in the sadness and fear she saw reflected within them.

The boy nodded to her, blinking back a muster of fresh tears that threatened to escape. "I'm sorry, Rayden. I didn't mean to be a problem. I just had to get away from the camp. I just couldn't stay there tonight."

"And you could have told me you needed to get away," Rayden said. "Now ... tell me what is hurting."

"Hurting? I...I am well," the boy replied, sounding confused. "I don't have any injuries."

"I am not talking about your body," Rayden said. With a closed right fist she tapped the middle of her chest lightly. "I mean inside ... here. Tell me. What is hurting? I can see it plain enough in your face. Speak of it. It is the only way to get it out of you."

The boy hesitated for a moment, but finally he began speaking. Like the skies opening up and raining down, he poured the things tormenting him out to Rayden.

She did not interrupt, listening carefully to his words. She learned that he harbored great fears of what might happen to him if something happened to her, or if she were to leave without him. The thought of being left at the mercy of the rebels evoked panic in his eyes.

What his parents had done, in giving him over to the priests of the bull-god for sacrifice, also tortured him. He told her of the betrayal he felt at being consigned to death by the family he had lived with every day of his life up until that terrible day.

He considered himself an orphan, with nowhere to call home. It soon became clear that the only tether he held onto was Rayden herself.

"I lost my own mother and father when I was not much older than you," Rayden informed the boy when he grew quiet, a deep sympathy abiding within toward his circumstance. "I once thought they would be there forever ... but the day came when both were gone, and my world changed."

She knew the kind of pain and emptiness he contended

with. In some darker moments, Rayden still found herself having to fight off such inner torments. Time helped to numb and drive back the aches, but they were always there, dwelling just under the surface.

Even though the boy's mother and father yet lived, something irrevocable had transpired when they had offered him willingly for the fires of sacrifice. They now stood dead to the boy, in the way that the physical deaths of Rayden's parents had affected her.

A gulf that could not be spanned had manifested in the boy's world, one that weighed both heart and spirit down with heavy burdens. With all of the hardships and dangers surrounding him, as they trekked through unfamiliar lands and faced perilous threats, life had undoubtedly become overwhelming.

"I have lost them. I have lost my home, everyone I knew, and now we may be killed or made slaves," the boy lamented. He paused, looking downward, and then added in a lower voice. "And I fear I will lose you. Without you, I am lost."

The boy's confession stabbed far into Rayden's heart. She had saved him from a fiery death and warded him on the journey, but the day would come when they would have to go on separate paths.

Rayden's world was no place for a younger boy like Hamilcar. He had a life to live and needed a healthy environment to grow into the man he would become one day. The path Rayden traveled, courting the deadliest adversaries and embracing the greatest hardships, would not serve the boy well.

"I will do everything that I can to find you a place that you can make a home," Rayden told him. "It will not be easy for you and it will take time. But you will never lose me as a friend. I could never forget you. None of us knows what tomorrow will bring, but my life is not one I would risk sharing with anyone. My road is one that must be walked alone."

"If I could only wield a sword ... or an axe ... like you,"

Hamilcar declared in a wistful tone, raising his eyes up to her.

Rayden smiled, reaching over and tousling his thick, curly hair. "Maybe one day you will, even better than I can."

The boy smiled at her words and then shook his head. "You are not being serious. I have never seen anyone use a sword or axe better than you."

Rayden chuckled. "Then you need to see more warriors in the world. There are many better than I with a sword or axe. I have even killed a few."

The boy laughed, shaking his head again. "Now that doesn't make any sense. How can you do that if they are better?"

"Sometimes it is a matter of the heart of the warrior and not the skill," Rayden said, thinking of a few fearsome opponents she had overcome, against all odds. "And I know you have a big heart. You would not be here with me now if you did not."

"You have helped me," Hamilcar said. "All through this journey. I wouldn't have survived it without you."

"And you have helped me," Rayden said, the words holding no shred of deception in them.

"I have never wielded a blade or weapon," Hamilcar countered, in a melancholic air. "I do not even know how to hold a weapon like the ones you have ... in the proper way."

"Do you think the use of weapons is the only value a man or woman can have?" Rayden asked. She shook her head. "You have much to learn, young Hamilcar."

"You were born to be a warrior, that much is obvious," the boy replied. "I have no idea what I was born to be. I only know I was not born just to be a god's sacrifice."

"You were born with gifts and a purpose," Rayden assured him.

"It is hard for me to see any gifts," the boy lamented. "I have really never been good at anything. How could I ever be a warrior like you? Among my friends, I was never the fastest, or the strongest. Far from it. I got pummeled more than once in the streets of Kartajen."

A frown grew on his face, and the boy heaved a sigh. She could tell the admission brought him embarrassment.

"It is true that some are born with great size, or exceptional speed, or other rarer gifts, but you are growing into a strong, healthy young man," Rayden told the boy. She leaned towards him. Cupping his chin with her right hand, she pulled his face toward her, looking the boy straight in the eyes. "All of our gifts are not apparent at first. Some emerge later in our lives. I believe in my heart you could learn the arts of a warrior ... and become a good fighter, even a great one, in time."

The boy looked surprised at her words, but before he could answer she continued. "It is not an easy road to become a capable warrior. The days are long and you must practice often. You will be bruised, sore, and sometimes injured. You will go to sleep at night thinking you will not be able to move in the morning. But if you keep traveling that road, you will gain the skills you seek. I do not see anything about you that would be an obstacle."

"You really believe that?" the boy asked after a few moments, with a trace of incredulity.

"I do," Rayden responded firmly. "And if you put your mind and heart to it, I will start to teach you. Beginning in the morning."

The boy perked up. "Really? You would teach me?"

"Yes, really. In fact, I took a Teveren blade when we freed the slaves from the ships, so that I could show you the use of it when the time was right," Rayden said with another smile, amused by his reaction. She got up to her feet and extended a hand toward Hamilcar, "I say the time has come. But tonight you need to come back with me to the camp and get some sleep."

She paused, her expression growing somber. "And you must promise that you will not wander off into the night alone. That was very foolish. I will not tolerate that again. The next time this happens we will have more than a conversation. It will not go well for you. May there never be a need for me to discipline you. But make no mistake ... I will, if you transgress."

The boy nodded to her, a shadow of fear passing across his eyes at the hard look in hers. Taking her hand, he stood up. The two started back toward the camp together.

A pace ahead of the boy, Rayden smiled to herself, breathing in cool drafts of the night air. Hamilcar's mood had lifted up considerably from where it had been when she found him, and she had confidence that he would honor his promise.

Given some of the fears she held for the boy when she had searched for him, a deep sense of relief pervaded her. Rayden knew she would sleep well that night after enduring so much angst.

Tomorrow would bring whatever it decided to, as it always did, so living in the moment served as the best approach. By the time they reached the camp, most of its occupants lay in slumber. Only the perimeter watch remained fully alert along with a few lingering at the sides of fires here and there.

The two found their own campfire and settled in for the rest of the night. After exchanging a few words with Annocrates, who still sat by the fire, Rayden watched the boy drift off before allowing herself to follow.

For the flicker of a moment, as she gazed upon him sleeping peacefully, she wondered what it would be like to be a mother to such a boy. She could imagine such a notion, but she knew that she could not act upon it.

She did care about Hamilcar, in a truly heartfelt way, but she had been called to a different path than most. Rayden reminded herself that if she had not walked that path, the boy would have suffered a horrific, agonizing death in the sacrificial fires of the bull-god. The fact that she did walk a different path and made choices that few others would had spared the boy's life, along with the lives of so many others across the years.

Looking at his calm face, his chest rising and falling in gentle fashion as he breathed, she had all the proof she could ever want that there was an important place and purpose in the world for those such as her. She had rarely doubted that in all her years, but the latest recognition gladdened her spirit. The hint of a smile rested on her own lips and the peace of satisfaction dwelled in her heart when Rayden took her own nocturnal journey of consciousness, gliding into the realm of dreams a short time later.

***

Tendrils of mountain air carried the sharp teeth of night's chill. Rayden pulled her cloak more tightly about her, taking a deep breath of the crisp air.

The taste of it felt good to her lungs, and along with the scent of pine, evoked memories of the land she once called home. The echoes of former times scattered and dissipated as Rayden kept her thoughts to the present. It would do no good to descend into melancholy, certainly not when grave dangers loomed in her path.

Three more days had passed, and nothing had changed. The Teverens would not attack. Rayden and the others who had scouted the enemy positions multiple times could glean their disposition clearly enough. Content to stay within the mountain pass, the Teverens knew time to be their ally.

The loose rabble of former slaves would break themselves on Teveren blades, spears, and shields, if they did not splinter apart first. Tensions spiraling, the voices of those such as Crassor had grown louder.

While rations were maintained, the rebels still had food in their bellies, but the situation could tilt any day with a fruitless day of hunting and fishing. The river might continue to yield some sustenance, but the game in the surrounding land was not inexhaustible.

Rayden's only respite came in the three morning sessions she conducted giving Hamilcar his first lessons in the use of the Teveren blade. The boy showed promise, displaying a cooperative attitude and willingness to listen.

In that sense he exceeded the majority of warriors she had worked with, so often caught up in matters of pride and ego. If Hamilcar maintained the kind of disposition she had seen during the three sessions, he would advance swiftly in his development.

While pleased with Hamilcar's training, Rayden needed to get away from the camp and tend to her own thoughts. She had to try and find a way to help the rebels out of their impasse. Sitting among them, watching their rising agitation and listening to reckless notions bandied about, she would never get the clarity of mind she sought and needed.

Setting off into the night, Rayden reached the base of a mountain and made her way up its wooded slope, until she reached a vantage from where she could see the distant fires of the Teveren camp. Brisk winds whipped about her form, tossing her locks to and fro as she gazed down the throat of the great mountain pass.

Stars glittered above, accenting a moon nearing its fullest state. She peered into the depths of the night sky, beholding its jewels and contemplating the mystery inherent within the majestic vision.

Whether places meant for gods or perhaps something as natural as the mountain she stood upon, the stars above cast their luminance night after night, keeping vigil over a world caught in the throes of shadow and turmoil. They had been there when the world began, and it would not surprise her if they were still there after it all came to an end.

The stars served as reminders of something much bigger

out there, though the greater vision remained cloaked to her eyes. She could not become lost in such thoughts. When the run rose and the stars vanished from view, the impasse facing the rebels would still loom.

Rayden blinked a moment later, thinking her eyes deceived. One of the stars appeared to be growing larger, or else it moved closer. The light curved and flowed, behaving nothing like any star she had seen before.

Astonished, she watched the light forming an image as it neared. In moments, a radiant human shape had manifested, set against the starry depths beyond.

Instinctively, Rayden took up her weapons and moved back a few paces. Unease gripped her, facing something not of flesh and blood.

She kept her body squared toward the descending light, not about to turn her back on the phenomenon. Courage involved the mastery of fear, not the absence of it. Eyes open and body in a balanced stance, she waited to discover if the thing drawing close was friend or foe.

"I hoped you would gaze upon the night. You did take your time though," a casual, masculine voice emitted from the genderless, human form. The next words that the apparition spoke carried a tone of bemusement. "Are blades really necessary, Rayden Valkyrie?"

Rayden returned her weapons to their familiar places, recognizing the speaker at once. Her voice carried a cold edge. "Dreaghen. Should I be happy you have finally decided to speak to me after sending me halfway across the known world? Your help would have been welcome many times."

She stifled the irritation welling up fast within. Rayden had sought the once-trusted sorcerer out for answers, only to be sent on a journey that had left her feeling even farther removed from any kind of resolution.

She held a deep mistrust of the things of sorcery to begin with, and Dreaghen had done nothing to mitigate that. If anything, he had soured her view of sorcerers even further.

"Yet you are here," Dreaghen responded.

"I am here by my own strength and honed iron," Rayden retorted. "And I'm about to be trapped in the massacre of these ill-fated men and women."

"Or you can be their salvation," Dreaghen replied in a calm air.

"That is easy for you to say, sorcerer, when your physical body is out of the reach of my fists," Rayden said. "Make yourself solid and come closer. We will see if you feel so comfortable."

"There need be no animosity between us, Rayden. The journey will bring what you seek. I have not deceived you, in any way."

"The journey is about to come to an end. Or are you not aware of a few thousand Teveren warriors blocking our way out of here? These rebels stand no chance against them."

"The Kartajenians are not so fond of these Teverens. Have you forgotten so soon?"

"What does that matter? Do you see any Kartajenians around here?" Rayden challenged the sorcerer, a harder edge to her voice. Her fury rose further with each passing moment.

"May I suggest that the Teveren force is there for a reason beyond blocking the way out of here?" Dreaghen countered. "Perhaps it is also blocking the way into here. That camp was not formed in response to your throng of rebels. Something else prompted it."

The sorcerer's words gave her pause, stilling the upsurge of rancor inside. "What are you speaking of, sorcerer? Don't play riddles with me. Speak plainly."

"Beyond that pass, not much farther, is a Kartajenian general with a sizeable force of capable fighters," Dreaghen stated.

"A Kartajenian force?"

"Of strong Hesperian warriors."

"Just beyond that pass?"

"Not even a half-day's march."

"And how does that help us?" Rayden asked sharply, though the ire within her ebbed a little at the unexpected news.

"The ones you are with are not strong enough in number to break through the mountain pass. The Kartajenian general is not strong enough to assail the Teveren camp alone. But there are choices now. Think upon them, Rayden."

Rayden listened with keen intent, understanding the implications posed by the sorcerer. "This news you bring does open a new door."

"The night is young," Dreaghen said, the hint of a suggestion in his words.

"Tonight?" Rayden asked, incredulous. "There may be trails or paths around that Teveren camp, but if there are I don't know of them."

"Never say I don't help you," Dreaghen responded, the tone of bemusement returning.

"Help me? How can you possibly?" Rayden started to counter when she heard the sound of twigs snapping behind her.

Rayden turned and looked off into the trees, giving a little start as she took in several glowing sets of eyes peering back at her. There had to be at least a dozen or more of the creatures among the shadows, all regarding her in silence.

She kept still, not wanting to provoke the creatures. Her hands readied to take up her weapons at the first sign of aggression.

"They will not attack. They are here at my behest to guide you," Dreaghen.

"After all I've been through you dare ask me to trust you now," Rayden said through clenched teeth. There were many ways to die a valiant death, but she did not wish to meet her end from a pack of wolves, alone at night on a windswept mountainside.

"Trust me. Or go back to the camp and wait for the rebels to tear themselves apart," Dreaghen said, his unruffled manner continuing to irritate her.

The wolves made no move forward and showed no signs of hostility. Reflecting the moonlight, their luminous eyes remained fixed upon her.

One by one, they started forward, spurring Rayden to brace herself. Emerging from the trees, they turned to the right and padded away, with the exception of a hulking black wolf that drew to a stop and kept its gaze fixed upon Rayden.

"They will not harm you," Dreaghen said. "Let them guide you. They will show you the trail around the enemy camp."

"A simple thing for you to say, when your body is far from here," Rayden countered. Yet the wolves were behaving in a manner unusual for wild beasts.

When the last of the wolves came out of the trees, the black wolf stared at her for a few heartbeats more, before turning away to join its brethren.

"Go Rayden, or return to the camp and await a certain doom," Dreaghan said with a hint of impatience.

She knew little time remained until the camp frayed apart or a Teveren threat manifested. To return would be to solve nothing, but her trust in the sorcerer had long since eroded.

"We will speak later, sorcerer," Rayden said, her ire curling her lips into the likeness of a snarl.

"We must," Dreaghen said. "The darkness plagues our homelands."

"What are you speaking of?" Rayden asked, a chill coursing through her blood at the enigmatic words. "Our homelands? What darkness?"

"I sent visions to you, in the hopes of speeding your return," the sorcerer said. "Villages burning, a danger prowling the forests, a field of dead warriors."

"That was you," Rayden said after a pause, her tone cold and threatening. She remembered the nightmare during her first night in the Divine City. She clenched her hands into fists, wishing she could batter the man who dared to invade her mind. "I remember that dream. It was not welcome, sorcerer."

"That dream?" Dreaghen asked, sounding surprised. "I sent you many."

Rayden laughed, though no humor could be found in the glare that she cast Dreaghen. "I only had one dream such as you describe. It appears you are not as powerful as you think you are, sorcerer."

The sorcerer grew silent for a moment, tilting his head toward the ground. At first it seemed that he spoke to himself. "Only one reached you, when you started on your journey back here. The darkness must have deflected my other attempts."

He looked up to Rayden. "I did not seek to invade your mind. I only sent the visions to you because it is a desperate time. It stood my only means of reaching you."

Taken aback at the contrite tone of his voice, Rayden paused. "What darkness is this? You have still not answered me that."

"The darkness that plagues our homelands, the darkness that blocked the visions I sent you, the darkness that drives the rise of the Teveren Imperator ... and the darkness that placed those with you in bondage."

Rayden's brow furrowed. "You speak in circles, sorcerer. This darkness is all these things? How can that be?"

"All roots of the same tree," Dreaghan replied. "Never forget that. But you must break this Teveren force if the former slaves you fight for are to have any possibility of surviving."

Rayden glared at the sorcerer. "If a darkness threatens our homelands now, why would you want to help me fight for those in the rebel camp? I'm one of few northerners walking amongst them. Even if all the northerners among the rebels were to leave, it would not diminish their strength by much. Why do you not tell me to leave the rebels and return to our homelands?"

She knew her own heart. She would not leave Hamilcar, Doros, Annocrates and the others in their dire hour. But she was curious as to what the sorcerer's response would be, perhaps giving her insight into the inner forces driving the mysterious figure.

"Many have a part in the service of darkness," Dreaghan said. "Many will have a part in the fight against it. But time is waning. You are wrong about one thing. If you do leave the rebels it will diminish their strength greatly. I have come to offer you a path to help save these former slaves from certain destruction. The question is, will you seize that offer?"

Her eyes narrowed, anger churning within her at the question. The tone of it sounded patronizing to her ears.

Dreaghen had evaded her question, offering nothing of substance beyond some generalities that could be interpreted a hundred ways. Further, the thought of cooperating with the sorcerer on any level, after what she had been through on her three-year odyssey, evoked abhorrence.

But the faint light of another possibility beckoned, when all other roads had seemed blocked. She had walked up to the mountainside in a fog of uncertainty, seeing no way out for the rebels. No matter how much fury she bore toward the sorcerer, she could not find it inside herself to walk away from a chance to change the dreadful impasse, no matter how slim.

Chapter 15

Without a word, she turned her eyes from Dreaghen and started forward. Breaking into a swift gait, she followed after the wolves, who were continuing onward a good distance ahead.

On her approach, the great black wolf turned its head and glanced toward Rayden. For a moment she wondered what it would do and was about to come to a stop, but the creature returned its focus to moving forward, loping along with its kind.

She followed the wolves along the slopes, passing through narrow, rocky stretches just wide enough for one person or wolf to stride upon. Despite their size, the creatures exhibited great balance as they navigated the thinner stretches of trail.

High winds beat against her, often at the cusp of perilous drop-offs, but she kept her attention fixed on her lupine guides. How Dreaghen arranged the aid of wolves formed a mystery she did not wish to explore, as much as she mistrusted the things of sorcery. But with her initial torrent of anger subsiding, gratitude rose within for the sorcerer's help.

The moon climbing ever higher in the night skies, the pack and their human companion continued along the trail until it finally widened and began descending from the heights. With a broader trail and downward momentum, the group picked up their gait considerably, until Rayden found herself close to a trot. Keeping her footing and breathing in a steady rhythm, she maintained her position at the rear of the wolf column.

Seeing the wolves ahead slowing to a halt, Rayden came to an immediate stop. The creatures turned and eyed her for a few moments, exhibiting no hint of agitation or threat. Springing forward, they bounded off the trail and headed into the trees.

The black wolf, the last of them to go, cast its golden eyes upon her for several moments before melting into the darkness. A few heartbeats later, no sound or trace of her four-legged guides lingered among the shadows of the lofty pines.

Trusting to their purpose in guiding her, Rayden continued forward. A few times she stared into the trees, wondering where her guides had gone, or if they might yet be watching her.

The wind whistled among the branches and rocks, the lonely sound accompanying her soft footfalls along the path. She had not gone more than a hundred steps when she came around a bend and discovered a jutting rock outcropping, overlooking a narrow valley.

Nestled within the darkness below, an array of firelights danced, marking the presence of a sprawling encampment on the valley floor. Its arrangement told her at once that the camp was not Teveren in nature.

She knew she had found the Kartajenians, exactly where the sorcerer said they would be. She could not yet forgive him for all she had endured, but the discovery of the Teveren's strongest and most dedicated enemy bolstered her spirits at once.

"Dreaghen, your vision goes far," Rayden commended the sorcerer under her breath. She started for the fires, making her way down the rest of the slope.

***

Kartajenian sentries gave a start when she appeared out of the shadows, a couple of them fumbling for their weapons in panic. Displaying a calm demeanor, her own weapons resting idle at her waist, Rayden hailed the men in an amicable tone and stated her peaceful intentions.

The moonlight revealing their expressions, she could see the looks of confusion and wariness on their faces as they silently evaluated her. Their gazes lingered on both her bodily form and her weapons. The next few moments would determine the state of their willpower and whether they survived.

The men did not relax their hold on their own weapons, even though she kept her empty hands in plain view. Their display of caution told her they did not regard her as a mere camp follower or prostitute, carrying about weapons as some kind of exotic, token possessions. Their somber expressions and alert stances spoke clearly that they would not find her ability to wield either axe or sword with skill to come as a surprise.

When they spoke, their accents told her that the men were from Hesperia, as Dreaghan had indicated, and not from across the seas. The development came as no surprise to her, from what she knew of the Kartajenian ways of war.

With the exception of their elite naval forces, the main part of any Kartajenian force was comprised from subject allies and other populaces. The citizens of Kartajen itself remained a ruling class, one that did not deem itself expendable as war fodder. That role was left for the likes of Hesperians, with the citizens of Kartajen viewing themselves only suited for the ranks of generals and their cherished navy.

Radyen stood silently in place, content to wait patiently while the men sent one of their number onward to inquire about the audience she requested. None of the sentries remaining behind tried engaging in any kind of banter with her, maintaining their posture of wariness.

She doubted all their thoughts embraced duty, but she

found herself impressed with their show of discipline. It told her a couple of things. Whatever general stood in command of the camp had instilled a solid order and held the respect of the warriors.

The man who had been sent to ask after the general returned a short time later. With a look and tone that told her that he had not expected the response, he informed Rayden that she had been granted an audience with the general.

Four guards escorted her from the sentry position deep into the camp. Taking positions around her with weapons at hand, they lead Rayden toward a large tent that she estimated to be somewhere near the center of the encampment.

Conveyed inside by the guards, one of them holding the front flap open for her, she found herself looking at a stout figure of about middle age. Head smooth and bare, he had a bushy beard that fell to the top of a brawny chest. Deep-set eyes surmounted by thick eyebrows peered toward her with scrutiny and wariness.

The guards flanked her, their weapons still out, and the general kept a distance. Taking no offense at their postures, Rayden had expected precautions in a region of conflict, even if she knew little could stop her were she there to kill the general.

"I did not expect a visitor tonight. But the report of a blonde-haired woman bearing blade and axe at my camp in the middle of the night, desiring an immediate audience with me, intrigues me," the general stated in calm fashion. "I know you have not come here with idle purpose. I have my own reasons for allowing this audience, but first I wish to learn more of your purpose and who you are."

His low-pitched voice held no accent, telling her that the man came from the great city of Kartajen and had likely been appointed by their Elder Council. As an appointed general, he would hold the authority to act upon her proposal, if he judged it valuable to his purpose.

"Thank you for being willing to see me at this late hour," Rayden said in a deferential manner. "I do have an important matter that compelled me to seek an audience with you."

"A northerner, yes? No mistaking your eyes, hair, and skin," the general stated. "The fact that you are a northerner is the main reason I granted you this audience. I know the people of the north have no love for my enemies. The empire's soldiers have raided the tribes on their border. They have burned villages. They have taken slaves."

He paused, eyeing Rayden, before continuing. "Yet my men told me you approached the camp from the south ... from Teveren territory. That mystery remains. By what name are you called?"

"I am called Rayden and I am a northerner, as you have guessed, but my travels have taken me very far away from my homeland, far to the south," Rayden answered. "I crossed the seas and had been finding my way home, when circumstances delayed me upon reaching Teveren lands."

"I will give you my name in return. I am called Mago. I am a Kartajenian, appointed by the Elder Council as a general to command forces in Hesperania. You have come far indeed for you to have crossed the Great Sea."

He halted again, staring toward Rayden. "The question I must have an answer for is why have your travels brought you from Teveren territory to my camp this night, Rayden?" the general queried, his eyes narrowing. A cloud of suspicion hovered between them, reflected in the general's piercing, unwavering gaze.

"I bring you a proposal," Rayden stated calmly. "That is my purpose for seeking an audience. I believe this proposal will be of great interest to you."

The wisp of a smile passed across the general's face, though the look in his eyes remained hard. "I am a man who deals in realities. I know it is not a request for my hand in marriage. A woman of your attractiveness could do much better than an aging Kartajenian."

The trace of jest in Mago's voice and eyes vanished, his look hardening again along with his tone as he continued. "I also know an experienced warrior when I see one. The very air about you betrays that. You are no stranger to killing. It is fortunate that none of my men sought to make sport of you."

"It is fortunate they did not," Rayden agreed, matter-of-factly. "I will say that your men conducted themselves with nothing but discipline."

"It is good to hear that my men maintain their discipline," Mago replied, nodding. "Perhaps they have some sense after all."

"It is clear that you have dutiful men under your command," Rayden said. "It gives my purpose for seeking you more confidence."

"Then tell me what purpose brings you to a Kartajenian camp in the middle of the night?" Mago asked, more pointedly. "Speak plainly, northerner."

She eyed the burly general, letting the silent pause bring greater focus to her next words. "Would it be of interest to you to know that there is a sizeable force of former Teveren slaves gathered on the other side of the pass? Former slaves from many lands armed with weapons and a deep desire to kill Teverens. Former slaves who have met the Teverens in battle and beaten them many times."

She saw a brief flare of surprise in his gaze and knew that the man had no knowledge of the rebel presence on the other side of the pass. Whether the general welcomed the news or not remained to be seen.

"Even if this is so, why would a rabble of ex-slaves be of any interest to me?" the general asked her, devoid of any hint of mockery. "What good does it do me? Even if we both share a desire to slay Teverens?"

"They are the lower teeth and you the upper," Rayden stated, keeping her gaze locked to the general's. "A set of jaws that can crush a host of Teverens between them. Grind them to destruction and lay clear the mountain pass for us both. For you to go southward, if you wish, and us to go north and leave that accursed empire behind."

"A set of jaws, you say..." Mago stated, his voice trailing off.

"Your forces coming up on one side of their camp and ours from the other. What we cannot do separately, we can do together," she said.

The general said nothing at first, staring into her eyes for several moments, expressionless. Despite no outward gestures, she knew by his deep silence that the grizzled man had taken her words into serious consideration.

"How many of you are there?" Mago asked.

"Over two thousand strong," Rayden answered. She then added, as a reminder. "Battle experienced."

The general eyed her and fell into a longer, heavier silence. She knew by the tension on his face that her proposal tempted him greatly, but he did not look to be the sort of man given to rash decisions. Saying nothing further, she endured the ponderous quiet and awaited his response.

"You would have to trust in us, I will not risk my warriors," Mago said, finally breaking the heavy silence.

Rayden nodded. "Do I have any other choice? Do those I am with have any other options? The only way to the north is through that mountain pass. A Teveren force we cannot dislodge by ourselves stands in the way."

"And that mountain pass opens up the enemy heartland, from where I stand," the general said. Rayden did not fail to catch the subtle tone of eagerness within his words.

"We are unable to break through the Teverens by ourselves, and from what I have seen your force also cannot," Rayden said, pressing the matter, the words carrying no insult.

She could see the general to be a practical, deliberate man and knew he held no illusions regarding his own situation. Like the rebels, he also stood at an impasse and she had just offered him a way out of it.

"Very well," Mago finally said, with a slow, purposeful nod. "I will have scouts verify your claim of this rebel force and its size. If you have spoken truly, we shall act in the way you advise.

"Form up your ranks in three days, just after dawn breaks. Offer battle to them. When the Teverens array themselves to fight and emerge from their camp, signal to us with three long, even horn blasts. If you are able to do that, we will enter the battle on the other side of their formation. The Teverens and their camp will be ours."

She held no worries about what his scouts would report. A shadow of anticipation in the general's face told her at once that he intended to carry out his part of the plan, once the rebel force's location and nature had been verified. He needed no convincing to realize he stood his best chance of breaking the standstill with the Teveren force by combining forces with a strong ally.

Striding forward a couple of steps, Rayden extended her arm with palm open toward the general and stood still. The guards who had been flanking her remained in their places.

The general showed no sign of alarm, stepping forward to meet her and extending his own right arm. The two clasped forearms in the manner of warriors, their firm grips mirroring each other.

"When dawn breaks, three days from now, await our signal," Rayden said, before releasing her grasp.

"When your signal comes, we will crush them between our jaws and open the mountain pass for the both of us," Mago replied, a sharp look resembling newly-honed blades glinting in his eyes.

Heart of a Lion

"You just escaped the Kartajenians, who would have killed you or burned you in the fires of sacrifice to their accursed bull-god," Annocrates said, his tone and look rife with incredulity and dismay. Several others nodded at his words, somber looks on every face. "And now you are wanting to entrust all of our fates to them?"

"Without them everyone in this camp will soon be dead, by one means or another," Rayden countered, not bothering to correct him that only children were hurled into the fires at Malech's altars. She swept her gaze across all the others. "Not a man or woman in this camp can even go back to being a slave. The Teverens will make an example of those who rose up to every slave in their lands. I too have seen the bodies crucified for leagues. The bodies of those from your ranks who fell into Teveren hands."

Images of decaying bodies and scavengers tearing away bits of flesh stabbed her mind again. Recalling the overwhelming stench from the decomposing bodies in the hot, midday sun, a wave of nausea washed over Rayden. She took a deep breath and stilled her mind, tamping the noxious, dark memories back down.

"The only way out of here for all of us is through that mountain pass," Rayden said. "And the only way we will do that is with Kartajenian blades striking the back of the Teverens."

A pensive silence fell over those gathered. "You are asking much of everyone here," Annocrates responded, after a few moments. "Our lives are in the balance of this counsel you give us, to cooperate with the Kartajenians."

Rayden caught the accusation in his words, but could not fault him for feeling the way that he did. Only she had looked the Kartajenian general in his eyes and taken the measure of the man. Over two thousand men and women were being asked to rely on her assessment, with violent death the consequence if she were wrong.

Asking thousands to trust their lives to her judgment of a single man was no easy task. Yet there were no viable alternatives. To do nothing meant death as well.

"I am giving you your only means to have a chance to avoid a brutal death at Teveren hands," Rayden said. "We cannot stay here forever. Time itself becomes more of an adversary with every day that goes by. All of you know that and see that, with every rise and fall of the sun."

"She deserves nothing but our gratitude," interjected Doros, eyeing Annocrates in a manner that told Rayden the woman stood poised for a confrontation. She looked to the others. "This is an unexpected blessing. Rayden has found a way forward where there was none before."

"I only express my distrust of the Kartajenians," Annocrates replied to Doros in a lower, conciliatory voice. "It is no ill-view of Rayden."

"I did not take your words as such and your mistrust has good reason," Rayden said. "I do not see the Kartajenians as friends, only as the enemy of my enemy. This general does not seek to help us out of any affection. He seeks to help himself. Do not forget that. We are a means to his own aims, and that is why he will honor his promise."

Annocrates listened to her words and nodded slowly. "What does he gain if the Teverens here are defeated? Are there not other Teveren forces? Ones much stronger than the force in the mountain pass?"

"This general seeks to strike at the heartland of the Teverens," Rayden said. "And if this force holding the mountain pass is overcome, he will find a soft underbelly to cut through and plunder."

"So this man wants to get into Teveren lands and we want to

get out," Doros remarked. "Seems simple enough."

"And it is why we can trust them to do their part," Rayden said. "They want to spill Teveren blood, set fire to Teveren buildings, and loot Teveren treasure. Without us, they are left stranded in their camp on the other side of the pass."

"Two more days?" Doros asked.

Rayden nodded. "Yes, after dawn, in two days, we must offer battle to the Teverens and draw them out if we are to have the aid of the Kartajenians."

"I wish we could strike at them today," Doros said, a simmering look within her eyes.

"As do I," Rayden said.

Doros looked to Annocrates and a few of the others who had listened to the discussion but not spoken. "I see no better chance for us. We all have seen what is happening among us. With each day it grows worse. We know the Teverens will send a great force from the south in time. We must call the full leadership council together and advocate Rayden's plan to all ... or we will all surely die on Teveren soil."

Several nods of approval met her words, including one from Annocrates. He stated, "We either tear ourselves apart, wait for Teverens to come and crush us with overwhelming force, or we take this chance. It is as Rayden has told us, the only chance we have to survive and seek a place to make a home for ourselves."

By the time the leadership council convened in full later that afternoon, Doros' plan of establishing a unified, supportive faction prior to the assembly bore immediate fruit. Rayden did not stand alone when telling of her meeting with the Kartajenian general and explaining the proposed battle plan to the greater council.

A number of the most respected men and women in the rebel force both understood and advocated the plan in support of Rayden. Even the surly Crassor spoke in agreement with the strategy, though Rayden suspected his consent to be less a matter of seeing the potential in the offered chance than an opportunity to break the monotony and spill Teveren blood.

Nevertheless, she accepted Crassor's support gladly. His favorable attitude brought along most of the more intractable and difficult ones counted among the rebel leadership.

By the end of the council, it was decided by near unanimous acclimation that the rebel force would array for battle at dawn, in two day's time. While glad that the rebels had heeded her, Rayden still realized that everything hinged upon the honor of one man; the Kartajenian general.

As if an afterthought, she rubbed her arm where she had clasped forearms with the general at the end of her audience with him. She remembered the unwavering and determined look in his dark eyes.

In two days, she would learn the full measure of the man, with profound consequences hanging in the balance. Her heart told her once more that he would be true to his word.

CHAPTER 16

The morning's chill had not receded entirely when over two thousand former slaves drew up in an extended line facing in the direction of the Teveren encampment. Presenting the broadest front that they could, the depth of their ranks ran shallow, no more than three lines deep at any point.

Rayden turned her head to the right. Doros stood near, a statuesque vision gripping her bow and staring forward with an iron-hard, unblinking gaze. A stony look sculpted on the woman's face, not even her two lengthy braids jostled the slightest bit.

Rayden suspected Doros to be harboring thoughts of blood vengeance. Most every former slave would be in a similar mindset, given the chance to shed Teveren blood and gain freedom in the north.

No matter how much ire dwelled within the men and women around Rayden, everything depended on the Teverens' taking the bait and the Kartajenian general honoring his promise. She could not yet worry about the latter, as nothing would happen if the Teverens chose to remain behind the palisades of their encampment.

A throng of former slaves standing out in the open would appear tantalizing to any Teveren commander. She did not see how the Teverens would pass up a chance to crush such a rabble, but Rayden could not be certain until she saw the Teverens forming up for battle with her own eyes.

The enemy camp remained a good distance away, but she knew their scouts were well aware of the rebel force. She had seen them moving, just after dawn's light revealed the great mass of rebel warriors on the stretch of land deemed suitable for a large clash.

A modest rise in the ground ahead prevented her from seeing a distant approach. The light rain of the night before and a layer of morning dew prevented any haze of dust from heralding an advancing Teveren force.

The land before her remained barren of enemies, time crawling by as she stared toward an empty horizon. Breezes swept across the low grass, sending shadowy ripples over unsullied ground. Touched with light gray hues, pockets of clouds rolled overhead, dotting an ocean of bright blue and casting drifting shadows below.

Any other day she would have found beauty in the tranquil scene. On this morning her axe and sword carried a thirst for Teveren blood that could not go unsated. A battle had to be won to set people free.

Periodically, shouts of anger and frustration rang out from the rebel line, warriors venting their ire at the lack of an enemy to fight. More than once, Rayden heard Crassor's voice among them, the fiery man hurling challenges and insults toward vacant space.

Rayden began to wonder if all were for naught. She could not blame the Teveren commander, who held a strong position and only had to let time wither away the rebel force perched at the gates of the mountains. She had hoped for a commander desiring glory and expediency, in crushing a numerically inferior foe.

The calls from the ranks about her grew in number. Turning

her head, Rayden could see the anxiety building in the faces around her, even Doros, with whom she shared a glance.

The sun climbed higher, warming the air and removing the dampness. Rayden began to wonder how much longer they should stand before conceding that the Teverens would not appear. She dreaded the march back to the rebel camp, carrying dissipating hopes when a ray of light had beckoned through the storm encompassing them.

At long last, the ground rippled with vibrations. Rayden straightened upright, her heart picking up its pace and sagging hope rekindling.

She peered to the horizon with a fresh scrutiny, a tingle running along her skin with the rumbling growing underfoot. She knew the sensations did not come from the land itself.

When the earth shook from a natural cause, the tremors did not sustain and grow in the manner of the ones happening now. A hush fell over the rebels, all eyes fixed toward the open stretch of ground to the north.

Movement broke the stillness before her. A dark line lifted above the edge of the horizon as thousands of Teverens marched into sight.

Her heart leaped inside. The enemy had come.

The morning sun glinted off helms and armor, accenting the splendid order displayed by veteran enemy ranks. Banners adorned with shining ornamentation of gold were carried high at several points, proclaiming the identity and legacy of those marching beneath them.

Their numbers much greater than that of the rebels, the Teverens tromped across the ground, an army brimming with confidence and deadly purpose. Looking upon the enemy, Rayden girded her resolve, knowing her fate now depended upon the honor of a single Kartajenian general.

Low horns resonated from within the enemy ranks. The

Teverens slowed to a halt and began taking up positions, creating a series of distinctive formations.

Force against force, the rebels stood no chance against the veteran Teveren soldiers. Without aid, the rebels would be cut to pieces.

Rayden looked again to Doros, Annocrates, and all of the faces around her. The weight of the moment pressed upon her without mercy, everything hinging on her accurate judgment of the Kartajenian general.

The moment of truth had arrived, and a miscalculation on her part would result in the death of thousands, not to mention the torture and death of any unlucky enough to survive the battle. Images flashed once more through her mind of rotting bodies in the heat of the sun, lining the lonely road she had traveled upon after leaving the port city of Iellia.

If she judged wrongly, the faces on those crosses would be the likes of Doros, Annocrates, and so many others she had grown affinity for over the past several weeks. The thought frightened her more than any grotesque beast she had ever encountered.

Yet courage involved the subjugation of fear, and she confined the dreadful thoughts to a place deep inside. Somber of face and resolved in heart, Rayden turned to her left and gave the appointed signal.

A younger man used both of his hands to brace the long, curving horn that he raised upward. Inhaling deep, he put his lips to the near end and set loose a sustained blast, the sound carrying across the field of battle and beyond, followed by a pause.

He then repeated the extended note twice more, as instructed by Rayden. Looking to her, he lowered the horn after the third and final blast.

The fate of over two thousand men and women loomed in the aftermath of the resonant signals. She watched the rigid formation of the Teverens and listened for any sound to break the air that would indicate the presence of the Kartajenians.

For several long and terrible moments, nothing stirred. But this time the rebels did not have to endure their anxieties as long as they had that morning.

Sudden movements within the enemy ranks and a number of horns sounding in the distance gave Rayden the first indications that the Kartajenians had arrived. A fiery energy filled her at the sight of the enemy shifting their formations, buoying her spirit and incinerating all lingering worries.

To the left and right of the enemy, Rayden saw fast-moving throngs of horsemen. Brandishing their weapons, the mounted warriors appeared to glide across the ground, flowing about the flanks of the Teverens. The newcomers drew out contingents of mounted riders from the enemy's flanks, initiating a dance of lethal grace.

A grin rose upon her face. As she had deemed, the Kartajenian general possessed honor, at least to the degree that he carried out his promises.

The Teveren ranks continued to shift about, horn blasts erupting from within their formations as they adjusted to meet the new development. Rayden saw that the time to close the jaws had come.

Rayden thrust her blade high into the air, crying out with the full force of her lungs for all to move forward to the attack. Her war cry taken up swiftly, a swelling roar manifested in the air.

A wave of vengeance, the rebels surged toward the enemy ranks. Striding through the grass, Rayden eyed the forefront of the Teverens.

A loose line of men holding javelins stood at the forefront of staggered rectangular formations of warriors carrying oval shields and spears. Beyond the first array of rectangular units, other formations of a similar shape were positioned in a way that covered the gaps of the first.

She knew what loomed, from a hail of javelins to a wall of shields and spears. The gap between the two sides shrinking, it would not be much longer before the rebels were within range of Teveren javelins.

Drawing closer to the enemy, many of those around Rayden began charging toward the Teverens. At first, only a few rebels broke away from their ranks, but more and more followed the lead of the early ones and began running.

In moments, the marching line lost cohesion. The air filled with a spirited din, a chorus of battle cries heralding the pending clash.

The air filled with the first wave of javelins hurled from the Teveren front line. Impaled with the deadly shafts, many rebel warriors fell to the ground throughout the rushing masses.

Rayden sprang into a full run, racing along with the other rebels and keeping herself at the forefront of the attack. An enemy javelin arcing downward drove into the ground just behind her, but no other missiles in the first wave passed close to her.

The trajectory of the javelins took a more level route with the gap closing fast between the two forces. Rayden espied an enemy soldier just as he threw his javelin straight at her.

Shifting to the right, she avoided the incoming missile. A warrior behind her caught the javelin on his shield with a loud thud.

The javelin-throwers melted back into the Teveren ranks, hurriedly using the gaps provided by the first rectangular formations. The two lines of combatants collided moments afterward, a crash of weapons and shields resonating like a booming thunderclap across the battlefield.

Loosing a war cry, Rayden swung her axe to hook the top of a Teveren shield. Yanking back with all her strength, she slashed downward with the blade in her other hand. Blood flew as iron cleaved the exposed neck of the Teveren soldier holding the shield.

She twisted at the last instant, the tip of a Teveren spear grazing the cloth of her tunic on her left side. She whipped the axe about, striking the enemy soldier holding the weapon. A stunned look upon his face, he slumped to the ground as she yanked her axe free of his side.

To her right side, Crassor beheaded a Teveren with one stroke of his blade. The Teveren soldier standing behind his headless comrade gave way after one look into the battle-maddened rebel's face. Crassor smote down the frightened man a moment later and pressed his advance into the Teveren ranks.

On her other side, Annocrates found himself beset by two Teverens at once. Rayden fell upon one from the side, cutting the soldier down with heavy blows from each of her weapons.

She had no time to see how Annocrates fared with the remaining enemy warrior, turning to intercept a spear thrust aimed at her gut. Her blade swept the onrushing iron tip away, an instant before it drove into her flesh. She brought her axe up from a low angle, taking the man squarely in the groin before she brought her blade back through to finish him off.

The rebels fought with a spirited frenzy, hacking and slashing their way forward through the enemy mass. Pressed on all sides, the Teverens were unable to concentrate the advantages of their cohesive formations.

Even their individual equipment had been suited for the style of fighting they could not bring to bear. Wearing single greaves on their left legs, which under other circumstances would have been their leading legs in a tight formation, their right legs remained exposed to the attackers moving among them. Rayden exploited more than one such unarmored leg in the chaos, in one instance sending a man to the ground upon severing his leg at the knee.

Most of the enemy had abandoned their long spears,

drawing out medium-length blades for close quarters fighting. Though trained, they proved no match for Rayden with their swords. She blocked their strikes with ease and rapidly found openings in their defenses, the count of dead enemies rising with lethal blows from axe and sword.

Unaccustomed to the kind of melee they were forced into, the Teverens' advantages became nulled. Forced to defend against the Kartajenians at their rear and harassed by mounted attackers at their flanks, the Teverens could not even assert their strength of numbers against the rebels.

Deep within the enemy ranks, Rayden suddenly found herself facing a distinctive-looking Teveren warrior. His helm featured a pair of flaring wings, between which ran a crest of red horsehair. A pair of knee-high greaves, upon which the images of roaring lions had been embossed, protected his legs.

His adept skill with a sword extended his life a few heartbeats longer, deflecting the first few strikes of Rayden's blistering attack. Executing a feint with her sword, she found an opening and brought the axe crashing into his side.

Falling to his knees after the blow, he did not see the killing blow when she brought her blade back down to chop into the area between his neck and shoulder. Eyes wide and mouth hanging open, he tilted over and fell to the ground, blood gushing from the wound.

A man wearing a wolf-skin fell to the ground at her side an instant later, hewn down by Crassor. He gripped the gold-adorned standard that the fallen man had been holding. Around him, rebels pressed forward with vigor, driving the Teverens back before a relentless onslaught.

With a look of disdain, he flung the standard toward a rebel behind him. "Take this thing! I'm not done killing today."

Turning, he loosed a bellowing shout and charged at the nearest Teverens. Rayden eyed the standard and its proximity to the man she had just slain. She understood its significance at once.

"Get that out of here now, where the Teverens cannot lay hands on it," she told the perplexed-looking warrior who had caught the standard. "In our hands, this weakens their morale."

Nodding to her, he took up the standard and headed away at a brisk trot from the fighting. Watching him departing for a moment, Rayden turned back to the fighting at hand. Like Crassor, she was not yet finished drawing the empire's blood.

The Teveren ranks lost their cohesion everywhere as the melee deepened and spread, eventually encompassing the entire battlefield. Kartajenians, former slaves, and Teverens mixed together in a swirling maelstrom of combat.

Shrieks of wounded men, clangs of metal, blasts of horns, clacks of weapons on wooden shields and all manner of sounds filled the air. The stench of voided bowels and bladders mixed with the pungency of opened guts.

Rayden's blade and axe drank heavily of Teveren blood. Deflecting and dodging blows, Rayden hewed one enemy down after another.

On one occasion she found herself fighting side by side with a strong Kartajenian warrior. Wielding a curved blade that widened toward the point, sharpened only on the inside edge, the man displayed great proficiency in delivering blows of both cutting and crushing natures.

Together, Rayden and the Kartajenian formed a deadly tempest. Working farther into the enemy mass, the two warriors left a swathe of dead Teverens in their wake.

As yet another Teveren soldier fell dead at her feet, Rayden looked forward and eyed a prominent figure standing just a few paces away. Like the one she had killed earlier, the man had distinctive headgear and attire, only significantly more ornate than the other.

Recognizing his high rank, possibly the commander of the entire Teveren force, she leaped over the dead body before her and loosed a piercing cry. The man's eyes spread wide, seeing her bearing down fast upon him.

He recovered from his momentary paralysis in time to catch her blade as it arced toward his neck, but he did not react fast enough to her quick sideways shift. He could not get his sword over to block the axe rushing down upon the exposed back of his left leg, the honed iron slicing through deep at the knee level.

Left with nothing to support his weight below the knee after her axe passed through, he screamed and fell heavily to the ground. Rayden brought her axe overhead and down into the face of the Teveren officer, sending bits of bone, flesh, and blood flying.

Enemy morale crumbled, radiating outward from where Rayden had slain the prominent man. A few Teverens fought on in desperate fear, while others sought mercy and begged surrender.

The Teverens fortunate enough to beseech Kartajenians found themselves spared, though enslavement awaited them. The ones pleading to former slaves met brutal acts of vengeance, hacked and cut down where they stood.

In a short time, only the whoops and cheers of victors, and groans and cries of the wounded and dying, filled the air. The battle over at last, the clash of weapons ceased.

Rayden had no appetite for meting out the revenge she saw transpiring everywhere. The former slaves showed no signs of being sated in their bloodlust, searching among the dead for any Teverens still exhibiting signs of life.

Not far from where she stood, Rayden watched Doros plunge a long knife into the neck of a badly wounded Teveren warrior. She wanted no part of the ongoing slaughter and hoped the rebels' fury came to a swift end.

Heart of a Lion

Walking among the bodies, she kept alert for any Teverens who might be posing as dead in order to get one last strike in at an unsuspecting enemy. She diverted from her purpose only once, to skewer a mortally wounded Teveren soldier with her blade, one who had begun to endure extended torture at the hands of a mob of rebels. Rayden showed the man the mercy that death itself withheld, taking its time with cruel indifference in claiming his ebbing life.

Seeing the angry looks at being denied their quarry, Rayden feigned misunderstanding of their intent. The teeming bloodlust sustained many heated expressions, but none of the would-be torturers were foolish or rash enough to seek trouble with Rayden. A few gave voice to their frustration, but fell to swift silence when her piercing blue eyes fell upon them.

War spawned all manner of cruelties, and Rayden had witnessed far too many to count over the years. She could not stop all instances of cruelty, but she did not like adding to that ignominious legacy of war. The torturing of a helpless, dying man from the ranks of the defeated could not be countenanced when she had the ability and proximity to stop it.

Having no desire to linger among the carnage, she proceeded onward. Her gaze roved the throngs of warriors ahead, Kartajenians and rebels alike. Many were picking carefully through the dead bodies, the collection of spoils already getting underway.

Rayden finally located the Kartajenian general. She eyed the burly man standing near a group of captive Teverens, the latter being watched over by a contingent of the general's warriors.

Seeing her, Mago smiled at her approach, exposing his yellowed, uneven set of teeth. "The underbelly of these bastards is exposed. I have you to thank for the chance to strike this great blow upon the Teveren scum today. The mountain pass is now open to both of us!"

Gripping his forearm in greeting, Rayden looked the general straight in his dark eyes. "You honored your word. That is all I can ask."

The general nodded to her. A look of respect that no false facade could mimic shone in his eyes. "As did you, Rayden of the northern lands. Your force arrayed when you said it would. Each of us had a part in this victory. You brought them out. We crushed them between us."

"We did, and this day we know triumph," Rayden stated. "I also know our paths must go separate ways now. You will soon be traveling south and we will be heading north."

"But not just yet. A camp awaits us both ... filled with treasures ... and undefended," the general stated with emphasis on the final word, the trace of a grin forming on his lips. "Let all the victors split the spoils. We both can make use of their foodstuffs, weapons and other supplies. There is plenty enough in the Teveren camp to go around."

Rayden knew the gesture did not derive from any sense of generosity. The general simply had no desire for bloodshed over the looting of the Teveren camp.

"Agreed," Rayden replied. "There is more than enough for both of us. Treasure hard-earned."

Clasping the general's forearm again, she felt a sense of relief that there would be no major conflict over the pillaging of the enemy's camp. What had been gained in battlefield victory could evaporate in a storm of chaos, greed and outrage.

"I wish you well, Rayden," Mago said. "Maybe the day will come when we can join forces again."

"Or maybe Kartajen will put an end to the Teveren scourge before I have a need to come south again," Rayden said.

"Then you may join me for a feast and the sharing of tales," Mago said, smiling. "I know I would like to hear of your adventures."

Heart of a Lion

"I would gladly fight alongside a man with honor such as you, though I hope the next time we meet it would be at a feast, free of a Teveren shadow," Rayden replied.

"Till that day we meet again, Rayden," he said.

"Till that day," Rayden agreed, clasping his forearm once more.

Turning, she left Mago and made her way back to Doros, accepting cheers and hails from some of the rebels. Their bloodlust ebbing, the spirit of celebration had begun to take hold.

When she found Doros, the woman's clothes and face were blood-spattered and a scowl filled her expression. Her bow had been returned to its case, but the long knife remained gripped in her right hand. The blade glistened with the blood coating its surface.

"I thought I would feel more joy after such a victory," Doros told her in a leaden voice. She didn't look at Rayden, but continued to eye the bodies on the ground all around them. "Yet I feel nothing but emptiness."

"It's over, Doros, we have a path open to the north," Rayden said. "We did what had to be done. Nothing is gained in becoming like those we defeated."

"It is not over until they are all dead!" Doros said, shooting a glare at Rayden. Powerful emotions burst and poured through her words. "They would see all of us hung on crosses and left to rot. They shattered my family. They enslaved us. They have killed friends, mothers, fathers, brothers, sisters, and the children of many here today. Why would you spare even one of them?"

"So that we never become like them," Rayden countered without hesitation. She held Doros' heated gaze without wavering.

At last, the look in the other's eyes softened, but only by a little. Her voice came controlled and steady as she replied, "I understand what you mean. You speak with wisdom. Even if I don't feel it in my heart."

"Let's get away from here," Rayden said. "It does us no good to stand in this field of death. Tonight we celebrate the victory of living through this battle. We mourn and honor those who have fallen. Tomorrow, we set our minds on heading north and finding a homeland for those who have fought so hard to gain freedom."

Doros nodded. Leaning over, she wiped her blade off on the tunic of a dead Teveren warrior and returned it to the sheath on the bow case.

When finished, she stepped toward Rayden. The two turned and walked together through the blood-soaked ground in silence, heading back to the rebel encampment.

CHAPTER 18

A bond forged through a hard-fought victory brought together both rebel and Kartajenian alike by the campfires that night. The flow of drink steady and abundant, including wine taken from the Teveren camp, raised the spirits of the celebrants.

Laughter, jests, and salutes to those who had fallen rose above the crackle of flames into the clear night sky. Life embraced and the thrill of triumph running through their veins, the warriors from the two forces mingled as kindred spirits, not as groups who would be going their separate ways when morning brought forth a new day.

At one of the fires, Rayden finished off another cup of Teveren wine, one of many she had imbibed since dusk. The libations bolstered her celebratory mood, all worries and cares consigned to another day.

Aroused in the glow of victory, she took notice of the Kartajenian warrior who had fought at her side during the battle. A grin spread on her face, the firelight enhancing the spark in her eyes ignited from within.

Spending a day surrounded with violence and death spurred a desire to embrace the joys of life. With the focus of a huntress, Rayden fixed her eyes on the Kartajenian.

Particularly strong-looking in appearance, he was one

whom she judged would hold up long enough to satiate her physical desires. He had already proven his worth many times over in the fighting and she decided to make an advance.

Like most men, he proved easy enough to lure away from the festivities. One extended look between them conveyed her intent, kindling a fire that begged for release.

Catching Doros' eyes as she walked away with the man, Rayden recognized both curiosity and surprise in her friend's look. She cast Doros a mischievous grin, the onset of anticipation sending a vibrant energy through her.

Leading the warrior well away from the campfires, Rayden guided him to a more private, secluded place where she could have her way with him. Eagerness reflecting in their movements, they disrobed between preliminary kisses. Shed clothes provided cover for the hard ground a few moments later.

The heat of fires replaced by the heat of bodies intertwined in throes of passion, Rayden indulged herself in ecstasy. To her delight, she discovered the man eager to meet the task, as vigorous in love as he had been in battle.

The intensity between them surging, Rayden rolled him on his back and took control, kissing him with fervor. She rose up and tilted her head back, the stars above mirroring the timeless sensation pervading her entire body.

Eventually, she leaned down and gave him a final, extended kiss. She got up and took a few moments to lace her sandals and don her clothes, before leaving the warrior spent and exhausted where he lay.

Having found the Kartajenian satisfying enough for her purposes, she rejoined Doros and a number of others back at the side of the campfire. When Doros gave her a quizzical look, Rayden grinned and nodded, laughing when she saw the other woman's eyes widen.

Life had more than enough hardships and sorrows to

endure. Moments such as those she had shared with the warrior had to be seized and embraced with vigor, a chance to transcend to a wondrous and vibrant state of being.

Rayden chuckled when Hamilcar wandered in, his eyes glassy and body swaying from indulging in far too much Teveren wine. Even with an absurd expression on his face, Rayden saw great beauty in the moment.

Hamilcar lived and experienced joy now because she and the others had won the battle that day. A radiant smile came to her face as she put an arm around the drunken boy and hugged him close, ruffling his hair playfully with her other hand.

Without thinking about it, she gave him a familial kiss on the top of his head. His life was worth fighting for; on any day and at any time.

He soon meandered off, in the company of a couple boys about his age that he had recently met and been spending time with in the camp. She watched him go with peace in her heart, knowing she had given him a chance at life when all others had failed him on that day before the altar of the Kartajenian bull-god.

Relaxing for awhile by the blazing fire, she listened idly to the conversations of the others still awake. Eyelids finally growing heavy, Rayden stretched out by the campfire and fell into the embrace of a deep, restful sleep.

***

The next day, the two victorious forces turned their attention from thoughts of battle to spoils hard-won. The Teveren camp proved abundant in foodstuffs and other supplies. Only wine was found in lesser quantities, a good portion of it already commandeered for the previous night's celebrations.

The cooperation with the Kartajenians proceeded as smooth as Rayden could have hoped for, with only a few minor incidents erupting. Mago and his officers were quick to help quell any signs of trouble, making it much easier for Rayden, Doros, and other rebel leaders to rein in their own.

With their path taking them north, Rayden urged Doros, Annocrates, and the others to spread word to gather up as many tunics and cloaks as possible, and anything else that might aid against the cold inevitably visiting all who dwelled in the north. Many Teveren-fashioned weapons, shields, and pieces of armor had already been gathered from the battlefield, but the looting of the camp turned up additional, significant quantities of each.

At the least, those who were going north would be well-equipped. In Rayden's eyes, they would all need to be. The tribes of the north could be unpredictable. There was no telling whether the mass of former slaves would be marching into a place of haven or the midst of a conflict.

Their ranks swelled further with an influx of newly-freed slaves. Most Teverens left within the camp had fled after the battle, but many who had been slaves returned, seeing their chance to gain freedom.

The Kartajenians gave Rayden's band no trouble with the new additions. There were more than enough surviving Teveren soldiers, including a number rounded up in the surrounding woods, to constitute a sizeable treasure.

More than once, watching the Kartajenians binding Teveren captives, Rayden found herself bemused that those with her did not even blink at the fact that the Kartajenians also practiced slavery. Their hatred of the Teverens overwhelmed any other feelings they might have had in other circumstances.

At long last, both sides had looted to their fill. The bodies of the dead Kartajenians and rebels were burned in great pyres, while the Teveren dead were left out in the open for scavenging beasts.

Great masses of smoke wafted up into the skies and the

scent of burning flesh filled the air, making Rayden wish for a quick departure. The pull of the north tugging inside, she was eager to be on her way, but did not begrudge the honor being given to the rebel and Kartajenian dead.

Had she been in command, she would have insisted on burning the Teveren dead as well. They had fought valiantly, most just men doing their duty as warriors.

Before the two contingents went their separate ways, Rayden and Mago met once more in the vicinity of the massive funeral pyres. Clasping forearms and looking into each other's eyes, they bid each other well.

Rayden watched the general stride away, wishing Mago good fortune in her heart. He had proven to be a man of honor, from the conduct of the battle to the arrangements with procuring Teveren spoils. She could not deny that he had practical reasons for his behavior, but he had done as he said he would do.

An uncommon trait in a cold, violent world, honor held one of the highest places in her heart when deeming another worthy of her respect. Mago now walked with both her respect and affinity, a man she could wield her blade for.

Finally, she turned and rejoined her companions, the vanguard of the rebel column having just started the trek northward. Moving into the mountain pass, Rayden walked alongside Doros near the forefront of the lengthy column.

Hamilcar followed just behind, looking a little awkward in the cloak he had picked up in the Teveren camp. Though an amusing sight, the fact remained that the youth would have a chance to grow into the cloak. Neither the bull-god's priests nor the Teverens had come to harm the youth.

For a little while, Rayden and her companions were content to walk in silence. Taking in the sights of towering, forested slopes to either side, Rayden felt a surge of inspiration.

Mountains a part of her northern blood, the sight of the

lofty peaks invigorated her weary spirit. The closest thing that she had to a homeland beckoned with nothing more standing in the way.

In just a few days she would see the people of the tribe that had effectively adopted her. She wondered how the Gessa had been faring in her long absence. She missed them and hoped that she found the tribe in a good state.

They were the closest that any group of people could come to being deemed a family for Rayden. Having lived among them for several years after the death of her mother and father, Rayden had formed powerful bonds of friendship with many women and men in the tribe. Leaving them behind for her lengthy quest south had been much harder than expected.

A few years had passed, and she knew there would be many changes. Children had grown and undoubtedly some in the tribe had died since she had last been among them.

She hoped Eigon still reigned as the tribe's chieftain. The more she traveled the world, the more she appreciated the wisdom and judgment of the man who had often been a father figure to her.

"How far do you see us journeying into the north?" Doros asked, bringing Rayden out of her thoughts. "Will we walk to the ends of the world itself?"

"Beyond the mountain pass we will be entering the lands of the Tega, unless something has changed since I journeyed south," Rayden answered.

"I'm sure they will be well-pleased at a horde of armed warriors arriving unexpectedly in their lands," Doros replied with obvious sarcasm, glancing to Rayden.

"Which is why we will seek counsel with their chieftain, as soon as we get there," Rayden said. "Our force is large enough to give them pause."

"If they don't ambush us first," Doros said.

"They would rather we pass through their land than suffer the bloodshed that attacking a force of this size would bring," Rayden said. "I plan on going ahead to speak with them when we are closer."

"You can be convincing," Doros replied, a grin forming on her lips.

Rayden rolled her eyes. "I only give speeches when I must. I prefer leaving that to others."

Doros turned and looked back at the column. "They still have a chance at freedom because you are convincing."

Rayden smiled, appreciating the compliment within her friend's words. "I do what I must. Now, we seek a place for this force to settle and create homes."

"Do you think we will find one?" Doros asked.

Rayden nodded. "With the Teverens growing in strength to the south, the tribes on the edge of the empire's lands will not like being perched on the border. Allowing a settlement containing some strength in it helps shield the tribes from intrusions. Whether from the Tega or another, I am confident we will find an invitation to settle these people."

"By putting us squarely in the path of any future Teveren invasion," Doros said, with a somber look. "So we become a shield for them."

Rayden shrugged. "It is the reason why a tribe may allow you to have some land to settle in peace. Better that than fighting another battle."

"There is that," Doros said, nodding. She looked back to Rayden. "Are their rivers in your homelands?"

"You miss your boats," Rayden said, breaking into another grin. "That is what you are truly saying to me, isn't it?"

"I think you are beginning to know me well," Doros replied, her cat-like eyes vibrant with a sparkle of amusement.

"I would hope so, after what we've been through together,"

Rayden said.

"We've shared a few moments, haven't we?" Doros said, smiling.

Rayden gazed ahead, taking in the blue sky draped behind the sun-kissed peaks. She thought back to the first time that she met Doros, standing in the shadows with her bow drawn, along the banks of the wide river.

"Yes, we've shared a few together," Rayden said, looking back to her friend.

"But you've had some better moments than I since I've known you," Doros said, laughing. With a raised eyebrow, she added in a lower voice, "Such as with that Kartajenian warrior, while the rest of us celebrated the triumph in battle."

Rayden smiled. "You have to live life. Death can end it in a moment, on any day."

"Didn't you want to bring him along with us?" Doros asked, grinning.

"I figured it would be best to give him some time to recover," Rayden replied with a wink, laughing herself.

"You do have an eye for attractive men," Doros said. A wistful expression crossed her face. "The things I would have done with him."

"When I choose, it takes more than that to gain my interest," Rayden replied. "But yes, he was pleasing to the eyes."

"I can agree fully with that," Doros said.

"You'll have to find one pleasing to yourself," Rayden said. "Live life. We have enough moments in our lives spent with things of an unpleasant nature."

"I like the way you see the world," Doros said. "You name things for what they are."

"I see things as they are," Rayden said. "There is no sense working to deceive yourself."

"No, there isn't," Doros agreed. "Our lives are too short and too vulnerable.

"All too true," Rayden said, her joviality fading as she thought of the great numbers of men and women who were no longer in the multitude heading north.

Fallen along the course of numerous battles, or crucified on the Boreus way, they had all started with dreams of reaching freedom, only to meet with death. To Rayden, it stood a miracle that Hamilcar, Doros, Annocrates and many more were still with her.

"What troubles you?" Doros asked, a look of concern on her face.

Rayden shook her head. "It is nothing. Let us put our thoughts to enjoying a feast at the end of this march."

"It is too early in the day to be talking about food," Doros said.

"Maybe one day we will go to the Western Isles together," Rayden said. "It is said great warrior queens rule there, and I am sure they would welcome a pair of fellow warrior women like us to the fireside of one of their feasts."

"A land ruled by a great warrior queen," Doros said, with a yearning air. "I hope that is not just a tale. I would like to visit such a place."

"Too many stories of great queens for there to be none," Rayden said. She grinned and shrugged. "I guess one day we will have to go see for ourselves."

Doros laughed. "You probably don't hesitate to think of going far to the east, to the distant lands where my mother came from."

"If we can travel there, why not?" Rayden said. "And why not beyond that if we wish? Everywhere, there are people with the kinds of hopes, dreams and ambitions that everyone in this column has. They may wear different clothes, speak different tongues, have different looks, but inside they all want what we seek. A life that fulfils them."

"I would love to travel to distant lands one day," Doros said. "To see things I have never seen before."

"Then travel to them," Rayden replied. "It is only a matter of putting your mind toward it."

"I shall," Doros said, nodding. "Once I find what has become of my brother, sister, mother and father. That will come next, once a place is found for all of us to settle. I cannot take journeys until I have answers."

"May it be that I can join you, once I attend to some matters in the north," Rayden said.

"I would love to have your company," Doros said, her face brightening. "Who wouldn't? You are the best sword in this entire army. Best with an axe too!"

"One who can fall just as easily as any in this horde," Rayden said. "One stray arrow. A sickness. The bite of a snake. There are many ways one can fall."

"Then let us watch each other's backs and see to it that neither of us falls," Doros said.

"You have just described the way of friends," Rayden replied, a warm smile dawning on her face.

"Then that is what we are," Doros replied. "Though I've felt that in my heart for some time."

"As have I," Rayden said.

CHAPTER 18

"One of the Gessa? You have the look of one who comes from even farther north than they," the tall, dark-haired man told Rayden.

Grogner, the chieftain of the Tega, had agreed to meet with Rayden and the small delegation that had proceeded ahead of the main column. An air of apprehension and suspicion permeated the air, as Rayden expected.

Over two-thousand well-armed warriors appearing on the edge of their lands had the Tega in an edgy state. Though the chieftain presented a strong facade, she could sense the worry lying just underneath.

"They took me among them when I was young and had lost my family," Rayden said.

Grogner nodded. "I have heard much of you, Rayden Valkyrie. From the tales I expected you to be much larger and to have wings."

"Tales exaggerate," Rayden said evenly.

"They say you are like lightning in battle and that you do not suffer even a scratch," Grogner said.

"I wish that were so," Rayden replied, chuckling. "It would make my recoveries after a battle so much easier."

"It is an interesting situation I see before me," Grogner

stated. "The storied Rayden Valkyrie, comes to the border of our lands with many hundreds of warriors in her wake. Warriors of many widespread lands. Out of Teveren territory too? How is that so? The Teverens do not take kindly to others."

She told him the tale of the slave uprising, her counsel to them and the movement to the north. Annocrates and Doros let her do most of the talking, but added a few pieces of information during the telling. Living on the boundaries of the Teveren empire, many of the Tega, including Grogner, spoke the southern tongue, so her two companions could speak directly with no need for translation.

"We seek no conflict with you or any northern people," Rayden said, when she had finished with the story. "We ask your help in finding a place where they can settle, or allow us to pass through your land unhindered to seek another place."

Grogner stared at her for a moment, a piercing gaze that carried great weight behind it. A younger chieftain, the man faced an early test in leadership. Rayden knew he wanted to appear strong to his people, while making the wisest decision.

"Strength like this can help defend the lands of the Tega, if the Teverens encroach," Rayden said. "None of the warriors I am with bear any love for the Teveren Empire."

"The Teverens will come to these lands sooner or later. Theirs is an appetite that no amount of feeding can satisfy," Grogner said, a dark expression passing across his face.

"I agree," Rayden said. "And two thousand more warriors will be of great value to you and your people when that day comes."

"Or a plague upon our people long before then," Grogner said.

"There is no land that is uninhabited? No land where a people could carve out a settlement and add to your strength?" Rayden asked. "Surely there is a place somewhere in the forests that is uninhabited."

Grogner grew quiet for an extended period. He looked to Rayden and then to her companions.

"Where would your allegiance be?" he asked.

"We seek to rule ourselves, we would have no masters, for that is what we have fought hard and lost so many to break away from," Annocrates said. "But we can offer allegiance in common cause and mutual defense. An enemy of yours is an enemy of ours. In other matters, we seek trade and friendship."

Rayden watched Grogner's face. Though still looking grim, he did not seem to dismiss the idea outright.

"What guarantee do I have? You and most of your people are not of the north," he said, looking to Annocrates and Doros. "I do not know your ways. You are of many people, with many customs."

"On my honor as a woman of the north you can trust them to do as he says," Rayden said. "I have fought alongside them for some time now. I have come to know them well."

She turned and looked to Doros and Annocrates, pausing. "I would put my own life in their hands. That is how much I trust them."

From the looks on Doros and Annocrates' faces, neither had expected such a powerful statement. Nor did Grogner, whose eyes carried a trace of surprise when she looked back to him.

"The only thing said to be greater than your skill on a field of battle is the honor you carry," Grogner said.

"I have no kingdom. I do not possess great riches," Rayden replied. "My honor and the value of my word are two of the greatest treasures I have."

"You speak highly of these people," Grogner said. "But I know that fighting alongside another proves the strength of their forging."

He fell silent again. Rayden said nothing further, content to await the verdict. His face remained like stone, betraying no hint of his inner deliberations. Finally, he raised his eyes back up to her.

"There are forested lands to the south and east of our territory where none dwell. You may build a settlement and rule yourselves, but we would share hunting in those woods. If a threat looms, I expect those in the settlement to stand with us at arms. I also expect to come to terms on having some of yours live among us, as assurance that there will be no uprisings in our lands. Perhaps both of us will become the stronger for this."

Rayden looked to her companions. "Are those terms agreeable?"

Annocrates and Doros gave firm assent to the terms. They gave no objection to the request from Grogner to harbor some representatives of the new settlement. Before the audience with the Tega chieftain, Rayden had told them such a request would be reasonable and likely, especially given the origin of the settlers as a force of rebels with the will to rise up in arms.

She looked back to Grogner. "One more question."

"Yes?" he asked.

"Rivers. Are there rivers in this territory?" she asked.

"Wide streams, rivers, yes, it is the way I can mark their boundaries clearly," Grogner said. "Teeming with fish too. They will provide a good bounty for the new settlement."

She glanced back to Doros. With no others observing the gesture, she cast her friend a knowing wink. Doros' eyes sparked with joy, though she kept her face solemn.

"It sounds like a wonderful place for many to build a new life," Rayden said. "Let us all come together in the spirit of a new friendship and common cause."

"It would be a great honor to feast with Rayden Valkyrie," Grogner said, shedding a little of the dour countenance he had displayed throughout the audience.

"Then let us drink an abundance of ale together, Grogner,

chieftain of the Tega," Rayden said. "It has been far too long since I had strong northern ale."

"You asked of rivers," Grogner said, with a chuckle. "Tega ale flows in rivers at one of our feasts. Abundance is what you shall have."

"I wish to experience this for myself then," Rayden replied with a smile. "As soon as it can be arranged."

"This very night you shall!" Grogner proclaimed with a lively air. He looked to Annocrates and Doros. "My new friends, bring your other leaders and we shall feast tonight. The rest of your people can camp on our border while you are shown where the settlement territory will be."

"Agreed," Annocrates said. "And I look forward to discovering this northern ale I keep hearing about."

"Whatever you have heard, it is an understatement," Grogner said. "There is no finer ale than that of the Tega. Not even the Gessa can match it."

He rumbled with laughter, casting Rayden a glance. She replied in a lighthearted tone, "I will be the judge of that, proud chieftain."

"You will see, Rayden Valkyrie," he said, before dismissing them.

Walking away from the chieftain and starting back for the place where the column had halted, Rayden found her assessment of the Tega chieftain a favorable one. Though a young man, he showed great promise. He had a strong presence, but carried no hints of having a hot temper or being inclined to recklessness.

Annocrates, Doros, and the others would be in a favorable situation. Doros would even have the rivers she had hoped for.

For the immediate future, a grand feast awaited with promises of copious ale. She could already taste the northern elixir on a tongue that had been parched from it for far too long.

She looked to Annocrates and Doros, grinning. "Enough

of the swill drank by Teverens. No more wine. Tonight you experience true northern ale, my friends."

Doros laughed. "If it is half as good as you keep saying it is, I shall be impressed."

"You will never want anything else," Rayden said, exuding a buoyant mood as they strode together.

For the first time in a long time, she would not be the foreigner in the gathering. The blood of the north ran in her veins and she could already feel the embrace of homecoming.

Every step she now took landed upon northern ground. The thought invoked a beaming grin, one echoing the bright sun enthroned in clear blue skies.

***

Rayden had dwelled among the Tega for only ten days when a couple of young warriors appeared in the temporary camp of the former slaves. When she had last seen them, the pair had been gangly teenagers crossing the boundaries between youth and adulthood.

While still encompassed in the glow of youth, the two had matured considerably. Both stood taller and stronger of body than the last time she had set eyes upon their forms.

Striding toward them, Rayden smiled and her spirits lifted. Her voice emerged jubilant. "Renna! Pallan! You are both welcome visions to these eyes! It has been far too long since we last met!"

"Rayden!" exclaimed the dark-haired one to her right, Pallan. A boyish echo still lingered within his glad expression. "We have missed you greatly in the years since you left for the south."

"And I have missed you, but we all must take our journeys in this world," Rayden said. "What brings you to the Tega?"

Her smile faded when the two young warriors grew somber and exchanged nervous glances with each other. Renna looked back to her, a hesitant air about him.

"We have come to ask you to return with us," Renna said.

"The Tega sent a messenger to let us know that you had arrived in their lands," Pallan added. "Eigon hoped you would return to the north soon. It is good that you have come back. We have kept a long watch for you."

"Why?" Rayden asked, puzzled, though the mention that Eigon still remained cheiftain of the Gessa came as welcome news.

The Gessa were not a tribe given to the kind of sentimentality she had witnessed in other groups of people on her travels. Like other northern tribes, they held powerful bonds of friendship among one another, but they were not overly expressive when it came to some emotions.

The looks in the eyes of the warriors told her of something far beyond a matter of the tribe missing her company. Even more troubling, their gazes contained the distinctive sheen of fear.

"Have out with it, I have faced more in this world than you two would ever believe," Rayden pressed. "Speak plainly."

"A war stirs with the Runi," Pallan responded.

"Out with it, that is not all," Rayden said more sharply, reading his face and the pensiveness she saw in his expression.

"Something roves their woodlands ... and something roves the mountains in our lands," Renna told her, looking worried.

"Something? What?" Rayden asked, looking between the two and growing impatient with their continued hesitancy.

"Something that leaves the bones and blood of skilled warriors in its wake," Pallan answered.

"And you cannot even tell me what it is?" Rayden countered.

"Only the fleetest of sightings ... and those from a distance," Renna said. "But whatever they are, they have never been seen before in our lands."

"They?" Rayden queried, brow furrowing.

"We do not know how many there are, but it is clear they

have come in number," Pallan said. "Some manner of beast. Not human."

"They are a plague upon the Runi and soon Eigon believes their shadow will fall over us in full," Renna added.

"They frighten the Runi enough to make war upon us," Pallan said.

Grave concern filled Rayden at their words. She looked to each of them, and nodded slowly.

"Of course I will go with you to Eigon, though I do not know what I may be able to do for the Gessa," she said. "This sounds like something far beyond the ability of one warrior."

She did not doubt the two warriors standing before her, but she wanted to hear the description of the threat from the lips of Eigon. Being the kind of man who faced adversaries openly, he would not seek to soften the danger or exaggerate it.

Her return to the Gessa coming sooner than anticipated, she knew there would be little time for saying goodbye to the others. She would have to go alone in a situation like that looming before her. With unknown threats daunting an entire tribe, one of the strongest in the north, there was no way she would take a boy or any of her new friends along.

***

Dawn's light filtering through the trees, Rayden and the two Gessa warriors started into the woods, heading north and east. Having donned a pair of trousers, exhanged her sandals for leather shoes, and wearing a light cloak on her back, she had readied herself for cooler mountain climes and denser forest terrain. The changing of her clothes had been another sign that she had reached the north at last, but a heavy heart weighed upon her.

After all she had been through with Doros, Annocrates, and the others, the departure seemed so abrupt, but time could not be spared. Whatever threat faced the Gessa stood imminent.

Heart of a Lion

She knew she would miss Hamilcar dearly, but this journey would be no place for a boy. Yet the parting stung in a way she did not expect when she bid him to the care of Annocrates.

While there were many among the former slaves who were much more skilled as warriors, the man had the right balance of strength and kindness to be a mentor. Hopefully, in the course of time, he could even become a kind of father figure to the youth.

Rayden's world far too unsuitable for Hamilcar, there had been no other choice than to go onward by herself. The pangs tugging at her insides nonetheless proved difficult to endure after they separated.

She entrusted an important message with Annocrates for Doros. The woman had a tough and stubborn heart. Rayden knew she would have tried to go onward with her, but she did not want Doros' fate weighing on her conscience. Doros had her own quest to pursue in the matter of her family and Rayden needed full clarity of mind to face an unknown menace.

In her heart, she hoped that their paths would cross again. She wanted to help Doros on her effort to find her family. But no man or woman, not even the most gifted of seers, could speak with absolute certainty on the future. Not a single day could be promised, even to the greatest of warriors in the entire world.

With a deep breath in and out, Rayden looked around, taking in the glittering vision of the sun's rays scattering through the trees. An older section of forest, little undergrowth existed beneath the dense canopy spread above.

The cooler touch of the air, the soft shadows, and the musty scents brought her comfort. The chirping of the birds in the boughs and the winds rustling the leaves carried the timeless song of the forest.

She knew she walked upon tribal ground once more and the thought brought her some comfort. After spending so long in other lands as a foreigner, she found succor in being among her own kind once more.

Rayden smiled to herself as she thought of Eigon and so many others that she would be seeing soon. She wished her return could be happening under better circumstances, but it would be wonderful to reunite with those she counted as friends.

Her step felt lighter as she thought of the people awaiting her. The burden she carried within her heart ebbed the nearer they drew to the lands of the Gessa.

The leagues passed and the nights transpired without incident. The company of the two warriors was pleasant enough, and she caught up as much as she could on the happenings within the tribe. Renna and Pallan were all too glad to answer her questions, and the time passed swiftly enough.

At last, she began to recognize some landmarks. Familiar peaks rose into the sky, and she began to identify several majestic trees that had witnessed many generations of men and women come and go.

Seeing a massive oak, its thick boughs spread wide in a manner that gave the ancient tree the appearance of welcoming her back, she grinned wide. No longer in need of any guides, she knew a direct path to her destination.

Picking up her pace, she gained on Renna and Pallan a short distance ahead of her. The two warriors exhibited looks of surprise when she passed them and took the lead. Looking back, she returned a wry grin as she proceeded onward.

Every step brought her a little closer to the only place offering her some sense of home. She could not arrive there a moment too soon, thinking of all the faces she had longed to see for quite some time.

Her journey had taken her much farther than she had ever imagined. Enduring all manner of obstacles and hardships along the way, she found at the end of three years that she had no more patience left.

Heart of a Lion

Rayden always found the boundary between day and night to contain a kind of magic like no other. Under a majestic sunset, amid great mountain peaks at the onset of twilight, she reached the outskirts of the Gessa village where Eigon made his principle residence.

Striding out of the trees, flanked by Renna and Pallan, she set her eyes on a number of thatch-roofed huts spread out in a cleared swathe of land. Tendrils of smoke climbed into the air and the laughter of children at play carried across the open ground. Sheep milled about in pens, settling in for the coming of night.

The first to take notice of the newcomers were a few of the village dogs. Bounding across the ground, their eager barks drew the attention of several men and women going about evening tasks.

Rayden grinned when she heard her name shouted in the distance, many faces now turning and staring in their direction. In moments, others emerged from the huts, a chorus of voices echoing with excitement and spreading the news that she had returned.

A crowd formed swiftly as Rayden and the two warriors neared. Children skipped and ran about, and a few trundled, some too young to remember Rayden the last time she had been in the village.

Looking to many familiar faces, all of them smiling in welcome, her heart soared. Even though she did not call any place a home, not since the terrible day of blood and fire that had seen her parents ripped out from her life, the Gessa had always made her feel like she belonged with them.

A tall, broad-shouldered woman with a tumbling cascade of auburn hair shouldered through the elated throng. A radiant smile on her face, she spread her arms wide and swept Rayden into a warm, lingering embrace.

"Tonight is a night to celebrate!" she exclaimed, joy filling her blue-green eyes. She blinked back tears, staring into Rayden's face. "I have missed you so much. I can't tell you how happy I am that you've come back to us!"

"Erethea, how I've missed you dearly," Rayden told her closest friend among the Gessa. "It has been too long of a time. Would I even recognize the boys by now?"

Erethea grinned and looked down. Two bright-eyed boys now stood at their side, one about five years of age and the other seven. Both had changed much since the last time Rayden had set eyes upon them, but their features told her who they belonged to. The younger had the look of his mother, while the older had the dark hair and gray eyes of his father, Jarut.

"They have grown a lot!" Rayden exclaimed, playfully ruffling their hair and drawing laughs from the two youths. "Going to be a pair of mighty warriors before long!"

"Jarut is well-pleased with the skill they have shown already," Erethea remarked, gazing upon her sons with a look of pride.

"Do you have a moment for others who are fond of you?" a strong, masculine voice interjected.

Rayden turned and beheld a towering blonde-haired figure. "Alcedan! I had hoped you would be in the village and not chasing down some boar in the forest."

The two grasped each other's forearms. Affinity and respect mutual, the bond forged between the two had been one hard-earned. From hunts to sparring, they shared a warrior's path, though Rayden's role took the shape of a mentor much more than a peer.

The younger man, while brimming with confidence and overflowing in strength, had always accorded her a respectful deference. Unlike many younger warriors with hotter heads, he always strove to learn when she bested him in weapons and fighting.

"I expect to see some improvement since last we sparred,"

Rayden told him, a grin on her lips.

"You shall, I have not been idle," Alcedan replied. "I believe you will be pleased."

"And if I am not, do not think my fondness for you will spare you from some bruises," Rayden said, smirking.

"I would be disappointed if you ever restrained yourself with me," Alcedan said.

"Have no worries of that," Rayden said, laughing as she slapped him on the right shoulder. A comrade at arms, he had undoubtedly improved his skills, and she looked forward to seeing how far he had come in her absence.

Her gaze roving past Alcedan, she took in a familiar figure approaching them. The people gathered around Rayden parted to make way for the man.

As tall and robust as Alcedan, his limbs still carried considerable strength, though the gray streaks in his hair and beard testified to many more years of experience. Eyes that had seen a multitude of births and bloodshed alike cast a gaze of paternal affection toward her.

"Eigon!" Rayden said, stepping past Alcedan toward the chieftain of the Gessa.

A smile broke through Eigon's thick beard. Spreading his arms wide, he hugged her tightly to him.

As she embraced him, Rayden remembered that first time he had wrapped his strong arms around her, so long ago, when she stood alone and in the throes of the deepest agony she had ever experienced, mourning the loss of her parents. That one embrace told a hurting young girl to keep moving forward and that not everything in the world had gone numb and cold. Being welcomed by those arms once more, Rayden basked in that truth.

"Been far too long, my sweet lass," Eigon said, laughing. "To see you back with us brings this old heart much joy."

"It is wonderful to see you again," Rayden replied, gazing

into a face that had looked out for the Gessa for so many long years.

"I wish it were under different circumstances," he replied, a little of the cheer fading from his expression.

"You know I would always come if I knew you needed me," Rayden replied.

"And you have come," Eigon said. "After a long journey."

"One that took me much farther than I thought it would," Rayden said with an air of chagrin.

"Walk with me for a moment, I would speak with you about some important matters before tonight," Eigon invited. Turning to the others, he raised his voice and commanded, "Leave us, and prepare ale and meat! This night is one for celebration!"

The surrounding men and women looked more than happy to obey Eigon, a number of cheers and exclamations sounding at the directive. Erethea, Alcedan, and the others expressed their joy once more at seeing Rayden before heading back toward the huts, leaving her in the company of their revered chieftain.

Rayden followed the older man into the fields beyond the huts, the tall grasses brushing against her trousers. The tranquility of the atmosphere contrasted with the look clouding the man's face. She knew the moment had come to hear of the tribe's threat from his lips.

"We will celebrate your return tonight," he began. "And I am certain that you have many tales to tell of your travels."

She grinned. "Maybe a few."

"Left a few lumps on stupid men foolish enough to try and take advantage of you, I imagine," Eigon said, giving her a wink, his mood brightening for a moment.

Her smile spread wider. "You know me well."

The levity faded from his eyes. "I do know you well. That is why I have had eyes looking out for you, for some time now."

"Renna and Pallan said something threatens the Gessa,"

Rayden said, getting to the matter at hand. "Both seemed frightened by whatever it is."

She knew by the look he gave her that Renna and Pallan had not overstated the situation. The Gessa faced a grave threat, one that even brought fear into the eyes of Eigon as he spoke with her.

The only other time she had witnessed such a look was several years before when his wife lay at the edge of death, gripped in an illness that he had been helpless to stop. Seeing that rare look in the chieftain's gaze brought a deep unease to Rayden.

"A great terror stalking the forests draws ever closer and madness seizes the tribes in its path," Eigon informed her. "War looms nigh."

"Renna and Pallan said something of war. The Runi?" Rayden asked, frowning. "Truly could it be the Runi as they told me?"

"The Runi," Eigon corroborated. "They told you true."

"It is difficult to believe the Runi would seek war with us," Rayden responded, both surprised and dejected at the confirmation. The Runi and the Gessa had enjoyed good relations for many years, and only the oldest among the two tribes could remember the last time there had been any conflict.

"It saddens me, but desperation moves them to recklessness," Eigon said. "The darkness sweeping through the woods in neighboring lands is like nothing any of us has ever seen."

"We do not need to be fighting amongst ourselves," Rayden said. She thought of the rising power she had witnessed on the other side of the mountains. "The time will come when we will need to stand together against Tevere. I have witnessed their power, their hunger and their cruelty. They will bring war to us in the future. The Runi need to ready themselves to stand with us, not fight against us."

"It is as I said, a desperate madness seizes them," Eigon replied. "Chaos spreads through the lands outside our borders.

We must defend our lands, though I do not think this shadow filling the woods of the Runi and the Marga will overlook us."

The dire news worried her. Rayden wondered what could possibly drive an entire tribe to war against another that it stood to gain nothing from.

The Runi were strong and proud, a people not easily cowed or intimidated. Anything that could terrorize the Runi would pose a serious threat to the Gessa.

"What is this darkness in the woods?" Rayden asked. "Pallan and Renna told me everything they knew, but that seemed very little."

A look of frustration came to his face and Eigon shook his head. "I cannot say. Nobody knows for sure. Blood and death are left in the wake of its passage, but no survivors. Even great warriors have failed so survive their encounters with it. There have been none that have come close to it and lived to say what it is, beyond rumor and wild-eyed claims.

"There are some hunters' tales of faraway glimpses of huge, two-legged beast creatures, said to be taller and broader than Alcedan, and unlike the wolf-men that roam the mountains. Those are the stories. But I can say this is something that none of us have faced before. A new darkness that acts with cunning and ferocity."

Rayden thought back to the words of the sorcerer. His voice sounded again in her mind, *'All roots of the same tree.'*

She suspected that whatever prowled the woods had roots of a darker, mystic nature. Nothing else would spread the kind of fear that drove an entire northern tribe to war against a neighbor it held no quarrel with.

In that moment, standing with Eigon in the meadow and night falling over the forests, Rayden sensed the tree that the roots were a part of. The bull-god accepting the offering of children hurled alive into fire, the rotting bodies of slaves lining a road for leagues and the gaping maw of an empire on the rise were just a few of many other roots feeding a monstrosity ancient and venomous.

In the face of such a terrible darkness, a single image arose within her mind. The greatest and oldest of trees could be cut down with an axe, even if it took hundreds upon hundreds of swings.

Rayden carried an axe at her waist and the willpower to wield it as many times as necessary. If the tree whose roots plagued her homeland and the lands abroad could be found, she would not cease hacking at its corrupted wood until the entirety of it toppled and fell.

"I know the look on your face well," Eigon said. "A storm begins to gather within you."

Rayden broke away from her thoughts and looked to the chieftain. With firm conviction, she declared to him, "I will stand with you and all the Gessa against this darkness. Whatever its origin may be."

"I never doubted that," Eigon replied. "But first we will have to prepare for war with the Runi. There is nothing I can do to stop their madness. I fear it is only a matter of days before they attack in force. Their warriors begin to gather from all over their lands. Though I wish there were another way to stop a war between our tribes, we must protect our own."

"Then I will be there to greet these maddened dogs when they set foot in the land of the Gessa ... with my sword in one hand and axe in the other," Rayden replied, her eyes like blue flames and resolve brimming within. "We will bring an end to their rashness. Let them come. After we have shown the Runi the folly of attacking the Gessa, we shall bring an end to the darkness spreading through these lands."

About the Author

Award-winning author and filmmaker Stephen Zimmer is based out of Lexington, Kentucky. His works include the Rising Dawn Saga, the Fires in Eden Series, the Hellscapes and Chronicles of Ave short story collections, the Harvey and Solomon steampunk stories, and the Rayden Valkyrie Tales. Stephen currently resides in Lexington, Kentucky.

Stephen can be found online at:
www.stephenzimmer.com
Facebook: www.facebook.com/stephenzimmer7
Twitter: www.twitter.com/sgzimmer

Transcend reality with Seventh Star Press!

On the following pages we would like to introduce you to some of our titles featuring Sword and Sorcery, Post-Apocalyptic Fantasy, Epic Fantasy, YA Fantasy, and more!

To get more information on Seventh Star Press and our titles, please visit:

www.seventhstarpress.com

or connect with us at:
www.twitter.com/7thstarpress
www.facebook.com/seventhstarpress

Single author author collections of short stories from Seventh Star Press!

Now Available!

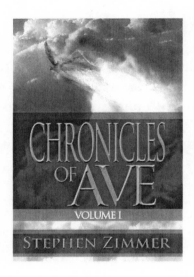

Have many action-driven fantasy adventures in the world of Ave in Stephen Zimmer's *Chronicles of Ave, Volume 1*.

Softcover: 978-1-937929-30-5
eBook: 978-1-937929-31-2

Grand Epic Fantasy from Stephen Zimmer!
Explore the world of Ave in the Fires in Eden Series from
Stephen Zimmer! Epic Fantasy for those who enjoy authors
like George R.R. Martin and Steven Erikson!

Softcover ISBN: 9780982565612

eBook ISBN: 9780982565698

Softcover ISBN: 9780983108627   Softcover ISBN 9781937929855

eBook ISBN: 9780983108610   eBook ISBN 9781937929862

Hellscapes, Volume 1
Venture through the infernal, where angels
fear to tread!

From Stephen Zimmer, a new horror
series set in realms where the inhabitants
experience the ultimate nightmare!
softcover ISBN: 978-1-937929-36-7
eBook ISBN: 978-1-937929-37-4

Want Sword and Sorcery?
Pick up the anthologies *Thunder on the Battlefield:*
Sword, and *Thunder on the Battlefield: Sorcery,*
from editor James R. Tuck!
(author of the Deacon Chalk novels)
Available in print and eBook!

 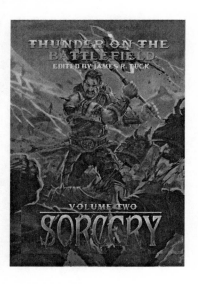

Thunder on the Battlefield: Sword
Softcover: 978-1-937929-24-4
eBook: 978-1-937929-25-1

Thunder on the Battlefield: Sorcery
Softcover: 978-1-937929-26-8
eBook: 978-1-937929-27-5

Explore post-apocalyptic fantasy worlds!
Read the Seventh Star Press anthology *The End
Was Not the End*, from editor Joshua H. Leet!

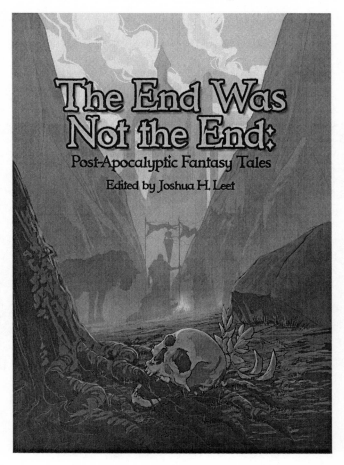

softcover ISBN: 978-1-937929-07-7
eBook ISBN: 978-1-937929-15-2

Gorias La Gaul adventures from Steven Shrewsbury!
Enter an ancient world of heroes, blood, and steel in the
tales of Gorias La Gaul! Hard-hitting Sword & Sorcery in
the vein of Robert E. Howard!.

Softcover ISBN: 9781937929800   Softcover ISBN: 9780983108634

eBook ISBN: 9781937929831   eBook ISBN: 9780983108641

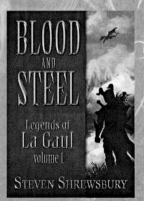

Softcover: 978-1-937929-28-2

eBook: 978-1-937929-29-9

Now available from Seventh Star Press! The Rising Dawn Saga, a series that explores the dystopian and the apocalyptic from author

Stephen Zimmer

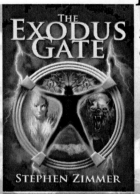

Book One: The Exodus Gate
Softcover ISBN: 9780615267470
eBook ISBN: 9780982565674

Book Two: The Storm Guardians
Softcover ISBN: 9780982565636
eBook ISBN: 9780982565681

Book Three: The Seventh Throne
Softcover ISBN: 9780983740247
eBook ISBN: 9780983740223

The Rising Dawn Saga titles feature cover art and illustrations from the award-winning Matthew Perry

From Bram Stoker Award-winning Editor Michael Knost!

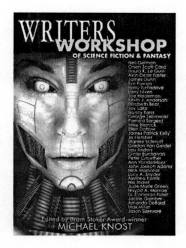

Softcover ISBN:
978-1-937929-61-9
eBook ISBN:
978-1-937929-62-6

Writers Workshop of Science Fiction and Fantasy is a collection of essays and interviews by and with many of the movers-and-shakers in the industry. Each contributor covers the specific element of craft he or she excels in. Expect to find varying perspectives and viewpoints, which is why you many find differing opinions on any particular subject.

This is, after all, a collection of advice from professional storytellers. And no two writers have made it to the stage via the same journey-each has made his or her own path to success. And that's one of the strengths of this book. The reader is afforded the luxury of discovering various approaches and then is allowed to choose what works best for him or her.

Featuring essays and interviews with:
Neil Gaiman, Orson Scott Card, Ursula K. Le Guin, Alan Dean Foster, James Gunn, Tim Powers, Harry Turtledove, Larry Niven, Joe Haldeman, Kevin J. Anderson, Elizabeth Bear, Jay Lake, Nancy Kress, George Zebrowski, Pamela Sargent, Mike Resnick, Ellen Datlow, James Patrick Kelly, Jo Fletcher, Stanley Schmidt, Gordon Van Gelder, Lou Anders, Peter Crowther, Ann VanderMeer, Joh Joseph Adams, Nick Mamatas, Lucy A. Snyder, Alethea Kontis, Nisi Shawl, Jude-Marie Green, Nayad A. Monroe, G. Cameron Fuller, Jackie Gamber, Amanda DeBord, Max Miller, Jason Sizemore.

Action-driven Fantasy from D.A. Adams!
Begin your journey into The Brotherhood of Dwarves, the
popular YA Fantasy series from D.A. Adams. An action-
filled saga where the dwarves are not just sidekicks!

Softcover ISBN: 9781937929916   Softcover ISBN: 9781937929923

eBook ISBN: 9781937929930   eBook ISBN: 9781937929-947

Softcover ISBN: 978-0-9837402-5-4 Softcover ISBN: 978-1-937929-78-7

eBook ISBN: 978-1-937929-90-9   eBook ISBN: 978-1-937929-77-0

YA Fantasy From Jackie Gamber!
The highly-acclaimed Leland Dragon Series from Jackie
Gamber! Strong character-driven YA Fantasy for those
who enjoy authors such as Christopher Paolini.

Softcover ISBN: 9780983108672

eBook ISBN: 9780983108696

Softcover ISBN: 9781937929893   Softcover ISBN: 9781937929404

eBook ISBN: 9781937929817   eBook ISBN: 9781937929435

Appalachian Gothic! Jason Sizemore's Irredeemable!
18 Tales of dark fantasy, science fiction, and horror

Softcover: 978-1-937929-59-6
eBook: 978-1-937929-68-8

Flowing like mists and shadows through the Appalachian Mountains come 18 tales from the mind of Jason Sizemore. Weaving together elements of southern gothic, science fiction, fantasy, horror, the supernatural, and much more, this diverse collection of short stories brings you an array of characters who must face accountability, responsibility, and, more ominously, retribution.

Whether it is Jack Taylor readying for a macabre, terrifying night in "The Sleeping Quartet," the Wayne brothers and mischief gone badly awry in "Pranks," the title character in "The Dead and Metty Crawford," or the church congregation and their welcoming of a special visitor in "Yellow Warblers," Irredeemable introduces you to a range of ordinary people who come face to face with extraordinary situations.

Whether the undead, aliens, ghosts, or killers of the yakuza, dangers of all kinds lurk within the darkness for those who dare tread upon its ground. Hop aboard and settle in, Irredeemable will take you on an unforgettable ride along a dark speculative fiction road.

Powerful fantasy from A. Christopher Drown
A clash of the realms of magic and knowledge!

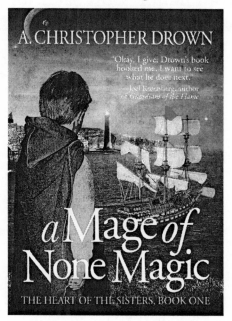

Softcover: 978-1-937929-53-4
eBook: 978-1-937929-58-9

Myth tells how magic came to be when the fabled gem known as the Heart of the Sisters was shattered by evil gods. The same tale speaks of the Heart being healed one day, unleashing a power that will bring the end of humankind.

While traveling to begin his magical studies, young apprentice Niel finds himself suddenly at the center of the Heart's terrifying legend. Caught in a whirlwind of events that fractures the foundation of everything he's believed, Niel learns his role in the world may be far more important than he ever could have imagined, and ever would have wished.

A Mage of None Magic begins an extraordinary adventure into a perilous land where autocratic magicians manipulate an idle aristocracy, where common academia struggles for acceptance, and where after ages of disregard myth and legend refuse to be ignored any longer.

A Mage of None Magic is Book One in The Heart of the Sisters series..

An Anthology of Animal Companions
from Editor Scott Sandridge!
Available in print and eBook!

Hero's Best Friend
Softcover ISBN: 978-1-937929-51-0
eBook ISBN: 978-1-937929-52-7

How far would Gandalf have gotten without Shadowfax? Where would the Vault Dweller be without Dogmeat? And could the Beastmaster been the Beastmaster without his fuzzy allies? Animal companions are more than just sidekicks. Animals can be heroes, too! Found within are twenty stories of heroic action that focuses on the furries and scalies who have long been the unsung heroes pulling their foolish human buddies out of the fire, and often at great sacrifice-from authors both established and new, including Frank Creed, S. H. Roddey, and Steven S. Long. Whether you're a fan of Epic Fantasy, Sword & Sorcery, Science Fiction, or just animal stories in general, this is the anthology for you! So sit back, kick your feet up, and find out what it truly means to be the *Hero's Best Friend*.